White Sky, Black Ice

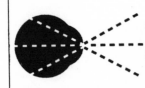

This Large Print Book carries the
Seal of Approval of N.A.V.H.

White Sky, Black Ice

a Nathan Active mystery

Stan Jones

WHEELER
PUBLISHING

Published in 2005 by arrangement with Soho Press.

Wheeler Large Print Softcover.

The text of this Large Print edition is unabridged.
Other aspects of the book may vary from the original edition.

Set in 16 pt. Plantin by Christina S. Huff.

Printed in the United States on permanent paper.

Library of Congress Cataloging-in-Publication Data

Jones, Stan, 1947–
    White sky, black ice : a Nathan Active mystery /
by Stan Jones.
        p.   cm.
    ISBN 1-58724-930-8 (lg. print : sc : alk. paper)
    1. Police — Alaska — Fiction.   2. Eskimos — Fiction.
3. Alaska — Fiction.   4. Large type books.   I. Title.
PS3560.O539W45 2005
    813′.54—dc22   2004028857

For Nunmuk, the packer

As the Founder/CEO of NAVH, the only national health agency solely devoted to those who, although not totally blind, have an eye disease which could lead to serious visual impairment, I am pleased to recognize Thorndike Press* as one of the leading publishers in the large print field.

Founded in 1954 in San Francisco to prepare large print textbooks for partially seeing children, NAVH became the pioneer and standard setting agency in the preparation of large type.

Today, those publishers who meet our standards carry the prestigious "Seal of Approval" indicating high quality large print. We are delighted that Thorndike Press is one of the publishers whose titles meet these standards. We are also pleased to recognize the significant contribution Thorndike Press is making in this important and growing field.

Lorraine H. Marchi, L.H.D.
Founder/CEO
NAVH

* Thorndike Press encompasses the following imprints: Thorndike, Wheeler, Walker and Large Print Press.

Author's Note

"Eskimo" is the best-known term for the Native Americans described in this book, but it is not their term. In their own language, they call themselves Inupiat, meaning "the People." "Eskimo," which was brought into Alaska by white men, is what certain Indian tribes in eastern Canada called their neighbors to the north; it probably meant "eaters of raw flesh."

Nonetheless, "Eskimo" and "Inupiat" are used more or less interchangeably in northwest Alaska today, at least when English is spoken, and that is the usage followed in this book.

But things are changing. To some extent, the authentic and indigenous "Inupiat" is superseding the imported "Eskimo," especially among younger and better-educated members of the culture.

Occasionally, the Inupiat use "Eskimo" in another way, in the same way that African-Americans use "nigger" among themselves. Sometimes this seems intended as a kind of ironic armor against white prejudice; sometimes it seems to reflect instead the internalizing of that prejudice. That usage also appears in this book, as when one of the characters refers to his own people as "dumb Eskimos."

In formal or public speech — such as journalism — "Inuit" is probably the most widely accepted collective term for the Eskimo peoples of Siberia, Alaska, Canada, and Greenland, but it is not an Alaskan word and so is not much used by the Inupiat of the state's northwest coast. Accordingly, it doesn't appear in this book.

A few Inupiaq words — those commonly mixed with English in northwest Alaska — appear in the book. They are listed below, along with pronunciations and meanings. As the spellings vary among Inupiaq-English dictionaries, I have used spellings that seemed to me most likely to induce the proper pronunciation by non-Inupiaq readers.

An Inupiaq Glossary

aaka (AH-kuh)   mother

aana (AH-nuh)   grandmother; old lady

Alipaa! (AH-la-paa)   It's cold!

angatquq (AHNG-ut-cook)   shaman

Arii! (ah-DEE)   I hurt!

innukaknaaluk (IN-you-kuk-NAH-luk)   the man-who-always-kills-people; a recurring figure in the folktales of northwest Alaska

Inukins (IN-you-kins)   gremlins

Inupiaq (IN-you-pack)   the Eskimo language of northern Alaska; an

Inupiat (IN-you-pat)	individual Eskimo of northern Alaska more than one *Inupiaq;* the Eskimo people of northern Alaska
kunnichuk (KUH-knee-chuck)	storm shed
nalauqmiut (nuh-LOCK-me)	white people
nalauqmiiyaaq (nuh-LOCK-me-ock)	almost white; a half-breed
niqipiaq (NICK-i-pack)	Eskimo food, especially meat
qaqsrauq (COCKS-ruck)	loon
qauqlik (COKE-lick)	head man, chieftain

Each story had a meaning beyond words and plot. Soon I was lost in a world not of my own making — an alien world that sometimes frightened me with its violence, its fatalism, its acceptance of the duplicity of man and beast. And yet, the very same tales told of the special reciprocal relationship between man and the animal world, of the devotion and love of Eskimos for their kin, and of the humor Eskimos find in their harsh world.

— Edwin S. Hall, Jr. and Claire Fejes,
The Eskimo Storyteller:
Folktales from Noatak, Alaska.

Chapter 1

Wednesday Morning, Chukchi

Ordinarily, Alaska State Trooper Nathan Active didn't get involved with deaths inside the Chukchi city limits. But the city cops were all out and he was flirting with Lucy the dispatcher when the call came in, so he took it.

"You better get over here, Nathan," said Hector Martinez. "Some kid shot himself across from the Dreamland and I want him moved."

"Who is it?"

"Don't matter who," Martinez said. "Just come get him. He's scaring away business." The bar owner hung up.

Active climbed the stairs to his office, took his fur hat and down parka from the hooks by the door, and went out to the eight-year-old trooper Suburban. The west wind that had set in yesterday scraped his face as he unlocked the driver's door and tossed in his briefcase.

A thin gray belt of cloud scrolled overhead, spitting snow at the narrow tongue of beach gravel and tundra that contained Chukchi's square unpainted wooden houses and its straggling dirt streets. He had arrived at work only an hour before, but already the Suburban's windshield was covered. The temperature was maybe six above, he judged as he brushed off the snow. The warm spell of the past few days was definitely over.

There were many things he had come to detest about Chukchi since the troopers had posted him there eighteen months before. But it was probably the west wind he detested most. *WEST WIND, COMES FROM WEST, OVER BERING SEA,*

It was the west wind's toothache-like persistence. God help you if you had to go gloveless in it, changing spark plugs on the Suburban or working an evidence camera. It gnawed at your hands and sprayed grit in your eyes. Inside a house at night you could hear it scratching bushes and weeds against the wall. You could feel it suck warm air out the cracks around the windows and push cold air under the door and through the electric sockets.

Well, he could persist too. Another year or two and he figured he would be promoted out of Chukchi to Alaska State Trooper headquarters in Anchorage.

Where his adoptive parents lived and where he had been raised. Where, thank God, the west wind never blew like it did here in Chukchi, the village where he was born.

He pulled out of the parking lot behind the Chukchi Public Safety Building, a three-story stack of fading brown plywood siding and blue aluminum roofing. He drove up Third Street, the only paved road in town, turned right at Lake Street, then drove east a block and stopped across from the Dreamland. The Chukchi police van was already there and two officers were walking toward something in a clump of willows maybe seventy-five yards out onto the tundra. The dispatcher must have reached the city cops by radio or caught one of them at home by phone.

Several Honda four-wheelers were pulled up beside Lake Street too. A gaggle of breakfast drinkers watched the proceedings from the steps of the Dreamland. They were probably the business "scared" away from Martinez's bar.

Active followed the city cops to where the dead man lay on his back near the edge of the Chukchi cemetery. He was young, his black hair was collar-length, and he wore a small mustache. His legs were

15

drifted over with snow but his head and upper body, more sheltered by the willows, were only lightly frosted.

There was a snow-covered rifle across his snow-covered legs, a bullet-sized hole in his throat, and a shadowy stain on the snow under his neck. Active was sure that, when they turned him over, they would find a much larger hole where the slug had come out.

"Mind if I take a look?" he asked one of the city cops, a white man named Mason.

Mason nodded. "Just don't touch anything till the chief gets here."

Active squatted and studied the rifle through its dusting of snow. It looked like an old 30-30 Winchester carbine, good for anything from seal to caribou, even moose. Most people nowadays had newer rifles that shot farther and hit harder, but 30-30s were still common in Chukchi, where nothing was thrown away if it still worked, or might do so again someday.

Active stood up. There were some liquor bottles lying around, mostly plastic "travelers" that could be hauled in a boat, plane, or snowmachine without breaking. But Martinez ran a package store next to the Dreamland, so the tundra nearby was always littered with bottles. How many of

16

them had the boy with the hole in his throat emptied in his last hours?

Active turned as footsteps crunched in the snow behind him. Jim Silver, the city police chief, stopped beside Active and studied the corpse.

Silver was a tall, paunchy man with an acne-cratered face. He had been around Chukchi since before Active was born. Active imagined that Silver would still be there, like the west wind, when Active was long gone.

"Another one, huh?"

"Looks like it," Silver said. "Third suicide since the weather turned cold."

"You know him?"

"I think so, but let me check." Silver squatted and patted the boy's coat pockets, then reached into one and pulled out a photo ID badge by one corner.

"Yep," he said after a moment's study. "George Clinton, one of Daniel's boys. Looks like he got himself a job at the Gray Wolf mine."

He waved the badge at Active, then tucked it back into the same pocket it had come from. "We'll move him pretty soon, we just need to get some pictures for the coroner. Not that there's much doubt what happened."

"Well, you don't need me. I'm only here because Lucy couldn't find you guys at first." Active started toward the Suburban.

"Actually, there is one thing."

He turned, knowing what was coming. Silver was white, and so were the other city cops on the scene. He, Nathan Active, was Inupiat Eskimo. Like George Clinton.

"You got a minute to go by and break the news to old Daniel?"

"Jim, I speak less Inupiaq than you do. You know that."

"Well, Daniel's English is pretty good."

"How about one of the other guys?" Active jerked a thumb toward the two city cops starting to work over George Clinton's body.

"I need them here for a while yet."

Active shook his head and shrugged. "Where's the house?"

Silver pointed across the tundra to the southeast. "That white one there, by the lagoon."

"You owe me, Jim."

"I owe you," Silver said.

Active walked back to the Suburban and pulled out his keys.

"Going uptown?"

He turned. A scrawny civilian in a Mariners baseball cap and a long dirty blue

18

parka had detached himself from the gang around the Dreamland steps and was walking toward the Suburban, a can of Olympia in hand.

"Not uptown, Kinnuk. I'm going down toward the airport," Active said.

"Great, me too," Kinnuk Wilson said in his high voice. He climbed into the passenger seat of the Suburban, cradling the beer between his knees.

Kinnuk Wilson was a part-time marijuana dealer who did just enough business to keep himself in beer. The troopers and the city cops tolerated him for two reasons. One, anybody who could get people to smoke pot rather than guzzle booze was doing everybody a favor, in the eyes of the Chukchi law-enforcement establishment. And two, Kinnuk Wilson liked to talk to cops.

The weird thing was, everybody in town knew he talked. But instead of dropping him through a hole in the sea ice some night, the bootleggers and the rest of Chukchi's riffraff kept talking to Kinnuk and Kinnuk kept passing it along.

Active could never figure it, but why look a gift horse in the mouth? He climbed into the driver's seat.

"You're going to see to old Daniel about

George, ah?" Wilson said as Active turned the key.

"Yeah, but you're not."

"No, I'll wait in your truck."

Active headed east on Lake Street, toward the lagoon. They bounced along in silence for a good ten seconds.

"Too bad about George, ah?" Wilson said.

Active said nothing. When Kinnuk Wilson had something to say, silence was the best way to get him to say it.

"It was his turn, though."

"His turn?" Active was immediately irritated with himself for breaking his vow of silence.

"Yeah, from the Clinton curse."

"The Clinton curse?"

"You never hear about it? You mind if I turn up your heater? *Alipaa* today." Wilson flipped the fan onto high without waiting for an answer. "You didn't know two of Daniel's other boys kill theirself already? Oh, yeah, I forget you was down in Anchorage with your white parents." He tilted the Olympia and swallowed, Adam's apple bobbing in the scrawny neck.

Active reached over and thumped the Oly can. "You know you can't be in here with that."

"It's empty anyway." Wilson rolled down the window and tossed the can onto the tundra.

"What about this curse?"

"Oh, yeah." Wilson rolled the window up again. "It start maybe fifteen years ago. There was this old man, Billy Karl, up on Beach Street. He used to make dogsleds."

Active nodded, turning the Suburban onto Fourth Street. Now they were headed south, parallel to the lagoon. It was freezing up as winter came on, the spot of open water in the middle shrinking like the pupil of an eye in bright light.

"Billy Karl have this kid named Frank," Wilson said in the stripped-down village English that was starting to sound as familiar to Active as the standard English spoken in Anchorage. Another reason to get out of Chukchi as soon as possible.

"Frank decide he want Daniel Clinton's wife, even though she's a lot older than him," Wilson went on. "She and Frank Karl were cousins or something, and you know them Karls always like to monkey around with their relatives. That's why they're so goofy."

"How do you know this?"

"George tell me about it when we're in fifth grade."

"Then I guess it must be true."

Wilson ignored the sarcasm. "Frank was no good, drinking and fighting all the time, and Annie — that's Daniel's wife — go to church a lot. So she won't have nothing to do with him. But Frank think it's because she want Daniel too much, and he start talking around town how Daniel better get out of the way.

"Finally one night, Frank get drunk and go over to Daniel's house with a rifle. He's out front, screaming and crying and shooting up in the air, threatening to come in and get Daniel and Annie and kill them both, or shoot himself. This is before Daniel have a telephone, so there's not much him and Annie can do. They and their kids are trapped in there."

They had reached Daniel Clinton's house now. Active stopped the Suburban in front. But he didn't get out.

Wilson pointed at the weathered plywood storm shed attached to the front of Clinton's house. "Frank go up to Daniel's *kunnichuk* there and start pounding on the door like hell. But Daniel put a board across it, so Frank can't get in. Then Frank start shooting through the door. Annie and all the kids get down behind some stuff in the back, so he never hit anybody."

Wilson looked from the *kunnichuk* to Active and back to the *kunnichuk* again. "But Daniel have all he can take. He put a slug in his shotgun, and he stick the muzzle right up against the *kunnichuk* door and pull the trigger.

"Well, he make a lucky shot. That slug punch a big hole right through Frank's guts and hit his spine. Frank fall dead right there."

"There." Wilson pointed again at the storm shed. "See them holes in the door of the *kunnichuk?* They say that's the holes Daniel and Frank make shooting at each other that night. The big one is from when Daniel finally kill Frank."

Active studied the door. The hole looked too big and smooth-edged even for a shotgun slug. But perhaps it would look like that after fifteen years of rain and wind and kids poking sticks through it. "So what happened?"

"The *nalauqmiut* cops decide it's self-defense, and they let it go," Wilson said. "But the Eskimos know it's not over. For one thing, Frank was the only boy that Billy had. The rest of his kids were all girls. Besides that . . . you know what an *angatquq* is?"

Active remembered the word from a

book his adoptive parents had given him to help him understand his origins. At the time, he had been more interested in Hardy Boys mysteries. "A shaman?"

"Yeah, that's right," Wilson said. "Early days ago, before the missionaries come, the *angatquqs* run everything. The old-time Eskimos thought they could do magic, and they were scared of them."

"Anyway, Billy Karl was supposed to be from a family of *angatquqs*, and lotta people always think he's one himself. So everybody wait to see how he will kill Daniel Clinton. They think it will be a real old-time Eskimo blood feud."

Active shifted to look at the holes in the *kunnichuk* door again, then turned back to Wilson. "But Daniel is still alive."

"That's right, Billy never kill him. One night there's big blizzard, and somebody knock at Daniel's door. When he open it, there's Billy. He look in and he see Annie back in there, and George and their four boys. He stare at each boy in turn."

" 'I won't take any revenge on you for what you did,' he tell Daniel. 'But you took my son from me and now your sons will take themselves away from you.' "

Wilson turned toward Active, then swung his gaze around the Suburban like

Billy Karl studying Daniel Clinton's cursed sons. Then he looked at Active again.

About fifty percent of what Wilson said was true usually. But it was braided with the untrue like the strands of a rope. Wilson's tale of curses and blood feuds didn't sound like anything in any of the books Active's adoptive parents had given him, or in the anthropology courses he had taken while studying criminology at the University of Alaska.

"Did you see this with your own eyes?"

"No, but everybody say it," Wilson said. "The oldest boy's about sixteen at the time and was sort of friendly with Frank Karl. He hang himself couple years later. Ever since then, them Clinton boys always kill themselves when they get to be about twenty. So far, the curse get them all. After George, Daniel only have one boy left."

"Billy Karl says a few words and Daniel's boys just start killing themselves?" Active asked. "Come on."

"It make sense if you don't think about it," Wilson said. "If you plant the idea in some dumb Eskimo's mind he's going to kill himself, he probably will."

"Don't say that, Kinnuk." Active said. "The Inupiat aren't dumb."

25

"Then how come we kill ourself so much?"

Active knew the argument was pointless. Kinnuk had absorbed the white man's contempt for the Inupiat, and it would take more than finger-shaking from a state trooper to erase it. But he took one more swipe at it. "It's called culture shock."

"I just call it dumb Eskimos." Wilson shrugged. "That's why Daniel and his boys believe what Billy Karl say."

"Your sons will take themselves away from you," Active repeated. Despair blew through Chukchi's streets like the west wind. He wondered if he could endure it long enough to get his transfer to Anchorage.

"Maybe if the first one didn't do it, the others would have a chance," Wilson said. "But them younger boys, seeing their brothers kill theirself, they start to know it's going to happen to them. Them dumb Eskimos feel themselves get smaller and smaller, pretty soon they're gone."

"Sounds like you've been there yourself."

"Sometimes I . . ." Wilson stopped talking and looked at Daniel Clinton's *kunnichuk* again. "Ah, I just go to that Dreamland and I get feeling good again."

"Don't touch anything," Active said, and

climbed down from the Suburban. When he glanced back, Wilson was pulling a fresh Oly from a pocket of his parka.

Active went through the *kunnichuk* and knocked on the inside door. He looked around while he waited, savoring the sharp, oily smells in the shed. Several parkas hung from nails on the walls, alongside some steel traps, a pair of caribou mukluks, and the hides of a marten and two foxes. Two red plastic jugs for snow-machine and boat gas sat on the floor in a corner. In another corner stood three rifles and two shotguns.

Active walked over and inspected them. No 30-30 Winchester carbine.

There was a noise behind the door, and an Inupiat woman opened it. She was in her early fifties, Active guessed. Her eyes were red and she clutched a soggy ball of Kleenex in one hand.

"Are you Mrs. Clinton?" he asked.

"We already hear about George," she said. "You don't need to come here."

"Well, I just need to ask a few questions for my report."

She let him into one end of a hallway that divided the house in half. At the opposite end was a partly drawn green curtain, and behind it a bathtub and a toilet.

27

"Daniel is in there." She pointed to a doorway off to the right. Active went in.

Daniel Clinton sat at a Formica-topped dining table with a cup of coffee in front of him. He had a round, mahogany face above a squat, solid-looking body. A small black-and-white television on the table was tuned to the state Bush channel, which was showing a *Wheel of Fortune* rerun. Clinton paid no attention to the coffee or the television. He was looking out across the lagoon to the white folds of tundra beyond. Unlike his wife, he was dry-eyed.

There was one other person in the room. A thin boy with long black hair, maybe fifteen, lay on a couch reading an Archie comic. If Kinnuk Wilson's story was right, this was Daniel Clinton's last son.

The boy looked up and said, "Don't look at me," as if reading Active's mind.

Daniel Clinton turned and saw Active. "You could go in the other room, Julius," he said. The teenager moved, but not to another room. Active heard the door out of the house slam, then the door of the *kunnichuk*. Clinton turned off the television.

"Thank you for coming to see us, Mr. Active," Clinton said. "I'm sorry if we bother you."

"I'm sorry for your trouble, Mr. Clinton."

"It's my fault, from something that happen long time ago," Clinton said. "You was gone in Anchorage with your *nalauqmiut* parents then."

Active wasn't surprised to find out how much Daniel Clinton knew about him. Since his arrival the year before, word had spread rapidly that the Chukchi baby adopted by white schoolteachers had grown up and come back as an Alaska State Trooper. Those who hadn't known his history had quickly dipped it from the river of gossip that coursed constantly through the streets of the village.

"I think I might have heard something about that," Active said, to let Clinton know he didn't need to talk about the curse if he didn't want to.

"Would you like some coffee, Mr. Active?" Clinton said. Obviously, Clinton didn't want to talk about it.

Active nodded and, when Clinton had poured him a cup, asked if George had acted different lately.

"No, he seem fine to me. He get a job at that Gray Wolf and he have some money, buy a new snowgo, he seem happy. He say he move out and get his own place pretty soon," Clinton said. "I start to think maybe George will be the one to make it. But I guess not."

The Gray Wolf was a huge copper mine that had opened a few months earlier a hundred miles north of Chukchi on Gray Wolf Creek. A Norwegian mining company named GeoNord ran it, but it was on land owned by Chukchi Region Inc., the Native corporation that all the Inupiat in the area belonged to. So the Norwegians hired a lot of Inupiat, and the work schedule was tailored to people who liked to hunt and fish: two weeks on, two weeks off, with the company paying for the plane rides back and forth to the Gray Wolf, or giving the equivalent in cash to those who preferred to ride their snowmachines.

"He just came back from the Gray Wolf?"

"Monday, I think. He hang out with his buddies, go down to that GeoNord office for something about his job, go rabbit hunting behind the lagoon, stay over at Emily Hoffman's, just run around. You know how it is with them young guys. I think he was going caribou hunting if that ice on Chukchi Bay ever get good again from this warm spell we had."

"Emily Hoffman?" Active wrote the name in his notebook.

"His girlfriend," Clinton said. "She's pregnant, I guess. I was thinking maybe she'll be his wife pretty soon."

"Do you know who he went to see at GeoNord?"

"He never tell me," Clinton said. "He just say he have to straighten something out. When he come back he just say everything is fine."

"They found a 30-30 rifle with him. Did he have one?"

"I keep one in my *kunnichuk*," Clinton said. "I could check if it's there."

"No, I looked on the way in," Active said. "It's not."

"He take that old 30-30?" Clinton said desolately in his husky, sibilant voice. "I teach him to shoot with that gun."

He looked out over the lagoon again. "I remember the first time I take him out on the ice for seal. It's spring day, sunny, blue sky, not much wind. We go out on snowgo, maybe fifteen, twenty miles where there's lots of airholes.

"I find pressure ridge by airhole that look like it get used a lot, and I put George up there to wait. He's just little guy, maybe eight or nine, but he lay there in his white parky real quiet for long time, watching that airhole.

"Finally that seal put his head through and I think maybe George will shoot too soon and that seal will fall back through the hole, maybe we lose it. But George don't shoot, he wait. Pretty soon that seal haul out on the ice and take one more look around before he go to sleep and that's when George shoot him. George hit him right in the eye and he don't even flop around, he just drop his head down like he's going to sleep.

"George, he look at me and he say, 'I'm a real Eskimo, now, huh, Pop?' "

Clinton stopped talking and picked at the edges of a triangular chip in the Formica. Someone had outlined the hole with a red crayon. "I never think he use that old Winchester for . . . for this."

Clinton stopped talking again and Active saw that now there were tears on his cheeks. Active closed his notebook and left.

Chapter 2
Wednesday Morning, Chukchi

"You still here?" he asked when he reached the Suburban. "That Oly is leaving this vehicle. It's your choice whether you go with it."

Wilson tossed the beer into the ditch in front of Daniel Clinton's house. "What did old Daniel say?"

"Police business, Kinnuk." Active started the engine and headed back uptown along Fourth Street. Fourth was on the back side of town. There weren't many houses, mostly just tundra pocked with rusting oil drums, dead snowmachines, and abandoned cars.

"Hey, wait a minute," Wilson said suddenly. "That's Pukuk." He pointed at a black-and-white mongrel barking beside the road. "That dog never leave Tillie."

"Tillie Miller? The old crazy woman?" Active remembered seeing her around town and hearing the city cops talk about her. As long as she was in city limits, she wasn't his problem, but he stopped the truck and started toward the dog with Wilson.

Before they reached Pukuk, they spotted Tillie's mukluks sticking out of the willows where the footpath from the Dreamland came out of the tundra onto Fourth. A couple of hundred yards north along the trail, the city cops were still gathered around George Clinton's body, the blue-and-white Chukchi ambulance now pulled up beside them.

At first Active thought Tillie might be dead too, but they heard snoring when they got close. She was lying on her back in the snow, and looked comfortable. One mittened hand cradled a half-bottle of the pure grain alcohol known as Everclear.

"What you gonna do, Nathan?"

"Maybe we should take her to the hospital."

"She don't look sick to me," Wilson said, stamping his feet against the cold. "Just drunk and asleep. Besides, the hospital won't take her anymore. They know how mean she is."

"Yeah, but she could have hypothermia." A gust of wind sucked a mouthful of snow off the tundra and spat it in Active's face.

He pulled down the earflaps of his hat and turned sideways to the blast.

"Sure, I heard of that," Wilson said. "It's when you get so cold you can't warm up. I'll try check." He dodged around Pukuk, who was yapping furiously in an effort to keep them away from Tillie, and slipped his hand down the neck of her caribou-hide parka.

"Nah, her titty's warm." He took the Everclear from her hand and put it in his pocket. "She's just passed out. She do this all the time. Her parky's good. We could just leave her."

"I don't think so, Kinnuk." Active went to her head, put his hands under her arms, and tried to lift her to a sitting position. She was, he discovered, built like a buffalo: short, but solid and heavy. He let her flop down again.

He couldn't arrest her, even for her own good. The courts had decreed that it wasn't a crime to fall down drunk in public in Alaska, however great the risk of being frozen like a Popsicle, watered by dogs, sucked dry by mosquitoes, or raped by passersby.

There was a limited exception for someone in imminent danger, but where would he take her? The city cops wouldn't help.

They were still busy with George Clinton's body and, like the hospital, preferred not to tangle with Tillie Miller.

"We could take her home," Wilson said, pointing. "That's her tent."

A hundred yards south and a block east, on Fifth Street, Active saw a wall tent with a wooden birdhouse mounted on the ridgepole, white canvas billowing in the wind.

"Poor old lady, the birds live better than she does," he muttered. But in Anchorage, she would have been one of the lost Natives who slept in the homeless shelters in the winter and in summer camped in Visqueen lean-tos along the creeks to poach salmon. Maybe a wall tent, a birdhouse, and a reputation as the meanest woman in Chukchi weren't so bad.

He crossed the road to open the clamshell doors at the back of the Suburban, then returned and put his hands under Tillie's arms again. Wilson took her feet and they staggered up onto the road and dumped her in. Pukuk was still yapping hysterically, so Active boosted him in too. He curled up on Tillie's chest and panted happily.

Active drove to the tent and went in to look around. A cot on one side, a table with a Coleman camp stove on the other, cardboard boxes filled with Tillie's food and gear, a small oil heater, a Coleman lantern hanging from the ridgepole, and a fifty-pound bag of dog food. He was surprised by the sense of order. Maybe Tillie wasn't as crazy as everyone said.

The cot was covered with caribou hides and a sleeping bag. He pushed off everything but the bottom two hides, and went back outside to the truck. They hauled Tillie in and laid her on the cot and piled the rest of the hides and the sleeping bag on her. Pukuk stretched out on the cot beside her, licked his crotch, curled his tail over his nose, and went to sleep.

They started to leave, but Active decided to check for himself that the old lady was warm under the hides and sleeping bag. He put his hand to the neck of her parka, chivalrously worked it around behind her head, and was wriggling it down to feel between her shoulder blades when she opened her eyes and spoke. The canvas of the tent creaked and popped in the wind, but he heard her clearly.

"Don't touch me, Goddamn you *nalauqmiiyaaq*," she rasped. Then she shut her eyes, rolled over, and resumed snoring.

Active knew a couple dozen Inupiaq

words. *Nalauqmiiyaaq* was one of them. It meant half-breed. Actually, it was a little worse than that. It pretty much meant "almost a white man." He heard it a lot.

"You're welcome, Tillie," he said. He shook his head and walked back to the Suburban.

When he got back to the public safety building, Evelyn O'Brien handed him the morning's mail.

The trooper secretary was a forty-something redhead whose husband sold Arctic Cat snowmachines. She was still attractive enough if you didn't mind a few extra pounds. Particularly on days like today, when her hair was a solid brick red. No trace of the gray that began to show toward the end of every month.

"Was your hair this red yesterday?"

"Shut up, Nathan."

"I heard Henri was back in town." Henri the Hairdresser commuted from Anchorage once a month to coif and color the women of Chukchi.

"Shut up, Nathan."

"Your secret is safe with me."

He flipped through the mail. Something from the state Division of Retirement and Benefits, something from trooper headquarters in Anchorage, a *Wired* magazine, a lingerie catalog addressed to "Box-holder," and a letter from the City of Nuliakuk.

He knew he should type up his report on George Clinton's suicide and send a copy to the city cops, a copy to headquarters in Anchorage, and a copy to his case file, which he hadn't started yet but planned to close as soon as he did, because this, thankfully, was Jim Silver's problem. Instead, he decided to read the letter from the City of Nuliakuk first. It was from Carlton Crane, the village's elderly and revered mayor. "Dear Mr. Trooper Active, please pardon my write you," it began.

As you will be know freezeup coming soon. Thats mean the snow-machine trail from Chukchi is opening again and thats mean ~~oar~~ our bootleggers start up again.

Last year, we ask Troopers three time to arrest our bootleggers, but they never arrest them. So we write again if you will come and arrest our bootleggers. Last year, they selling to kids and ~~all~~ old ladys, not just drunks, and we want them arrest before they do it this year.

39

We having our city council to special meeting Thursday at 3 oclock, and we invite you to come and tell us about arrest our bootleggers. Now theres Eskimo Trooper in Chukchi, I tell city council maybe troopers will help us.

Active folded the letter and put it back in the envelope, wishing there was something he could do for the old man. Liquor was legal in Chukchi but not in Nuliakuk, which was eighty-five miles up the coast at the mouth of the Nuliakuk River. And that was the root of Mayor Crane's problem.

In the summer, when the only way to get from Chukchi to Nuliakuk was by plane or a long, cold boat ride on the ocean, liquor wasn't much of a problem. Long cold boat rides were too much work for bootleggers, so that left airplanes. Arnold Frost, Nuliakuk's lone public safety officer, just met them at the village's beach airstrip, searched the luggage, and dumped out any liquor he found. It probably wasn't legal, but so far no bootlegger had hired a lawyer to bring an illegal-search-and-seizure case against Arnold.

After freezeup, however, Nuliakuk was a few easy hours by snowmachine from

Chukchi, day or night. The liquor traffic became impossible to police. Now it was late October and the snowmachine trails were opening up again, so Mayor Crane wanted Active to come up and cart away the local bootleggers before they started up in earnest for the winter.

If Nuliakuk had had a year-round problem, he might have been able to wangle some help for the mayor. But, because liquor came in only during the frozen part of the year, Nuliakuk averaged less violence than most other villages around Chukchi. When someone had punched the buttons on the bureaucratic calculator in Anchorage headquarters, Nuliakuk had missed the cut for the next undercover sweep, which was due in January.

Active grabbed the Chukchi region phone book from his desk and found Carlton Crane's number at home.

"Oh, thank you for calling," the old man said when Active identified himself. "Can you arrest our bootleggers? Yesterday they try to sell bottle to my grandson. He's only eleven. I can show you who they are."

"I know you can," Active said. "But it's not so easy for the troopers. We have to have something that will stand up in court."

"I will stand up in court."

"I know you will, but that's not enough for the courts," Active said. "We would have to send in an undercover trooper and let him live there until the bootleggers trust him enough to sell him some liquor. But that would cost too much. The state doesn't have so much money now that Prudhoe is running out of oil."

The old man was silent. Active heard only the slight wheeze of his breathing.

"We have to spend our money in villages that have more bootleggers," Active said. "Nuliakuk only has them in the winter."

"Our winters are pretty long," Crane said.

"Did you hear about our liquor election next week?"

"I hear," Crane said. "Tom Werner talk about it on radio."

"Well, if the ban passes, then we can keep liquor out of Chukchi," Active said. "That will mean the bootleggers can't buy it and take it to Nuliakuk. Maybe things will get better."

"Maybe they will," Crane said. "But best thing would be if you could arrest our bootleggers."

Active said goodbye to the mayor, turned on his computer, and started the report on George Clinton's death. Somebody in headquarters might actually read it, so he started with an explanation of how he happened to get involved in a city case, then described his conversation with Daniel Clinton. He decided to leave out the Clinton curse. Headquarters probably wouldn't be impressed by gossip from street riffraff like Kinnuk Wilson. But he did mention reports that other sons of Daniel Clinton had committed suicide.

When he finished, he grabbed the *Wired* and started down the hall.

Just then the office phone rang. Evelyn O'Brien answered and listened for a moment.

"You better watch out, Nathan," she said. "Lucy says Tillie Miller is on her way up."

"Oh, God." He took the phone. "Why didn't you stop her? What did she say?"

"She said, 'Where that Goddamn *nalauqmiiyaaq* cop?' " Lucy said.

That word again. "Maybe she didn't mean me. I'm no half-breed."

"That's your opinion," Lucy said.

He decided to stick with his original plan so he put down the phone and started down the hall.

Unfortunately, he had to pass the stairwell to get to the men's room. There was Tillie, almost to the top, and snorting like the buffalo she resembled.

"You stop, Goddamn you *nalauqmiiyaaq*," she grunted. He stopped. She climbed the last three steps and faced him.

"What is it, Tillie?" he asked, forgetting momentarily that she was deaf, at least according to the city cops.

"That *qauqlik* kill that boy," she said. "You catch him." She turned and stumped off down the stairs.

"Wait, what boy?" He followed her downstairs, pulling at her sleeve and feeling foolish. She didn't stop, turn, or speak until they were outside. Then she faced him again. "That *qauqlik* kill that boy. You catch him, Goddamn you *nalauqmiiyaaq*."

He stared into the wide brown face and the unreadable black eyes. She jerked her sleeve free, turned, and walked away up Third Street.

He went back in and walked over to the dispatcher's office.

"Does she come in here a lot?"

"Not much," Lucy said, grinning. "I think she likes you, *nalauqmiiyaaq*."

"She used a word I don't know, being a mere *nalauqmiiyaaq*. It sounded like 'coke-lick,' sort of."

44

" 'Coke-lick'?" Lucy said. "Doesn't sound like any Inupiaq word I ever heard."

"OK, that's not exactly what it sounded like. It sounded like she was hawking, getting ready to spit, at the same time."

"Let me call my grandma," Lucy said, donning her headset and poking buttons on the console.

"*Aana,* it's me," she said into the headset. "Nathan wants to know an Inupiaq word. Coke-lick, but like you're hawking to spit at the same time."

She listened, then looked at Active. "She says you should learn Inupiaq, then you won't be such a *nalauqmiiyaaq*. She'll teach you."

"Tell her the first lesson I want to learn is what 'coke-lick' means," he said.

Lucy relayed, then listened again.

"She says, will you give her a ride to bingo tonight in your trooper truck?"

Active grimaced. "OK, OK."

"She says, with the flasher on?"

Now he groaned. "Yes, with the flasher on."

Lucy told her grandmother the good news, then listened again. She looked at him. "*Qauqlik,* does that sound like it?"

"That's it."

"She says it's an old-timey word, it

means 'chief,' and you come at eight o'clock." Lucy punched a button on the console and took off her headset.

Lucy hoped Nathan would banter with her some more. But he just stood there thinking, his fingertips pressed to his forehead.

His face was so hard to read, with its wary deep-set eyes under the buzz-cut black hair. Sometimes it was a face that seemed completely closed. But there was something soft about the lips, a softness that seemed to say Nathan Active needed something. Or someone.

"So Tillie thinks you're the chief of the half-breeds, huh?" she asked, hoping the teasing would draw him out.

But he just rolled his eyes, turned, and started for the stairwell. He must have something on his mind, she decided.

Perhaps George Clinton's suicide was bothering him. The suicides bothered her too, but she had learned to push them out of her mind. There were so many. Nathan would probably learn too, when he had been in Chukchi longer.

As he disappeared up the stairs, she put her headset back on and punched in Pauline's number.

"Why did you do that?" she asked when her *aana* answered. "What will he think?"

"He won't think nothing," Pauline said. "He'll just think old lady needs ride to bingo."

"Don't you say anything!"

"I never tell him nothing," Pauline said. "I just want to meet him, see what he's like."

Active climbed the stairs to Jim Silver's third-floor office. The police chief was filling out paperwork, drinking coffee from a Styrofoam cup, and listening to "Mukluk Messenger" on Chukchi's public radio station.

The person-to-person messages were KSNO's most popular feature, an irresistible if unplanned mix of gossip, news, and entertainment.

"To Sis in Chukchi, from Eleanor in Nuliakuk," the announcer read. "Please get a case of Pampers at Arctic Mercantile and send them up by air. The store here is out and little Herbie really needs them."

"Poor Herbie." Active dropped into the chair in front of Silver's desk.

Silver looked up from his paperwork. "Ah, Nathan. How did Daniel take the news about George killing himself? Coffee?"

"Black," Active said. "I guess I'd say Daniel took it stoically. Not that I broke it to them. They'd already heard about it somehow. Anyway, Daniel didn't say much except that he figured it was his fault from something that happened a long time ago. He didn't say what it was, but Kinnuk Wilson says there's a curse on the family."

Silver grunted, went over to the coffeepot, poured some into another Styrofoam cup, and handed it to Active.

"You know, I find I don't care for coffee from your regular type of cup anymore," Silver said, sitting behind the desk again. "During my challenging, lucrative career in law enforcement, I've come to feel it takes Styrofoam fumes to unlock the full flavor of the bean. What do you think?"

"I think I'd like to hear about the Clinton curse."

"Yeah, the curse." Silver frowned reflectively. "You know, after the first Clinton boy killed himself and people started saying it was because of the curse, I figured old Billy Karl was the only one who could get it out of the other boys' heads. So I went and asked him to lift the curse. Probably the first time in the history of Chukchi there was an official police request for the practice of witchcraft. Probably the last time too."

"What did he say?"

"He didn't say anything. He was in his workshop, steaming the runners for a dogsled he was making. He just looked at me and turned Kay-Snow up louder."

"Hard guy," Active said.

"I thought maybe it would stop when he died a few years back, but it seems like the curse has a life of its own," Silver said. "Now we've got another Clinton boy killing himself."

"I guess."

"You guess what?"

"I guess George killed himself. But maybe there's another possibility."

Silver put down his coffee, leaned back in his chair, and crossed his arms. "Such as what?"

"Maybe somebody shot him."

"I know somebody did." Silver unfolded his arms, leaned forward, and pointed his index finger at Active, like a gun barrel. "George Clinton shot George Clinton. Just like Andrew Harker drowned Andrew Harker last August and Franklin Berry hanged Franklin Berry last month and some other kid is going to shoot himself or hang himself next month or next spring.

And if he doesn't do it himself, one of his buddies will do it for him when they're out drinking together, then tell me about it and ask me to let him kill himself. Or some kid will get drunk and fall out of a boat and drown, or he'll fall off his snow-machine and freeze to death on the trail, or he'll poison himself sniffing gasoline."

"You been out here too long, Jim?" Active asked. "You know what happens when white people stay in the Bush too long: They go crazy or they turn into drunks. Usually both."

"Sorry." Silver sighed, rubbing a corrugated cheek. "I've got two weeks off and a ticket to Hawaii for me and Jenny after the booze election next week. I promise to come back a better human being."

Silver opened one of the files on his desk and thumped the stack of papers inside. "What's got you so revved up about George Clinton? Everybody we've talked to, not to mention the physical evidence, tells the same story: His buddies and him meet at the Dreamland and drink all night. They leave at closing time, they split up. He walks over to the willows by the cemetery, where, I might point out, two of his brothers repose, likewise deceased at their own hands. He fishes his father's rifle out from where he hid it behind a tombstone, he points it at his Adam's apple, and pulls the trigger, which, I might also point out, relieves us of the necessity of explaining how the killer, if it wasn't George himself, got the 30-30. Case closed, right?"

"Well," Active said, "Daniel keeps that old Winchester out in his *kunnichuk,* which as far as I can tell doesn't even have a lock anymore. Anybody in town could have taken it about as easy as George. Did you talk to his girlfriend? Did she notice anything funny with him lately?"

"Haven't found her yet," Silver said. "I guess she's pregnant?"

"Yeah, that's what Daniel told me," Active said. "He thinks they were going to get married. You think she could have shot him?"

"Not a chance," Silver said. "Emily's just a kid. She could never cook up something like this. And if she did, she'd be knocking on my door in ten minutes to tell me about it. Look, it's a city case. Don't complicate it, huh?"

"OK, OK, just a couple more things," Active said. "How many suicides have you seen where they shot themselves in the Adam's apple?"

Silver reflected for a while. "I don't recall anybody ever shooting themselves in that exact spot," he admitted finally. "In the heart, in the temple, one in the crotch that bled to death before he could get to a doctor, though I always thought his wife did that after she caught him fooling around with her sister. Lots of them in the mouth, but nobody in the Adam's apple. But, look, it's almost impossible to hold a rifle to your temple, especially if you're drunk. And maybe George was afraid if he put it in his mouth, his lips would freeze to the barrel."

"He's about to shoot himself and he's worried about freezing his lips?"

"Maybe a guy would want to look normal in the casket," Silver said. "Maybe a guy would want to be able to change his mind at the last minute without having to rip his lips off. Come to think of it, I can't hardly remember anybody shooting themselves outside in cold weather. Usually, if it's cold, they'll do it inside. Maybe I never saw an Adam's-apple shot before because nobody ever shot himself outside in cold weather before."

"But maybe . . ."

Silver held up his hand and shook his head. "But the biggest problem with all this is that somebody would have to be trying to make a murder look like a suicide. That's way too cute for Chukchi, Nathan. Murder's pretty basic around here. A guy kills his buddy, then either kills himself or heads for my office. I remember one guy that beat his girlfriend to death, then put her body out in the *kunnichuk* for cold storage. Nobody even knew she was dead till he got tired of tripping over her and turned himself in three days later."

"All right, one more thing and I quit," Active said. "Tillie Miller paid me a visit."

"Lucky you," Silver said. "Any damage? She's got a vicious right hook."

"No, she must be in her nonviolent phase. She climbed up the stairs and blew dragon's breath on me and said, 'That *qauqlik* kill that boy.' "

"*Qauqlik?*" Silver said. "I don't recognize it."

"Neither did I. I guess the old-time Inupiat used it but you don't hear it much anymore. Lucy got her Aana Pauline to translate. It means the head man or chief, apparently. Tillie said a *qauqlik* killed George Clinton."

"She actually said the name? George Clinton?"

"No, she just said, 'That *qauqlik* kill that boy.' "

"Then how do you know she meant George Clinton, if she meant anything?" Silver said. "She's just a crazy old drunk. She could have been talking about something that happened thirty years ago, or she could have been talking about something that happened in a story her grandmother told her in whaling camp when she was a little girl, or she could have been talking about a dream she had while she was passed out."

"I know," Active said. "But there's one more thing. On my way back from Daniel Clinton's house, I found Tillie passed out in the bushes on Fourth Street. Right where that footpath from the Dreamland comes out of the tundra. You can see the cemetery from there. In fact, I could see you guys still at work on George. So Tillie could have seen something from where we found her. She could even have been right at the scene, maybe taking a rest on one of the graves, and seen it up close."

"Could be," Silver said. "More likely, it was just the Everclear talking. All I know is, there wasn't one shred of evidence on or around George Clinton's body that he was killed by anybody but George Clinton and I'm sure the autopsy is gonna show he was fairly drunk."

Active started to speak, but Silver raised a hand to stop him. "Look, in Chukchi you should take things at face value. I'd be the first one to tell you a cop has got to follow his gut, but mine's not twitching a bit on this. And it's a lot bigger than yours."

"I guess you're right," Active said with a shrug. "You know the town a lot better than I do."

The police chief drank from the Styrofoam cup and looked out the window onto Fourth Street. "What does your boss think about it?"

"Carnaby? He's down in Anchorage for a few days," Active said. "My report's in the file, like it's supposed to be."

"Well, may it rest in peace. Just like George Clinton."

Chapter 3

Wednesday Evening, Chukchi

The message light was blinking on his machine when he got home that night.

"This your *aaka*, Nathan," his birth mother said, the usual tease in her voice. "Your Uncle Jake send down fresh muktuk from Barrow. You better get over here, you want to be a real Eskimo."

He had heard on KSNO that Barrow had landed three bowheads in the fall hunt. Now whale parts were working their way through countless family trees to villages all over the Inupiat part of Alaska.

He hoped Martha Active Johnson wouldn't explain to him how the Active family tree ran through cousins, brothers, aunts, grandmothers, and in-laws all the way to Uncle Jake in Barrow. Martha would expect him to remember it if he wanted to be a real Eskimo and he was pretty sure he didn't. What he wanted to be was a real Alaska State Trooper, with a real transfer to Anchorage as soon as possible.

Still, he was starting to like whale hide with the fat still on, as long as the muktuk was fresh and cooked right. Especially when the alternative was making his own dinner, meaning another Mexican Fiesta from the freezer.

Not only that, staying in would mean spending time in the tiny, plywood-sided house the troopers rented for him. One small room served as the kitchen and living area. The furnishings consisted of a two-place dining table, a dung-yellow studio couch, two gray metal bookshelves, a gray metal office desk, and his computer, stereo, and TV. The bathroom was larger than an airline toilet only because it contained a tiny shower. The place had a cramped bedroom with a queen-size mattress but, mysteriously, no bed or box springs. Some fiscal year, no doubt, headquarters would approve his requisition for a new bed, but for now he slept on the mattress on the floor in a down trooper sleeping bag.

"Men!" Evelyn O'Brien had sniffed one day when she brought by some paperwork for him to sign. "You don't live in a place, you camp."

Besides everything else, the sewer was frozen again. The malodorous Arctic institution known as a honeybucket stood beside his toilet, and served the same purpose. More buckets under the sink drains in the bathroom and kitchen let him shave and wash dishes. But no contrivance he had been able to think of would allow him to bathe at home. He could shower at the Rec Center for five dollars, but Martha wouldn't charge anything.

He rounded up his bath things, put them in a gym bag, and went back out to the Suburban. He would be all right, as long as he didn't get trapped in a one-to-one conversation with Martha. He started the Suburban and headed for her house.

When he was born, Martha Active had been only fifteen, interested mainly in partying and sleeping around. So she had turned him over to two of her teachers at Chukchi High. Officially, his adoption by Ed and Carmen Wilhite had been *nalauqmiut*-style, complete with lawyers, court proceedings, and documents on long paper. In practice it had operated more as a village adoption, even after the Wilhites moved to Anchorage. They had let him keep his mother's last name and he saw her from time to time when she came to the city. She sent him Christmas and birthday presents and Carmen made him send her thank-you notes.

In time, Martha had tired of bars and strange beds. When he was five, she had graduated from high school and gotten a job as a teaching aide.

When he was ten, Ed and Carmen had dragged him to Chukchi to visit his birthplace and mother. But when the Wilhites saw how much he resented the woman who had sent him away, there were no more visits. He hadn't set foot in the place again until his first, dismaying assignment came down from trooper headquarters.

Still, the cord that tied him to his mother had never quite broken. The presents from Chukchi kept coming, even though he didn't write thank-you notes anymore. The Wilhites kept in touch with her and told him what she was doing. He assumed they kept her posted on his progress too.

About the time he was old enough for Little League, she had married Leroy Johnson, an electronics technician at the nearby air force radar site that had peered across the Chukchi Sea for Russian missiles and bombers until the Cold War ended. Two years later, the Wilhites reported, Martha and Leroy had produced a son.

And now, Martha seemed to have settled

into Chukchi's version of married, middle-class comfort. Leroy, who delivered stove oil for the local Chevron dealer, hunted and fished more than a lot of Inupiat. Martha now headed the teacher-aide program at Chukchi High. They lived in a modern house on a quiet back street with a new Ford Ranger in the driveway and three snowmachines — one for each Johnson — in the yard. Active parked the Suburban in front, went past the Ranger into the *kunnichuk*, and knocked on the inner door.

Leroy, Jr. opened it. The rich smell of boiled muktuk billowed out.

"Hey, Nathan," the twelve-year-old said. Sonny had inherited his mother's dark hair and eyes, but, thanks to Leroy, his skin was light enough to make it clear he was the product of two races.

"Hey, Sonny," Active said. In Chukchi, juniors were known as Sonny until the seniors died. Then they got to use their real first names.

"Your tip worked. I got to Phleebhut on Space Quest," Sonny said.

The boy ran off to a computer in a corner and resumed his game. Active walked over and watched the screen for a moment, trying to imagine his half-brother ending up like George Clinton. Was it possible? The house seemed so full of love. There was no curse on this family, not now, but who knew what time and Chukchi would do to them? Well, Martha and Leroy both worked and neither drank now, so maybe the Johnsons would be all right.

He turned and walked to where Martha and Leroy were seated at a big dining table with a heavyset Inupiat woman he didn't know. She wore a light calico parka with a pattern of tiny blue-and-red flowers on it, known locally as a *kuspuk*. She was older than Martha, he judged, but not old enough to be an *aana*, like Lucy's grandmother.

On the table sat a bowl of muktuk, some mustard, a jar of peanut butter, and a box of Sailor Boy pilot bread. A pot of coffee simmered on Martha's fancy propane-fired cookstove.

"Nathan, my baby!" Martha said. "Come get your muktuk! This my Cousin Clara, Clara Stone." Active nodded to the stranger and took a seat at the table.

Martha got up and fetched him a plate and cutlery from a row of cupboards along the wall near the stove. He helped himself to a chunk of muktuk and two big round pilot bread crackers. He spread mustard on the muktuk, sliced off a piece, bit into it, and savored the taste: fatty and succulent, like a pork roast, but with a slightly nutty flavor behind it.

Leroy ate his muktuk Inupiaq-style. He took a strip from the bowl, clamped his teeth on one end, and stretched the muktuk out tight with his left hand. With his right, he slashed downward with an Old Timer clasp knife, slicing the muktuk strip in two, and began chewing. The four-inch blade, Active calculated admiringly, had passed less than an inch from the tip of Leroy's nose.

Cousin Clara, for some reason, wasn't having any muktuk. She just sipped her coffee and fidgeted.

Martha followed the same practice as Leroy, except it was even more alarming to watch because she used the *ulu*, the traditional Inupiat woman's knife improved by the incorporation of white man's steel. It was shaped like a big piece of pie, with a bone handle at the apex and the sharpened edge on the outer arc. It flashed in front of her face like a guillotine as she ate the blubber.

Active couldn't imagine how the technique could be acquired without the loss of facial parts, but he hadn't seen any evidence of missing lips or noses in Chukchi. Evidently it was so simple even children and drunks could master it. Probably just a matter of getting up the nerve to try it, he decided.

He chewed his own muktuk — cut the Anchorage way, lying safely on a plate — and thought again what an odd match Martha and Leroy seemed.

Leroy was short and wiry, red-haired, and didn't talk much, especially if Martha was around. He was seven years younger than his wife, but when he wasn't out fishing, hunting, or hauling stove oil, he seemed content just to bask in her energy.

For Martha Active was like a sun in her house. She was just forty-one, no sign yet of middle-age fat, the black hair still glossy. Her face was smooth, except for laugh lines around the mouth and the sparkling black eyes.

A knowing grin usually played around those eyes and that mouth. Martha was always teasing, just as when she had left him the message about being a real Eskimo. But there was a point to her teasing. Her house ran smoothly, without anybody ever quite being aware that it didn't happen by itself. Active had never heard her make a direct request of Leroy or Sonny, but neither had he known either of them to refuse to do things her way.

He remembered when Martha's new propane stove had arrived the month before. For a week, it sat in the middle of the kitchen in its shipping carton. For a week, Martha said, "My Leroy will put it in for me." For a week, Leroy was busy with other things.

One Saturday, while Active was over to do his laundry, the matter had come to a head, or as close to a head as things ever came in Martha's house. He was drinking coffee with Martha when Leroy, who liked to sleep in on weekends if he wasn't hunting or fishing, finally got up around noon. He came to the door of the kitchen in a bathrobe, a towel over his shoulder.

"Sweetie, do I have any clean underwear?" he asked.

"Of course," Martha said. "Your T-shirts are on the top shelf and your shorts are on the bottom, just like always."

"No, they're not," Leroy said. "I looked in the closet."

"Oh, I guess I forgot to tell you," Martha said. "I moved them."

"You moved them? Where?"

"I put them in the new oven. Seem like if

64

we're not going to cook with it we could use it for a closet, ah?"

A sheepish-looking Leroy crossed to the oven, took out a set of underwear, and left the room without a word.

"I think my Leroy will put that stove in now," Martha had said with a huge grin. When Active had showed up the next day for Sunday dinner, Martha was cooking with gas, her old oil-fired range nowhere to be seen.

Maybe they weren't such an odd match after all, he decided. Two people with Martha's energy probably would have ended up killing each other. And two as mellow as Leroy probably would have ended up in abject poverty, with an oil cookstove.

He found himself grinning as he remembered the affair of the gas range. "Hey, Leroy," he said. "This new stove sure cooks nice, huh?"

"I guess," Leroy said with a pained look.

"So what have you been up to?" Active didn't hunt or fish much, so he found it hard to talk with Leroy, who thought of little else.

"I was going across to the Katonak River for whitefish today, but I didn't go," Leroy said. "I don't know if I can handle that ice on Chukchi Bay yet."

"Still soft from the warm spell, huh?" The conversation was veering toward weather, which bored Active even more than hunting and fishing. But it looked like he was caught. "Why stop at the Katonak? I thought the fishing was better over on the Nuliakuk."

"Kay-Snow said there's another fish kill over there," Leroy said.

"Did they say what it is this time?" Active finished a piece of muktuk and swallowed some coffee. He put peanut butter on a piece of pilot bread and took a bite.

"They say it's all that rain we had in the fall," Leroy said. "The ground is too wet to soak it up so a lot of minerals are flushing into Gray Wolf Creek and it carries them into the Nuliakuk."

Leroy pushed his plate back, wiped the Old Timer with a napkin, and studied the blade intently. He pulled a small whetstone from a sheath on his belt and began stroking it with the Old Timer. Leroy's hands were always busy.

"Too much rain?" Active asked. "I thought when we had that dry spell last summer they said it was low water killing the fish."

"Yeah, the water in the Nuliakuk was so low even the normal amount of minerals was too much. That's what they said."

"And they're saying it's not the mine this time either?" Active asked.

"That's what they say." Leroy stopped whetting for a moment and drew the Old Timer's blade along the hair of his forearm. He inspected the result, squinted, spat on the whetstone, and went back to work.

"They say the environmental controls at the mine are good and it's not affecting the creek," he continued. "I dunno, though. I never heard of any fish kills up there before the Gray Wolf started."

"Well, I suppose GeoNord knows what it's doing. Plus the Department of Environmental Protection watches them pretty close."

"I guess," Leroy said.

Martha cleared her throat. "You guys done talking about fishing? Cousin Clara want to talk to you, Nathan." She nudged the other woman.

He braced himself. Cousin Clara no doubt had a daughter or a niece who was lovely, lonely, accomplished in the domestic arts, and embarked on a suitable career. In short, a fitting daughter-in-law for Martha Active Johnson.

"That Aaron never come home yet," Cousin Clara said, suddenly and anxiously.

"What?" Active asked.

"That Aaron never come home yet," she repeated. "He say he come home this morning."

"I'm lost," Active said. "Who's Aaron? Where did he go?"

"Her husband have a camp over by Katy Creek," Martha said. "He go there Monday, tell Clara he stay couple nights, hunt caribou, get his trapline ready for when season open, then come home this morning."

Active had never been to Katy Creek, but he had gathered from casual conversation it was north across Chukchi Bay, near the mouth of the Katonak River.

"I tell her not to worry," Martha said. "Aaron is late before. I tell her he's just waiting for the ice to get good."

They both looked at Cousin Clara.

"He say he come home Wednesday morning when ice is hard from cold night," she said with a stubborn frown. "It's Wednesday night now."

"I think maybe Aaron could have come back today," Leroy said. They looked at him. "I saw a couple of the older guys go across by snowmachine this morning all right. I think if they could do it, Aaron could. He knows the ice better than anybody."

Despite his upbringing in Minnesota, Leroy's speech had picked up traces of village English. As far as Active could make out, Leroy tried to be like Chukchi's expert old Inupiat hunters in everything he did, even talking.

"Did you check with Search and Rescue?" Active asked Cousin Clara. "Did she check with Search and Rescue?" he asked his mother.

"I talk to them," Cousin Clara said. "They say he's probably just waiting for the ice to get good. Then they say they're about out of gas money. Some kind of problem with their physical year."

"Could that be fiscal year?" Active asked.

"That's what I say, their physical year," Cousin Clara said.

"You could try check, ah, Nathan?" his mother said.

"Well, Search and Rescue is supposed to decide when to start a search," Active said. A hunter a half-day late in Chukchi was barely late at all. Carnaby would fry him if he burned up travel money checking on this one. "We troopers are supposed to

69

leave it up to them. It's in our interagency agreement."

The two women stared at him. Leroy stared at him. The only sounds were the simmering of the coffeepot and whoops, whistles, and explosions from Sonny's computer game at the other end of the room.

"He say he come home Wednesday morning," Cousin Clara said again. "He tell me that when he call from the Gray Wolf."

It took a moment to click. "The Gray Wolf? Mr. Stone works at the Gray Wolf?"

"Yes," Cousin Clara said, speaking slowly and patiently. "I tell you already: He get off Monday and he call me and say he ride his snowgo to Katy Creek, stay couple days, hunt caribou, then come home Wednesday morning. Now it's Wednesday night."

"How did his snowmachine get to the mine?"

"How you think? He ride it there when he go on shift two weeks ago," Cousin Clara said with a pitying look at Active. "He always ride back and forth to mine in winter. Then he can hunt on the way."

Cousin Clara rattled a question at Martha in Inupiaq, speaking too rapidly

70

for Active to follow. Leroy, whose Inupiaq was pretty good, smiled and looked at his coffee. Martha giggled and shook her head.

"What did she say?" Active asked.

"She ask me if you went mental from being at Anchorage too long," Martha said.

"Can a plane land at Aaron's camp?" Active asked Cousin Clara.

"That Cowboy can," she said. "He take us up there sometimes."

"Cowboy Decker? We have a contract with him," Active said. "I could take a look tomorrow."

"You don't have any problem with your physical year?" Cousin Clara asked.

He smiled and shook his head, then looked at Martha. "Can I use your phone, *aaka?*"

He went down the hall to Martha and Leroy's bedroom, pulled the skinny Chukchi region directory out from under the phone on the nightstand, looked up the number, and dialed.

"Cowboy," he said. "This is Nathan. Can you take me up to Nuliakuk tomorrow morning, maybe around eight o'clock? The city council wants to talk to me about bootleggers."

"Sure," Decker said. "We'll take the

71

Cessna. I got a load of soda pop for the store up there anyway. I'll give you a seat rate instead of the charter rate."

"No, bring the Super Cub."

"The Super Cub?" Decker protested. "I can't haul you and the pop in the Super Cub, and it'll take twice as long. And cost the troopers more."

"I need to land at Katy Creek on the way and check something."

"OK," Decker said. "The Super Cub it is, then. You're paying."

"Just make sure the invoice shows it as a charter to Nuliakuk," Active said. That way, his freelance search-and-rescue work wouldn't show up on the books.

Active hung up and dialed Evelyn O'Brien's home number.

"Evelyn," he said when the trooper secretary answered. "It's Nathan. I'm going up to Nuliakuk tomorrow for a city council meeting. But I'm leaving real early and I won't be in the office before I go. Will you call Mayor Crane and let him know I'm coming? In fact . . . do they have a fax machine in Nuliakuk? . . . Good. Look, after you call him, write the mayor a letter saying I'm coming, sign it for me, and fax it to him too, will you? Just make sure the paperwork's all there."

He went into the bathroom and showered. Then he went back to Martha's kitchen for another helping of muktuk and pilot bread. He was enjoying the warm feeling that muktuk always spread through his body when the telephone in Martha's kitchen rang. She answered, then handed it to him.

"It's that Lucy," she said, a frown in her voice.

"Nathan," the dispatcher said, "where are you? My Aana Pauline says you didn't pick her up for bingo."

He looked at his watch, and groaned. "I'm on my way."

"Don't forget to turn on your flasher," Lucy said.

He hung up and looked at his mother. "I have to go. I promised to give Pauline Generous a ride to bingo."

He went down the hall to the bathroom to collect his shower things. He was rolling up his towel when his mother spoke from behind him.

"Is that Lucy going to bingo too?"

"I don't know. I don't think so." He dropped the towel into the gym bag. "Why?"

"Somebody tell me you talk to her at work sometimes."

God, how did women find these things out? "I talk to everybody at work. It doesn't mean anything."

Martha watched silently as he dropped a plastic bottle of shampoo into his gym bag, then pulled it out, tightened the cap, and dropped it in again. "Lucy's pretty, ah?"

In his mind's eye he suddenly saw her. Hair like a raven's wing, the face an impossible study in reflected diagonals: mouth curving up at the corners, upturned almond eyes, slanting brown cheekbones.

"I'm too busy with work to notice things like that."

"That's good. You'll get ahead that way."

He dropped in a stick of deodorant and a bar of soap in a red plastic case. "What if I did notice Lucy?"

"I guess she's nice, for a village girl."

"You mean an Inupiat girl? Should I look for somebody white, like you did with Leroy?"

"Maybe it's better if she's Eskimo, but white's OK. Main thing is, you should look for girl like you," Martha said. "Smart, went to college, good job. Village girl will never do anything but have babies, play bingo, and get fat."

"Would a village girl give her baby away like an extra pup?"

74

Instantly, he regretted his lapse of control. He knew he should let his mother undo the past, or at least think that she had, but he could never leave the sore spot untouched for long. She put her head down and he knew she was crying.

"I'm sorry," he said. "I didn't mean to say that."

"No, no, you're right, Nathan," Martha said, tears glistening on her cheeks. "You were my baby and I gave you away. But . . ."

"We don't have to go through this again, *aaka*. It always comes out the same."

"But I did it because I loved you. I knew I couldn't take care of you right," she said. A switch had been thrown and now there was no stopping her. "So I found somebody else to do it. Weren't Ed and Carmen good to you?"

He pulled out his handkerchief and handed it to her. "Of course they were, but they're not Inupiat. Now I don't know what I am."

"That was bad time for me, just drinking and sleeping around," she said. She wiped her eyes and put his handkerchief in the pocket of her slacks. "I thought Eskimos were all going to hell like me. It's white man's world, that's what I thought. So I

75

gave you to white people. That's one reason I marry Leroy after I straighten out, because he's white."

"And now?"

"Now I see Eskimos can learn like white people," she said. "You're smart. Sonny, he's learning to program that computer you give him. Tom Werner's smart. Look what all he do for us, leading our corporation and getting the Gray Wolf and everything. And now maybe he will get liquor banned in Chukchi."

"Maybe he will."

"Anyway, Nathan, I'm sorry if I mess up." She looked at him. He looked down and fiddled with the zipper of the gym bag. "I always try to take care of my responsibility best way I can. When you're born, that seem like giving you to white people."

"I know you did what you thought was right."

"And now that you're back up here, I try to see you end up with good wife. That's mother's responsibility too, ah?"

"It's my responsibility, *aaka*. But I promise to submit her for your approval when I find her." He smiled and touched her shoulder.

She was silent, still studying him.

"What is it?"

"Are you careful, Nathan?"

"About what?"

"About, you know." She reached out into the hall, where her parka hung from a hook. She pulled a box from one of its pockets and handed it to him.

"We give these to the kids at school if it seem like they're fooling around," she said.

"*Aaka!* I don't need these. And if I did I'd get them myself. You don't get them from your mother!"

"You take them," she said. She dropped the condoms into his gym bag and zipped it up. "You don't want baby before you're ready to take care of it, like me."

A few minutes later, he stopped in front of Pauline Generous's tiny log cabin and turned on the flasher. The yard held a dead Datsun pickup and two snow-machines, also apparently long dead. Three stove-oil drums sat by one wall. A fourth rested on a wooden cradle, with a copper tube running into the house.

A little old bowlegged lady in a red calico parka came out and climbed in beside him.

"About time you get here, *nalauqmiiyaaq*." She glared at him, her eyes huge behind thick-lensed glasses.

He turned off the flasher. "Be nice," he said.

"Hmmph!" she said. He turned the flasher back on, and started toward the Lions Club bingo hall.

"You know Tillie Miller?" Active asked.

"Everybody know Tillie. I think she's my cousin, maybe."

"You think she's mental?"

"Everybody think she's mental," Pauline said. "I think maybe she just get mean from can't hear so long and drink so much. Lonesome, probably."

"You think I should listen to what she says?"

"You should always listen to what old lady says, *nalauqmiiyaaq*. How you like Chukchi?"

Chapter 4

Thursday Morning, Katy Creek

Active stopped the trooper Suburban in front of Cowboy Decker's house on Second Street. He knocked at the door and waited, grateful for the overnight improvement in the weather.

Morning was breaking sharp and cold under a flint blue sky. It was twelve below, according to KSNO, but the west wind had eased off and consequently it felt warmer than yesterday. Still, twelve below was twelve below. He knocked again. Another wait, and the pilot came to the door barefoot, in Levi's and a T-shirt.

"Hiya, Nate," Decker said in his loud confident bray. "Come on in. What time is it, anyway?"

"A little before eight, like I said on the phone last night," Active said. "You gotta get off Village Standard Time, Cowboy."

Decker pulled back the curtain from a small window over the kitchen sink and peered out. The rising sun bathed his face, picking out silver pinpoints here and there in the morning stubble.

"Damn fine flying weather!" He turned back to Active. "What time's your meeting with the city council anyway?"

"Three o'clock."

"Geez, what's the rush? It's only about an hour and a half to Nuliakuk, even in the Super Cub. You want to take the Cessna, it's under an hour."

"No, no, I need to go by Katy Creek on the way. Remember?"

Decker shrugged again. "It's your nickel."

The pilot made a cup of instant coffee under the hot-water tap, stood over the sink, and ate two slices of pizza from the refrigerator. There was no sign of Decker's wife, who taught fifth grade at Chukchi Elementary. Active guessed she had already left for school.

Decker finished dressing, grabbed his flight case from the floor by the door, and they set out for the airport.

Cowboy's real name was Bill. His uniform was a leather bomber jacket, steel-frame glasses, and a baseball cap. When he wasn't flying or eating, he kept a cigarette clamped between strong yellow teeth. He was about forty-five, Active guessed.

"Too bad about Daniel Clinton's boy

80

killing himself, huh?" he asked as the Suburban bounced along.

"Yeah," Active said. "Too bad."

"I heard it was his turn, though," Decker said. "The Eskimos say there's a curse on the family."

"You believe that, Cowboy?"

"I don't believe in anything but having plenty of airspeed, altitude, and avgas," Decker said. He laughed hoarsely at his own Bush-pilot humor.

They reached the airport. Active stopped the Suburban beside Lienhofer Aviation's red-and-white Super Cub.

Decker took off the bomber jacket, pulled a pair of insulated coveralls from the back of the Super Cub, and worked them on over his Levi's and T-shirt. They were stained with oil and gave off a sharp tang of avgas. He put the bomber jacket back on, over the coveralls.

Decker slipped his flight case under the front seat, then untied the Super Cub. He removed the insulated engine cover, pulled a catalytic preheater from the engine compartment, snuffed it, and stowed both behind the passenger seat. He checked the gas tanks and the oil, and said, "I think it'll probably fly."

Active put his evidence kit in back of the

passenger seat, on top of Decker's stuff, then crawled in. The uncomfortable little Bush plane was so narrow that his seat was behind the pilot's, as if they were astraddle the same horse. They put on headsets so they could talk over the roar and rattle of the Super Cub in flight.

Decker cranked up and they taxied out to the runway. The kite-like craft rolled only three hundred feet before lifting off into the cold air.

Decker turned out to the north and climbed to cross the bay toward Katy Creek. The bay's protected waters were frozen, but, off to the west toward Siberia, the ocean was still open, and perfectly calm in the morning air. From the north shore of the bay, the coastline ran northwest until it vanished into blue gauze where sky and sea merged.

Due north, over the tops of the Sulana Hills, Active could see the jade coils of the Katonak River, newly frost-edged, snaking away into the white folds of the Brooks Range.

He wasn't sure when Chukchi bothered him more. Yesterday, it had been close and gray and mean, but at least it had seemed easy then to stick with his plan to stay un- involved and get out at the first opportunity. Today, the Arctic opened itself before him, blue and limitless and intoxicating, and he felt himself being pulled in. It was the same sensation of weightless vertigo he felt when he contemplated the lips and eyes of Lucy Generous.

At the north shore of the bay, he asked Decker to drop down and head for Aaron Stone's camp on Katy Creek.

"What are we looking for?" Decker asked through the intercom, lowering the plane's nose.

"Aaron Stone," Active said. "He went to his camp for a few days and didn't come back on time. His wife, Clara, asked me to check on him. On my way to Nuliakuk."

The country crawled past below. Countless small lakes, one band of seven caribou, scattered singles and pairs. The stunted spruces that passed for trees around Chukchi cast long spears of blue shadow across the tundra in the slanting light of the Arctic sun.

A cabin here and there, a few snowgo tracks, but no sign of a man on a snowmachine, or on foot. It was still too soon after the thaw for most people to cross the ice from Chukchi. And it was too early in the winter for many workers at the Gray Wolf to have started using their snowgos, as Aaron Stone did, to travel back and forth.

Decker followed the shoreline to the mouth of Katy Creek, then flew upstream to buzz Aaron's cabin. Three frozen caribou carcasses lay beside it, but there was no snowmachine out front, no smoke from the chimney.

Decker circled, lined up on a barren stretch of creek bank near the cabin, and set the Super Cub down. The Bush plane's fat tundra tires easily negotiated the inch or two of new snow on top of the hard-frozen older snow and tundra beneath.

The Super Cub bounced to a stop and they got out. Decker pulled the engine cover from behind the passenger seat and draped it over the nose of the plane to keep it from cooling down in the cold air.

They walked to the cabin, and found the door padlocked. "You got a key?" Decker asked.

"No," Active said, peering in through a window. "We can just break it."

"Hang on," Decker said. He walked around the cabin, looking up into the trees. "Here we go," he said. "These guys always leave one around somewhere." He reached up into the crotch of a spruce and retrieved a small silver key. Active, feeling slightly shown-up, said nothing.

Aaron's cabin measured twelve feet by sixteen, three sheets of plywood by four, with silver-backed fiberglass insulation between the studs. An oil stove squatted in a back corner, with bunk beds lining the nearest walls. To the left of the door, wooden Blazo crates had been nailed together for shelves, with a Blazo-burning camp stove sitting on top. In the middle of the cabin stood a card table with three folding chairs and a square five-gallon can of Blazo fuel for seats.

On the card table, they found some dried salmon, half a bowl of frozen chili, and a box of pilot bread, along with a half-empty Jack Daniel's bottle and a carton of Lucky Strikes. On one of the folding chairs lay an empty cardboard box that had once held twenty cartridges for a .308 Winchester rifle. A trashbox beside the shelves held, among other things, another Jack Daniel's bottle, this one empty.

"You been in here before?" Active asked.

"Lots of times," Decker said. He lit a cigarette.

"Anything look different?"

"Nah, it's all about the same," Decker said. "I don't ever remember seeing any liquor up here before, but I never really looked." He kicked the trashbox. The Jack Daniel's bottle rattled against a chili can.

Active surveyed the rest of the cabin. A sleeping bag was unrolled on one of the bunks, a pillow at the open end suggesting it had been slept in at least one night. Spare clothes and some camping gear were jumbled on another bunk, and an old shotgun leaned in a corner. There was no rifle.

They went back outside. Snowmachine and sled tracks, dimly visible under the most recent layer of snow, radiated from the camp in various directions. There was no way of knowing which to follow, even if following one from the air had been possible.

"What do you want to do, Nate?" Decker asked around his cigarette.

"Let's look for him," Active said. "He didn't take much gear, so he wasn't planning to go far, maybe just out on his trapline."

The pilot dropped his cigarette in the snow and climbed into the plane. Active stood uncertainly by the wing.

"Get in," Decker said.

Active shook his head. "Hold it a minute." He dug into his evidence kit for plastic bags, went back into the cabin, and slipped one down over the Jack Daniel's bottle on the table without touching it. He worked a ballpoint pen into the mouth of the bottle in the trashbox and dropped it into another plastic bag.

Then, quickly but thoroughly, he searched the cabin, looking in the duffel on the bunks, the shelves in the cooking area, every place in the cabin that might hold — what? He didn't know, but he didn't find it.

He left the cabin, walked to the Super Cub, and stowed the bottles behind his seat. He turned to find Decker watching, a quizzical expression on his face. Active shrugged. "Can't hurt," he said.

Active climbed in and they took off. Decker spiraled the plane outward from Aaron's cabin, each loop a half-mile from the last. Active scanned the tundra to the plane's left, and Decker searched to the right. Thirty minutes passed, then an hour. They saw nothing of a snowmachine or a man on foot or a makeshift camp or any sign of life at the other cabins in the area.

"Nate, if we don't head for Nuliakuk soon we'll have to go back to Chukchi for more gas," Decker said.

"If we don't go to Nuliakuk, how long can we keep searching here?" Active asked.

"Hour and a half, two hours," Decker answered.

"Keep searching," Active said.

But the search lasted only another ten minutes.

"Hey, Cowboy, come around again," Active said as they passed over a stand of spruces on a little knoll at the end of a kidney-shaped lake.

"You see something?"

"Maybe," Active said. "Down in the trees there."

Decker circled, slowed the Super Cub to sixty miles per hour, and floated toward the grove, fifty feet above the treetops. Active directed the pilot right and left so that they passed over the thing in the spruces. Pretty clearly, Active saw a dogsled, empty except for a Blazo box lashed to the stanchions at the rear. He could just see the back of the snowgo the sled was hitched to, and the suggestion of a large T-shaped object on the seat of the machine.

"Can we land?" Active asked.

"I'll have a look at the lake," Cowboy told the trooper in the back seat. "Kinda touchy this time of year, especially with the thaw. Ice might still be kinda thin."

The wind had broomed the snow on the lake into long parallel dunes. He lined up on a strip of bare ice between two dunes and flew down it at fifty-five, as slow as you could trust a Super Cub to fly.

The ice looked good. Gray-green, with a few cracks webbing the surface. Not black and perfect like ice was when it was new and thin and deadly. Not beautiful, as the Eskimos called the ice that would kill you.

He came around again and bounced the Super Cub's wheels off the surface once, twice. He circled and made another pass at fifty-five, studying the ice. It showed no sign his wheels had ever touched it. No cracks, no dark spots from water welling up to signal he'd broken through.

"Let's give 'er a shot," he said through the intercom. He circled, lined up on the bare streak again, and gently set the plane onto it. The ice felt good. Solid, no sign of unusual drag, as there would be if the wheels were breaking through.

Still, it didn't hurt to be careful. He kept some throttle on and taxied rapidly along the bare streak until he reached the end of the lake, where he drove the main wheels up onto shore. "No substitute for solid ground," he told the trooper. He pulled a knob on the control panel and the engine coughed to a stop.

The lake and woods were silent and deserted, except for a raven that flapped in to watch from the top of a dead spruce. *"Tularuk,"* it called.

Active got his evidence kit from behind the passenger seat, Decker threw the cover over the plane's nose to keep the engine warm, and they walked to the clump of trees on the snowmachine trail, the snow crunching deafeningly under their boots. Decker took one look, paled, and turned away.

"That him?" Active asked the pilot's neck and shoulders.

"Yeah, it's Aaron," Decker said.

Aaron Stone lay on his back on the seat of the snowgo, arms flung out as if starting a swan dive into the lake of blue sky above. He wore a parka with a fur ruff on the hood, a baseball cap, and a green Refrigiwear snowmachine suit. His leather-and-rubber Sorel boots still rested on the running boards of the Yamaha. His eyes were covered by mirror sunglasses; his waxen face looked surprised under a light covering of snow. There was a small hole in his throat and a lot of blood on the snowmachine seat under his neck. There was so much blood it had dribbled off and puddled on the running boards around his Sorels.

A .308-caliber semiautomatic Winchester hunting rifle with a telescopic sight lay beside the trail just ahead of Aaron's Yamaha. Across the machine's skis lay a bare spruce branch, with a fork at the tip. It appeared that Aaron had stopped in the spruce copse, propped the stock of the rifle on the Yamaha's windshield, put the muzzle to his throat, and pushed the trigger with the spruce branch. He had then fallen backward on the seat, while rifle and spruce branch were thrown forward by the recoil.

Active studied the trail before and behind the Yamaha, and the snow beside it.

"Two suicides in one week," Decker said from behind him. "That's kinda weird, even for Chukchi. Must be something in the water, huh?"

Active turned and saw that the pilot had recovered his normal color and some of his normal bravado.

"Here's something else that's weird," Active said. "Look at the trail here. Stay back, stay back, just look from where you are. You see those old snowmachine tracks under the new snow? Now look around

91

Aaron's snowgo. You see any boot tracks under the snow?"

"No," Decker said. "So?"

"Wouldn't a man want to stand beside his snowgo a few minutes and think it over before he killed himself? Maybe take a leak, have a last smoke? And see that spruce branch on the Yamaha's skis there? He probably used it to push the trigger, right?"

Decker nodded.

"Well, look at this tree." Active pointed at the only spruce within reach of the Yamaha's seat. "See, no sign a branch was broken off. So where did he get it?"

"He could have pulled it off another tree back down the trail," Cowboy said. "Maybe that's where he took his last leak and had his last smoke."

"Of course he could," Active said. "But why wouldn't he just shoot himself there? Why would he bring it here?"

"You think somebody killed him and made it look like he did it himself?"

Active shrugged.

Decker pulled out a cigarette and lit up. "That kind of stuff never happens around here, Nate. Somebody gets drunk, gets mad, blasts his woman or his best friend, then turns himself in. Nobody in Chukchi ever plans anything more complicated than a hunting trip."

Active was silent as they surveyed the scene again. "Yeah, you're probably right, Cowboy. It's probably just another suicide. Can you put him in the Super Cub?"

"Not with you, and probably not at all the way he's frozen with his arms spread out," Decker said. "We need the Cessna."

"Well, go get it," Active said. "Call Evelyn from the airport and tell her to set up an autopsy. And get her to call Mayor Crane and let him know I won't make his city council meeting."

"You're not coming?" Decker said. "You're going to stay here by yourself with the . . . with Aaron? What if something happens? What if the 206 is out on a trip and I don't get back tonight?"

"I'll walk to a cabin, or drive Aaron's Yamaha." Active pulled a Nikon from his evidence kit. "I've got a couple hours of work here and I want to get it done before dark. If I leave now, somebody else may come down the trail here and disturb the scene. Or our friend there might decide to have a snack." He pointed at the raven in the dead spruce.

The bird launched itself from the top of the tree and circled them. *"Tularuk,"* it chuckled twice. Then it winged away. Decker shuddered.

Active looked at the pilot. "The raven is the only animal that laughs. That's what the *aanas* say, Cowboy." COOKA BURAS DO TOO

Chapter 5
Thursday Evening, Katy Creek

The short Arctic day was dying in a spray of salmon and rose on the southwest horizon when he heard the snowmachine coming. He looked around as the buzz got louder, but couldn't tell the direction. He walked rapidly into the indigo shadows of the spruce grove, leaving his evidence kit open on the snow beside the Yamaha. He removed his right glove, unsnapped the holster of the .357, and waited. The buzz stopped coming from everywhere and came only from the north.

Soon the noise became a light bouncing down the trail through the twilight. Active pulled the .357 from its holster and held it behind his right hip. Somewhere in an undisciplined corner of his mind, he noticed that the grip of the revolver was very cold and hoped that this would be over soon, so he could put the gun back in its holster and the glove back on his freezing right hand.

The light stopped behind Aaron Stone's

Yamaha and the other machine sputtered into silence. The driver, visible now that the headlight was off, had a rifle slung across his back. He stood up on the running boards, stared for a long time at Aaron Stone, then looked straight at Active in the spruces.

"It's all right, Mr. Active," the driver called out. "You don't need to shoot me. My grandson send me to tell you that Cowboy not coming back tonight and you can stay at my cabin."

Active holstered the gun, put his glove on, and stepped out of the grove, trying to think what to say first. Finally, he took off the glove again and extended his hand to the driver, a small old Inupiaq with a trace of mustache and chin whiskers. "Nathan Active," he said.

"I'm Amos Wilson." The old man pulled off an elbow-length fur mitten, letting it dangle from a cord looped around his neck, and shook Active's hand. "Harold send me message on Kay-Snow, say you're stuck out here by yourself, I should come get you. He don't say why, but he tell me not to be surprised about anything I find. I guess this what he mean." He looked at the corpse on the Yamaha. "Did Aaron shoot himself?"

"We're not allowed to talk about our investigations," Active said. "I'm sorry." The old man looked quickly at him, then away.

"You said Harold told you I was here?" Active asked. "Who's Harold?"

"Harold Wilson, my grandson," Wilson said. "I guess he have another name they use sometimes, but I always call him Harold."

It dawned on Active. "Kinnuk Wilson is your grandson?"

The old man looked aside, then down at the snow between the toes of his caribou mukluks. "I always call him Harold."

"But Kinnuk sent you? How did he know where I was?"

The old man was silent for a long time. "I always call him Harold."

Active shrugged. "Harold sent you? How did he know where I was?" he repeated.

"I guess that Cowboy tell my grandson and he remember I come here last night. Harold's message on Kay-Snow say you're at Qaqsrauq Lake. That what we call this place, *qaqsrauq*. You know what is, *qaqsrauq?*"

Active shook his head. "My Inupiaq isn't very good. A bird of some kind?"

"*Qaqsrauq* is loon. Loons live here in

summer, so we call it Qaqsrauq Lake. I don't think white man map have name for it."

"You came up last night?" Active asked.

"About four o'clock this morning. When ice is thick from cold."

"Did you see anything . . . about this?" Active nodded toward the corpse.

"No, I go to my cabin, sleep little while, then go north when it get light. I never come this way until Harold send me message about you."

"No other snowmachines came or went?"

"No, just mine."

"Any airplanes?"

"I see that Cowboy's Super Cub couple times, think maybe he's caribou hunting, but I guess he's bring you," Wilson said. "That's only one."

"Can you tow Aaron back to your cabin?"

"I guess so," Wilson said. "But plane can't land there, so we have to bring him back in morning when Cowboy pick you up."

"Let's leave him here then," Active said.

"We could put this over him." Wilson pulled a canvas snowmachine cover from a wooden box lashed to the rear of his own sled.

The old man looked away while Active tied the cover over Aaron Stone. Then the trooper stepped onto the runners at the tail of the sled. Wilson started the snowgo, swung around in a big circle, and headed back up the trail.

In a few minutes, he pulled up in front of a cabin that, like Aaron Stone's, stood on a bank above Katy Creek. He left the Arctic Cat idling, its headlight shining into a window, and disappeared through the door. Active could see him moving about inside, holding a camp lantern up to the headlight's beam, pumping air into the pressure tank, inspecting its wick.

Active studied the dome-shaped little dwelling. Except for the stovepipe poking through the roof and the door and window, it was made of sod, squares of tundra laid like bricks.

The lantern came on inside. Wilson came out and shut off the Arctic Cat. "I call it my beaver house," he said.

They went in. Wilson pulled some pilot bread and a can of beef stew from a shelf under his camp stove. "I'm sorry I never catch any caribou yet," he said. "We have to eat white man food. Did you see the herd when you're up with Cowboy today?"

"No," Active said, seating himself on a

steel cot against one wall of the cabin. "Just a few singles and small bands."

"Well, maybe I will find some to-morrow." Wilson put the stew in a pan and lit the camp stove. "You mind if we listen to radio, Mr. Active? I think it's time for 'Chapel of the Air.'"

Active, already munching pilot bread, nodded. The program was famous all over the north half of Alaska, as much a staple of Bush life as mosquitoes or satellite TV. Wilson clicked on a big battery-powered Zenith Transoceanic that stood on the counter near the hissing camp stove. An antenna wire ran up the wall behind it and through the roof.

". . . but first we have this message from the president of Chukchi Region Inc.," the KSNO announcer said.

"Hello, this is Tom Werner," said a new voice. "I'm talking to you to ask you to vote yes in a few days when we have our election to ban the sale of liquor in Chukchi. When I was drinking, I could not be a good father, a good husband, a good hunter, a good worker for our corporation, or a good Inupiaq. I don't drink now, and I'm still not perfect, but I'm better than I was and my family is happier. Now that we have the Gray Wolf mine to provide our young people with jobs, they don't have to leave us to find work. But we need to make Chukchi a better place for them to live and raise the next generation. We can do that by banning the sale of liquor when we vote on Tuesday. We don't need any more suicides taking our young ones away. This liquor is like an *innukaknaaluk*, killing off our culture, and we have to stop it. My Inupiaq is not very good so now my wife, Mae Werner, will talk to you in our language."

A woman came on and spoke in Inupiaq. From what Active could make out, she repeated what her husband had said, then talked of her own experiences as the wife of a drinker. Her fluent Inupiaq was like music, even though most of it got past him.

When she finished, a blizzard howled from the radio. Then a door slammed and cut off the sound of the wind. "Come in, friend," drawled the Reverend Jaron Palmer. "Welcome. Welcome to 'Chapel of the Air.' "

Active still wore his parka and snow-machine suit. Wilson's lantern and camp stove hissed, the wood stove in the corner crackled. He leaned back against the wall of the cabin and listened to the reverend.

"Have you ever had your eyes opened?" Palmer was asking. "That's what happened to John Newton, the man who wrote our first hymn tonight. He was an English sailor in the dark days of the slave trade and he was on his way home from Africa when a terrible storm came up, the worst storm this expert sailor had ever seen."

Reverend Palmer paused and the blizzard became just audible again. But now it sounded like a storm at sea.

"Now John Newton was a man who laughed at God," the drawl went on. "Yes he did! He thought he didn't need God. He drank and he blasphemed and he knew the very flesh in which he trafficked! Yes, he did, he lay with helpless slave women while they were shackled in the hold of his evil ship!"

Now the storm was so loud the reverend had to shout to make himself heard.

"But that day in the tempest, John Newton's pride and his scorn stood for nothing. No, they stood for nothing and he cried out in his terror, 'The Lord have mercy on us!' "

The reverend was silent as the wind howled from the radio, then faded.

"And God put out his hand and he stilled that wind and he calmed that fevered sea," the reverend said. "Yes, he did! The ship was saved. And John Newton turned away from his old habits. He became a minister and he fought the slave trade. And many years later, he wrote this wonderful song about his salvation that the Nuliakuk Singers are going to perform for us tonight. Yes, he did!"

Active closed his eyes as the Native voices took up "Amazing Grace." The day in the cold with the dead man had drained him. How pleasant it was to be inside again, and to be warm.

He was standing on the seawall along Beach Street on a cool, gray spring day. The current swept past Chukchi thick with ice, the outfall of the Katonak and Isignaq rivers as breakup came on. The ice hissed and tinkled as the floes ground together.

George Clinton and Aaron Stone walked by. They looked at him briefly, smiled, looked at each other, and jumped into the current only a few feet from where he stood.

"Stop," he shouted. He jumped in after them.

To his surprise, the water felt warm. And despite his clothing, he could move through it easily.

As the three of them rushed toward the open

sea, he tried to swim to George Clinton and Aaron Stone. But the current was too strong. It whirled the three of them farther and farther apart, until Active could barely distinguish the two dead men's heads from the sleek, black heads of the seals swimming among the floes. "George! Mr. Stone!" he called.

"It's all right, Mr. Active," they shouted in unison, smiling and waving understandingly. Their voices were tiny in the distance. "It's all right."

"George! Mr. Stone!" he called again. But now he had lost them completely in the ice.

"Are you all right, Mr. Active?"

He awoke with a start, breathing hard.

"You were talking in your sleep," Amos Wilson said. He studied the trooper for a moment, as if waiting for him to describe the dream. "We could eat," he said finally. "The food is ready."

They ate pilot bread and stew and drank Tang and listened quietly as the Reverend Palmer finished his sermon.

"I'm almost out of water, Mr. Active," Wilson said. "Not even enough left to wash these dishes. I have to go get ice out of Katy Creek so it will melt tonight or we will not have coffee in the morning. You can go to sleep if you want."

"No, I'll come with you if it's all right," Active said. "Maybe I could help."

They went out of the cabin and Active breathed deeply in the cold air as Wilson loaded the sled for their expedition. It was full night now, stars glittering, a small high moon bathing the snowscape in dime-colored light.

Wilson started the Arctic Cat, Active climbed on the runners of the sled again, and they bounced down the bank to the bed of Katy Creek. Active threw back his parka hood and slid the zipper to the middle of his chest, letting the frozen air burn away the last traces of his dream.

Wilson drove down the creek a few hundred yards and stopped on a bend where the ice was bare. "Wind always blow snow away here," he said.

He spread a blue plastic tarp on the bed of the sled, then walked out onto the ice with an ax in his hand, studying the moonlit surface as he went. Finally, he dropped to his knees. Active knelt beside him. The ice looked to be two or three feet thick and was webbed with pressure cracks.

Wilson found a place where two of the largest cracks formed a V. About eighteen inches from the crotch of the V, he chopped a cross-crack with his ax. Now the V was a triangle. The old man worked the legs of the triangle with his ax, and in almost no time a chunk of ice eight inches thick was free in the hole. Wilson hit it in the middle with his ax, breaking it into smaller pieces they could grip and pull out of the hole.

"You could carry it to the sled," Wilson said.

Active, happy to have an assignment, zipped his parka up and trudged back and forth with armfuls of ice while Wilson worked his ax. At last, Wilson stopped and looked at the ice chunks on the tarp. "That's enough," he said.

He closed the edges of the tarp over the ice, then lashed the bundle down with rope from the jockey box at the rear of the sled. He sat on the seat of the Arctic Cat and lit a cigarette. "When I'm young, I never need to rest," Wilson said. "Now I do."

Active sat on the front of the sled and leaned against the bundle of ice, pleasantly warm from his loading duties. "When Tom Werner was on the radio, he used a word I don't know. *Innuka . . . innuka . . .*"

"*Innukaknaaluk?*"

"That's it. What does it mean?"

"Oh, it's just a word from them old Eskimo stories," Wilson said. He was silent and Active thought he didn't want to explain. But then he started up again. "It mean man-who-always-kill-people. But I guess Tom Werner mean bottle-who-always-kill-people, ah?"

"I guess." Active unzipped his parka, flipped it open, and laid his head back on the ice. Overhead, lambent curtains of aurora billowed in the solar wind. "In the stories, what happens to the man who always kills people?"

"Usually some orphan will come to the village and they have big fight."

"And the orphan kills him?"

"Not at first. *Innukaknaaluk* is very strong. First few times they grab each other, look like he will throw orphan on sharp rock and kill him. But orphan always twist away. Last time, orphan throw *innukaknaaluk* on his own rock and kill him."

"Then what happens to the orphan?"

"Then the people take him in. Maybe he'll marry village girl and live there. Have kids, go hunting. Not be so poor and lonely anymore."

The old man smoked in silence. Active got off the sled and walked out onto Katy Creek. He squatted to study the crater Wilson had made in the ice.

"You think it's too late for my grandson, Mr. Active?" Wilson called from behind him. "You think Harold will . . . will . . ."

Amos Wilson's voice trailed off, as if he was picturing Kinnuk Wilson in Aaron Stone's place on the sled in the spruce copse.

"I don't know, Mr. Wilson." Active stood up and turned toward the sled. "I feel there's a lot of good in him."

"Thank you, Mr. Active," Wilson said after another long silence.

Chapter 6
Friday Morning, Chukchi

"Who killed him, Nathan?"

Active slammed the doors of the ambulance. Blue smoke rolled from its tailpipe and rose into the air as it pulled away from Lienhofer Aviation's Cessna 206 and headed up Third Street for the hospital.

"Who was it, Nathan?"

Now he turned at the sound of the familiar high voice. "What are you doing here, Kinnuk?"

"That Cowboy say he'll bring you this morning. I decide to come around."

"And see what you could find out?"

Wilson didn't speak, but he raised his eyebrows in the Inupiat equivalent of a nod.

"So what makes you think somebody killed Aaron Stone?"

"That Cowboy say . . ."

"Did Cowboy see it with his own eyes?"

"No, but . . ."

"That Cowboy says lots of things. Do you believe them all?"

"No, but . . ."

"Then you should listen to what I say," Active said. It was obviously time to muddy up the gossip river a little. "And I say we won't know what killed Aaron until we ship him to Anchorage for an autopsy."

Cowboy Decker fired up the Cessna 206. The propeller kicked snow and grit and a Butterfinger wrapper past them. They turned their backs and hunched their shoulders as the pilot taxied the plane away, toward the Lienhofer hangar.

"There was no evidence of foul play at the scene," Active said as the storm subsided. "You know what that means?"

"Sure, it mean he kill himself," Wilson said. "Kay-Snow always say there's no evidence of foul play when somebody kill theirself."

"Yeah, I guess they do," Active said. He climbed into the Suburban and rolled down the window. "You need a ride?"

Wilson nodded, walked around to the passenger door, and slid in.

Active pulled away from the airport. "Where you headed?"

"The Dreamland," Wilson said. "I'm out of Olys."

"I have to talk to Clara Stone. Do you know where she lives?"

"Sure," Wilson said. "It's that house on Beach Street with all the caribou heads."

"Yeah, I've seen it. I guess Aaron was quite a hunter."

"I guess," Wilson said. "Before he work at Gray Wolf, he hunt caribou for money. Thirty-five dollars, he bring you whole carcass. I think he do all right, except he give lots away to old people."

They bounced along in silence for a while. "Thanks for sending your grandfather to get me from Qaqsrauq Lake," Active said finally. "How did you know I was there?"

"When I'm little, my grandfather always take me up there to Katy Creek. Yesterday when I catch ride with that Cowboy, he tell me where you find Aaron Stone. It sound like Qaqsrauq Lake to me."

"Pretty smart. Maybe you should spend less time at the Dreamland and more time using that smart head of yours."

Wilson was silent.

Active stopped the Suburban in front of the Dreamland. Two drunks sat on the deck in front, sharing a bottle in a brown paper bag. "Your grandfather loves you a lot."

"I know," Wilson said. "He take care of me when Dad go to prison for shooting Mom." He climbed out and sat down beside the drunks. One of them handed him the bag.

Active parked the Suburban in front of Aaron Stone's house, got out, and studied the trophies lining the eaves above the tarpapered walls.

Or were they an advertisement? Antlered caribou heads stared down like gargoyles. Some looked ancient, the skulls stripped of flesh by maggots and ravens and polished white by weather. Peeling strips of fur hung from others. Still others looked almost alive. The fur was intact and the eyes gleamed dully behind half-closed lids.

An Inupiat woman came out of the house, climbed on a Honda four-wheeler, and drove away. Active knocked and Clara Stone let him in, her brown face as rigid as a whalebone mask on a museum wall.

"I'm sorry for your trouble," he said.

She nodded and led him through the *kunnichuk* to the kitchen. "You want coffee or something?" She motioned at the dining table. It was covered with dishes sheathed in aluminum foil or plastic wrap. "Everybody bring food over when they hear about Aaron."

"Just coffee." He slipped off his parka, hung it on the back of a chair, and sat down. "Do you have someone to stay with you?"

She turned on a burner under a pot on an electric stove. "My daughter is coming in from Nuliakuk this afternoon with her kids. That will be good. Those grandkids sure keep me busy."

She sat down across the table and stared at her hands. "I hear you think somebody shoot Aaron."

"My report isn't done yet, but I think it will say there was no evidence of foul play at the scene."

She absorbed the information in silence. Her expression didn't change, but tears appeared on her cheeks. Active handed her his handkerchief. She took it absently and held it in her lap.

He wondered if what he had said was a lie. There was nothing that amounted to proof of foul play at the scene — maybe. But what about the spruce branch that didn't seem to have come from any of the trees near Aaron Stone's snowgo? What about the lack of boot tracks around the

113

machine? Did those things amount to evidence of foul play?

"It's my fault," she said finally. "I should have let him get that snowgo."

"But he had his snowmachine with him when . . . he had it at Katy Creek."

"That's his old snowgo," she said. "He want new snowgo this fall when freezeup come, but I tell him we don't have enough money. He never know I'm really getting him new Yamaha for Christmas."

"I don't think he would hurt himself just because of a snowmachine," he said. She didn't react. "Otherwise did he seem all right? Did he have any problems at work?"

"He never talk much about work, but he seem happy," she said. "I think he's glad he don't have to hunt caribou to sell anymore. He never feel right about that, so he like it when Gray Wolf hire him. Then he can give away more."

The coffee pot began to simmer. She got up, poured a cup, and pushed it across the table.

"Only thing he ever complain about is how I won't let him get new snowgo," she said. She dabbed her eyes with Active's handkerchief. "He always say, 'Look like I'm the woman in this house now. Next thing I'll be sitting down to pee.' I sure laugh when I think how he's gonna see that new snowgo Christmas morning."

She blew her nose into the handkerchief, then balled it up in one hand. "I guess I better call the Yamaha shop now and cancel my order." The tears came again. "*Arii*, I sure miss him."

"I really don't think he would kill himself because of a snowmachine."

"I don't know. There's so many people killing theirself around here, I never know what they're thinking. Maybe they would do it because their snowgo was too old."

"Usually they do it because they get sick inside," Active said. "Their drinking gets out of control, they feel like they're nobody, and they give up. Did Aaron drink much? We found whiskey bottles at his camp."

The woman's head jerked up and she stared at him, hard.

"Aaron never drink," she said. "Never! He always say liquor is like poison, especially for Eskimos. I used to drink little bit when I'm young girl. But Aaron say I have to stop if I want to marry him, so I never drink again. If there's whiskey at our camp, somebody else leave it. Maybe somebody visit him?"

Active was silent, studying Clara Stone's eyes. "Maybe so," he said finally.

The door to Jim Silver's office was unlocked, so Active stuck in his head. "Busy?"

"Oh, just catching up on my paperwork and marveling at the number of people who have told me that you think somebody murdered Aaron Stone," the police chief said. "Coffee?"

"Black."

Silver pushed back from his desk and lumbered over to the coffee pot. "I'm further marveling to think you'd shoot off your mouth about it to the likes of Cowboy Decker. You might as well put it on 'Mukluk Messenger.'"

"Exactly," Active said. "And now I'm telling people there's no evidence of foul play at the scene. That way, everybody will get confused and go back to talking about the weather." He dropped into the chair in front of Silver's desk and shrugged out of his parka. "Except the killer, if there is a killer. He'll get nervous and screw up. I hope."

Silver set a Styrofoam cup in front of Active and shook his head. "For my money, there's no killer except in your head. But let's not get into that. Just tell me what you found over there at Katy Creek that moved you to unburden yourself to Cowboy Decker."

"Actually, it wasn't on the creek. It was by a lake a few miles south of Aaron's camp." Active walked to a map on the wall behind Silver's desk, studied it, then jabbed down a finger. "I think this is it. I don't believe it has an official name, but people call it Qaqsrauq Lake."

Silver swiveled his chair and looked at the spot. "Loon Lake." He shrugged. "I've heard people talk about it, but I've never been there."

Active described the scene at the spruce copse, flinging out his arms to portray Aaron Stone's frozen T on the seat of the Yamaha.

"But how could a killer set up the scene like that and not leave a trace?" Silver said when he finished. "Did he fly in and out like a raven?"

"Maybe he used a snowmachine." Active dropped back into the chair in front of Silver's desk and the chief turned to face him. "He runs into Aaron on the trail. They stop and talk like people do when they meet out in the country. He bums a Lucky Strike off Aaron. They have tea from

117

Aaron's thermos. He asks how Aaron likes the .308, he picks it up to look through the scope, he turns around and shoots Aaron in the throat."

Silver thought it over. "Yeah, and leaves signs a blind man could read. His and Aaron's boot tracks, a hole where Aaron fell in the snow, blood all over the place. It would look like he butchered a caribou." He snapped his fingers. "Wait a minute, I'll show you."

Silver walked to a row of file cabinets against a wall and surveyed them, his hands on his hips, his belly hanging over his belt. "Shit, what was that guy's name? Oh, yeah." He reached into a drawer marked "T–Z" and pulled out a folder.

He walked back to the desk and scattered the contents in front of Active. "Tobias Westerman. Doctor from the hospital. Accidentally shot in the chest with a twelve-gauge by the pharmacist while they were ptarmigan hunting up at the north end of town three years ago. Look at all that blood."

Active studied the red snow. "Yeah, but this wasn't an instant kill. See how he thrashed around in the brush and sprayed blood everywhere? In Aaron Stone's case, the bullet destroyed the spine. I bet he didn't even twitch as he fell back."

"Maybe," Silver said. "But there would have to be some blood, plus all kinds of tracks in the snow."

"Yeah, but our guy's not done," Active said. "He cleans up the mess so it doesn't show unless you're standing on it. He pulls his snowmachine around in front of Aaron's rig, ties a rope to Aaron's skis, and tows him a few miles down the trail. He sets up the suicide scene and goes on his way. The snow and the thaw and the wind do their work and now you couldn't find the scene of the crime if you crawled along the snowgo trails with a magnifying glass and tweezers."

Silver swept the Westerman photos back into the folder. "I guess it's possible. But who would do it? And why? People around here don't plan to kill anybody. They just get drunk and it happens. And like I said the other day, nine times out of ten they head straight over here to tell me about it. Speaking of which, was there any sign Aaron was drinking?"

"Yes and no."

"Why don't we start with yes?"

"We found a couple of Jack Daniel's bottles in his cabin," Active said. "One empty, one half full."

"That's a pretty strong yes, I'd say. What's the no?"

"Clara Stone says Aaron never drank," Active said. "Ever. So maybe he had a visitor who left the bottles behind. Maybe the same guy he met up with on the trail."

"Yeah, and maybe he didn't tell his wife everything. Some guys don't, you know." Silver walked to the file cabinet and dropped in the Westerman folder.

"Maybe," Active said. "Anyway, I'm going to have the bottles checked for fingerprints."

"Good luck. The crime lab in Anchorage is backed up two or three weeks, last I heard. But if they do recover any prints, I'll lay odds they'll all be Aaron's." Silver walked to the window and stared down at Third Street. "This mystery guy of yours would have had to be sober and plan way ahead and plant those bottles and . . . nah, I can't see it."

The phone on Silver's desk rang. He answered it and listened for several seconds.

"Yeah, I heard the same thing," he said. He listened again. "He's right here. Ask him yourself."

He handed Active the phone. "Roger Kennelly," he said, rolling his eyes. Active was not sure if the eye-roll was for the KSNO newsman or for himself.

"Can you give me a statement on Aaron Stone's death?" Kennelly said. "I hear he was murdered."

"Now, where would you hear something like that, Roger?"

"Everybody's talking about it."

"And did everybody see it with their own eyes?"

"No, but . . ."

"Then don't believe everything you hear," Active said. "Start your tape."

There was a pause and some clicks. "Go ahead."

"The Alaska State Troopers are investigating the death of Aaron Stone, whose body was found yesterday in the Katy Creek area," Active said. "At this time, the evidence does not suggest foul play."

He paused and cleared his throat. "How's that?"

"No evidence of foul play?" Kennelly said. "Are you saying it was another suicide?"

"I'm saying there was no evidence of foul play."

"So it was an accident then?"

"I'm saying there was no evidence of foul play."

"Gee, thanks a lot, Nathan," Kennelly said. "You're lucky the troopers don't pay you by the word."

Active handed the phone back to Silver, who hung it up and stared at him.

"See?" Active said with a wave at the phone. "More confusion, delivered to every radio in Chukchi, courtesy of Roger Kennelly."

Silver shook his head, looking disgusted. "At least you told him the truth, even if you don't believe it yourself. No evidence of foul play."

"OK, just a couple more things," Active said.

Silver held up his hand and scraped his chair back. "They'll have to wait. I'm going to George Clinton's funeral. You want to come?"

"His funeral? How can they have his funeral already? The autopsy can't possibly be finished."

"There won't be any autopsy."

Active stared at the chief. "But you said . . ."

"I know. But the coroner decided there wasn't any reason to do one and so the state won't pay."

Silver walked to the door and took a parka from a hook. "And the city's got

122

budget problems, like everybody, so I decided I couldn't justify the money either. And why drag it out for his folks? It's a suicide. Like all the others."

"But . . ."

Silver opened the door and looked at Active. "But the only question right now is, do you want to go to the funeral with me or not?"

"Sure, sure."

"Good deal," Silver said. "We can take your Suburban. They're gonna bury him on the bluff across the lagoon and my van doesn't do too good on that road over there."

Active got his parka and followed the chief out of the office. "Aren't his brothers buried in the cemetery by the Dreamland?"

"It's full. That's why they started the new one on the bluff a couple years ago." Silver paused to lock the door, then headed downstairs.

"Anyway, there were a couple more things about Aaron Stone," Active said.

"You're worse than the west wind, you know that?"

"Suicide is for twenty-two-year-olds like George Clinton," Active said. "Aaron Stone was fifty-five. How many guys that age have you seen kill themselves?"

"Not many, maybe not any," Silver said. "But so what? Every winter, there's a couple days when the temperature hits a new low. It doesn't mean the climate is changing, doesn't mean the Great Perhaps is punishing us sinful children. It just means every so often, the old record's gonna get broken."

Chapter 7

Friday Morning, Bluff Cemetery, Chukchi

They came out of the public safety building and inhaled involuntarily when the air hit their faces. In unison, they dived into the Suburban and slammed the doors.

"Jesus, what a day for a funeral," Silver said. "It must be twenty below. Not a new record, I guess, but at least the graveside services should be brief."

"Let's hope," Active said. He started the Suburban and turned on the heater. The air it blew out was cold, but not quite as cold as outside. "How do they dig a grave after freezeup, anyway? They build a fire to thaw out the ground or something?"

"No," Silver said. "They dig them before freezeup."

Active twisted in his seat to look at the police chief. "Really? How many?"

"Usually about a dozen."

"How do they know how many?"

"I don't know how they know. Long experience, probably. Can we go now?"

Active put the Suburban in gear. It lurched forward, then died. "Needs to warm up more," he said, restarting the engine. "So, do they ever use all the graves up before breakup?"

"Geez, you're morbid," Silver said. "Yeah, sometimes they use them all up. Can we change the subject now?"

"But what if somebody else dies?"

"They put the coffins in a shipping van behind the hospital and pray the ground thaws before the departed do."

Active shuddered.

"Sometimes, it's better not to know the details," the chief said. He was silent for a moment, then chuckled.

"It did come in handy once, though," he said. "I had a guy who slashed his girlfriend's throat with her own *ulu*, but he didn't want to confess. So I arrested him, told him the jail was closed for repairs, and threw him into the van with her and a couple of other corpses that had piled up over the winter. Came back a couple hours later, and he was ready to talk."

Active shook his head. "Sounds cruel and unusual to me."

"Well, he didn't know enough to ask for a lawyer and I didn't offer," Silver said.

Active raced the engine of the Suburban.

It sounded like it was ready to go. "Where's the service?"

"St. Mark's."

He put the Suburban in gear again. This time the engine stayed alive, and he pulled away from the public safety building. "No kidding. I didn't know the Clintons were Catholic."

"Yeah, going way back," Silver said.

"And they're giving him an official funeral? I thought suicide was kind of a touchy issue for the one true church." He turned onto Temple Avenue, jammed on the brakes to let a snowmachine cross, then drove on. St. Mark's was three blocks west, on Second Street.

"Father Sebastian is one of Annie Clinton's nephews," Silver said. "Besides which, if the Catholics got too persnickety about suicide around here, they'd be out of business. Like I said, sometimes it's better not to know the details."

"Speaking of details, George Clinton and Aaron Stone both worked at the Gray Wolf," Active said. "How many times . . ."

"Don't say it," Silver snapped. "How many times have two suicides in a row been people who worked at the same place? I have no idea. Never, probably."

"Plus, this is two suicides in a week," Active said. "That's a lot for a town of twenty-five hundred."

Silver put a big red weather-cracked hand on the trooper's shoulder. "Look, Nathan, there's always loose ends. But you've got to let this go or you'll end up as crazy as a white person who stays in the Bush too long."

He pulled the hand off Active's shoulder and punched him with it. "Anyway, here we are."

Active stopped the Suburban in front of a weathered gray two-story building. St. Mark's looked big enough for its work of saving souls, but perhaps too old and tired for the job. The lot in front was becoming crowded with snowmachines, four-wheelers, and a few cars and pickups.

"Come on," Silver said. "I don't know why, but I always go to these things."

They climbed the stairs to the second floor, slipped into the chapel, and stood along the back wall. Red-tinted windows bathed the mourners in a peaceful ruby light and the word "sanctuary" came into Active's mind.

Daniel and Annie Clinton, Julius between them, sat on a bench at the front. George's coffin, covered by a white parka, stood beside them in the aisle between the two banks of wooden pews.

"Where do you like to sit?" Active whispered.

"I don't," Silver said. "I just stand back here. Being an unbeliever, it's against my religion to take up a pew that should rightly go to one of the faithful."

The room was starting to fill. People crossed themselves as they entered, then took seats or stood along the back and side walls. Perhaps two hundred and fifty people were crowded into the chapel by the time an Inupiaq in priest's robes came out to stand before the coffin.

"That's Annie Clinton's nephew I was telling you about," Silver whispered. "Sebastian James."

Active studied the man. He looked young and serious. Active wondered how he could face the burdens of ministering to the human soul in a place like Chukchi.

"Comes from a village upriver, but he went to Notre Dame," Silver whispered. "Very smart guy. Chukchi's lucky to get him."

Active looked around the chapel as Father Sebastian led the congregation through the funeral service. Some of the young women had babies inside their parkas, signified by humps on their backs and scarves tied around their waists. One of the humps started to cry, and the mother jiggled in place in an effort to quiet the baby.

When the cries continued, she lifted up the hem of the parka and worked the hump around to the front. The cries ceased and Active surmised the baby had been hungry.

"We expect the old people to die," Father Sebastian concluded finally. "But when the young die, it hurts us. The young people are the hope of the future and the hope of the old people."

He switched to Inupiaq. As far as Active could make out, he said the same things as he had said in English.

Then the mourners sang hymns in Inupiaq and some took communion.

Father Sebastian opened the coffin, and people filed past for a last look. Several took snapshots. Daniel Clinton bent over the coffin and kissed his son good-bye. He straightened up and Annie Clinton bent down, then collapsed on her knees and made a high, keening sound. Daniel and Julius helped her up and led her away.

Active followed Silver downstairs. The people from the service were milling around in the parking lot. He saw Evelyn O'Brien from the trooper office sitting in a pickup with her husband, and Kinnuk Wilson watching from the edge of the crowd, an unreadable expression on his face. He glimpsed Pauline Generous and wondered where Lucy was.

Six young men brought out George Clinton's coffin and loaded it into the bed of a pickup at the door of the church. It pulled away and the crowd followed with snowmachines, four-wheelers and cars. Active steered the Suburban into line at the back of the procession.

"Have you had a serious talk with Carnaby about these theories of yours yet?" Silver said as they crossed the bridge over the lagoon.

"Not really," Active said. "What am I going to say, except that I'm investigating an unattended death that looks like another suicide?"

"Nathan, you're on thin ice here. Your boss needs to know if you think there's a problem at the Gray Wolf."

"Who says there's a problem at the Gray Wolf?" The bridge ended and Active steered the Suburban onto the rutted track that led towards the foot of the bluff. "Everything I know is in my reports. Besides, if he is mad, what can he do, send me to a remote location? I'm already here."

"What's the deal with Carnaby, anyway?" Silver said. "He's kind of senior to be in a Bush post like this. Punishment for the Howell bust?"

Patrick Carnaby had run the troopers' Central Investigative Unit in Anchorage until a raid on a crack house turned up one Clayton Howell, president of the Alaska Senate. A high-priced San Francisco lawyer beat the cocaine charges against the politician and the Central Investigative Unit was disbanded after the state senate passed a resolution denouncing its "gestapo tactics." A superior court judge barred the troopers from further investigating the senator and Captain Patrick Carnaby, the unit's commander, became Sergeant Patrick Carnaby, head of the Chukchi detachment.

"I think it's more for safekeeping, although I understand Senator Howell was led to believe otherwise," Active said. "One of my buddies from the academy works at headquarters. He hears the feds are going to take Howell down anyway. Then the honchos will bring back CIU and Carnaby too."

"Maybe, but I never heard of a cop yet

who played dodgeball with the establishment and won," Silver said.

When they got to the bluff, the pallbearers already had George's coffin out of the truck and were wrestling it up the hillside. Active and Silver followed and, when they reached the top, heard the priest finishing the Lord's Prayer. The coffin stood beside an open grave and a tidy pile of sand and gravel.

"That didn't come out of the grave," Active whispered.

"Nope," Silver said. "It's borrowed from the city's stockpile of road sand. They brought it up by snowmachine last night."

The pallbearers lowered the coffin into the ground. Then they lowered the vertical beam of a big white cross into the grave and positioned it at the head of the coffin.

Father Sebastian dropped in a handful of dirt, then the mourners followed suit.

"Daddy, could I help putting the rocks on?" a tot piped as the earth rattled onto the coffin. His father nodded and the boy threw in a handful of gravel from the pile.

Finally the pallbearers picked up shovels and the grave filled rapidly. Little groups of people stood chatting, occasionally laughing quietly, as the work went on. Off to one side, a group of women sat on the tundra in their parkas and recited the Hail Mary. "Holy Mary, Mother of God, pray for us sinners now and at the hour of our death," they chanted. Then they switched to Inupiaq. It sounded like the same prayer.

"Which one's Emily Hoffman?" Active asked.

Silver scanned the crowd, then shook his head. "Don't see her."

"George's girlfriend doesn't come to his funeral? Doesn't that seem strange?"

The police chief shrugged. "I hear she's drinking pretty hard. Maybe she's at the Dreamland."

"You ever interview her?"

"Never found her, and now I guess it doesn't matter." Silver hunched down inside his parka as a particularly icy gust whistled over the bluff.

"Well, if just hypothetically speaking George Clinton had been murdered and you couldn't find his girlfriend, wouldn't that . . ."

Silver nudged him and pointed back the way they had come. "Look, it's Tom Werner."

Active turned and looked down the trail. A man in a green-and-white Gray Wolf parka, the hood thrown back, was just coming over the brow of the bluff. A woman followed close behind on the steep narrow trail through the tundra.

The man had a cigarette in the corner of his mouth and wore sunglasses with bright blue lenses. His black hair, just starting to frost with gray, swept back to his nape in a fifties-style ducktail. Some mixture of white and Inupiat genes had conspired to give him a smooth olive complexion and Levantine good looks that still surprised Active every time he saw the president of Chukchi Region Inc.

Werner and the woman topped the bluff and Werner flicked his cigarette into the snow. He spoke briefly to Father Sebastian, who listened intently, then nodded.

"Tom Werner wants to talk to us," the priest said.

Werner stepped up to the grave and put one hand on an arm of the cross. He stood quietly while the mourners gradually fell silent.

"I know it's cold and there's a basketball game on TV this afternoon, so I'll be short," he said. "My wife, Mae, is going to translate for me, and I know she'll poke me if I go on too long."

He smiled and Mae Werner smiled, raising her eyebrows. The crowd chuckled.

"Good luck shutting that guy up, Mae!" someone called.

"You must have heard one of my speeches when I was in the legislature," Werner said. The crowd chuckled again, then was silent.

"What I want to say is that this" — Werner motioned to George Clinton's grave — "this doesn't have to keep happening. One would be too many, but this is two in a week. We have to stop it."

"That's right, Tommy," a woman in the crowd murmured. Active didn't see who spoke, but the voice sounded like Annie Clinton's. Werner paused as his wife spoke rapidly in Inupiaq. An ancient *aana* in a caribou parka standing a few feet from Active nodded vigorously at Mae Werner's words.

"I bet everyone here has had a loved one who went just this way," Tom Werner said, pointing again at the grave. This time someone in the crowd moaned. A man, Active thought.

"Just this way!" Werner boomed in a sudden, startling shout. "Just this way! Some of you remember when my own brother went." A few older people nodded. Mae Werner translated.

"Just this way he went!" Tom Werner

continued in another shout. A girl near the front sobbed. Werner paused. A gust rolled up the bluff from the lagoon and rippled the wolf ruff of his parka. The crowd settled down.

Several miles east, the afternoon Alaska Airlines jet from Nome rolled onto the final approach for Chukchi and turned on its landing lights. The threshold of Runway 25 lay almost at the foot of the bluff a hundred yards down the lagoon from the cemetery. It looked as if the pilots planned to land on the funeral.

"We can stop it," Werner said. "Some people blame it on the white man, because he brought the liquor and gave it to our grandparents." The crowd murmured agreement.

"That's true, but the white man doesn't pry open our teeth and pour it down our throats. We do that ourselves!"

"That's right, Tommy!" several people in the crowd shouted. Werner paused for his wife's translation. The old *aana* near Active listened to the Inupiaq translation, nodded vigorously again, and muttered something to an equally old Inupiat man standing beside her.

"We do it ourselves!" Werner shouted when his wife was done. "Yes, we do it ourselves! But we can use the white man's own invention to stop this!" He paused as his wife translated. Behind the little gathering, the noise of the approaching jet grew.

"I'm talking about the vote," Werner said. "We have a chance in a few days to vote Chukchi dry and keep this liquor, this *innukaknaaluk*, out of our region."

He paused again for Mae Werner to translate, but the whine of the Boeing 737 drowned her out. She turned to watch as the plane roared past. Like all Alaska Airlines jets, it had a huge Inupiat face painted on the tail. The old Inupiaq gazed down at the little funeral with sympathy and encouragement, Active thought, but not much hope.

The jet's tires hit the runway with a screech and twin puffs of smoke, then the noise died off. Mae Werner translated her husband's last words, and he resumed in English.

"I know we can't stop all of the drinking, but we can stop a lot of it," Tom Werner said. "Maybe if we all go out and vote on Tuesday, we won't be coming to any more funerals like this."

As Mae Werner translated, he moved to the head of the grave and rested a hand on each arm of the cross.

"Boys like this one should be marrying their sweethearts and making their own families," Werner said. "And older men like Aaron Stone should be out hunting their caribou and playing with their grandchildren, just like we Inupiat have always done!"

He stood silently, as if thinking what to say next. The crowd waited expectantly.

"I guess I'm through now," he said. "You know what to do next Tuesday."

He bowed his head and looked at the grave as Mae Werner translated. When she was done, he shook hands with Daniel Clinton, then Annie, then Julius. He stared into the boy's eyes for a long time, then squeezed him on the shoulder and released his hand.

Julius just stood there, his hand still out, watching as Werner took his wife's arm and they started on their way. He didn't move until the Werners had dropped out of sight over the brow of the bluff.

"Hell of a show, huh?" Silver said. "Almost made me want to go up and get saved."

Active looked at Silver, annoyed for once by the police chief's cynicism. "You don't take him seriously?"

Silver grimaced. "Don't mind me. I'm

too much of a smart-ass for my own good sometimes. We all owe a lot to Tom Werner. You should have seen this place before he got the Gray Wolf going."

The crowd began to stir again and the pallbearers went back to work with their shovels. When the coffin was covered, the Clintons — Daniel, Annie, Julius, and some others Active didn't know by name — gathered at the cross and took pictures of each other.

The crowd broke up. Active and Silver made their way down the hill and crossed the bridge back to Chukchi. At the public safety building, Silver climbed into the police van and went home. Active went back to his office, turned on his computer, and wrote his report on Aaron Stone.

He left a note for Evelyn O'Brien to call Mayor Crane at Nuliakuk and say he'd try to make the next city council meeting. He flipped through an issue of *Wired* and played a few rounds of solitaire on the computer. He went down the hall to the bathroom, came back, and dialed the phone on his desk.

"Pauline, it's Nathan," he said.

"Isn't it terrible about Aaron Stone?" the old lady said. "I hear at Senior Center he don't kill himself, somebody shoot him.

Maybe Inukins steal his gun and shoot him with it?"

He groped for the word, then remembered. Inukins were the Inupiat version of gremlins, tiny people who lived in the tundra and caused mischief for the hardworking Inupiat as they hunted caribou, picked berries, or trapped fox and lynx. "I heard those rumors too, *aana*," he said. "But did you hear my statement on the radio? No evidence of foul play is what I said on the radio."

"No evidence of foul play? I know what that mean from Perry Mason. It mean it look like Aaron do it himself, or have accident. But I think Inukins can make it look however they want."

"Maybe so, *aana*," Active said. "Anyway, how was bingo the other night? You going tonight? I could take you in my trooper car."

"What you want, *nalauqmiiyaaq*? I'm too old for young guy like you. You find girl your own age, like my granddaughter Lucy. She smart, pretty, work hard, cook good, I think be joyous in bed. Much better for you."

"No, no, *aana*," Active laughed. "I just want to ask you something about Tillie Miller. I was wonder . . ."

"You ask me about Tillie Miller before, *nalauqmiiyaaq*," Pauline interrupted. "How come you so interested in her? She too old for you too. You mental, Nathan? That's what happen, Eskimo boy adopt out to *nalauqmiut* parents. Live at Anchorage too long, go *kinnuk*."

"Wait a minute. *Kinnuk* is the same as mental?" No wonder Amos Wilson had insisted on calling his grandson Harold.

"That right," the old woman said. "Like that Wilson boy. Kinnuk is mental, just like you will be if you fool around with old lady."

"I don't want to bed Tillie, *aana*, I just want to talk to her," Active said. "But I don't know how. Does she ever talk to people? Does she have a friend or a granddaughter like Lucy that she talks to?"

Pauline was silent. "I find out, tell you tonight when you pick me up for bingo," she said finally. "But I call your *aaka* first, make sure you're not mental. If Martha say you are, I don't come out tonight, even if you turn on your flasher. I call police."

Chapter 8
Friday Afternoon, Chukchi

GeoNord's Chukchi offices took up part of the middle floor of a green three-story plywood cube near the airport. Chukchi Region Inc. owned the building and used the rest of it for its headquarters.

Active walked into the tiny lobby and pushed the button for the elevator. It didn't come or make noise, so he walked up a flight of stairs to the GeoNord reception area. What was apparently the receptionist's desk bore a sign that said "Back at" with the hands of a cardboard clock underneath set to two P.M. He turned and inspected the office.

Big black-and-white photographs from the Gray Wolf covered one wall. There was an aerial of the treeless bowl in the hills that cradled the mine and several shots of Native workers.

Progress for the Chukchi Region and Its People, said a sign in the middle of the photographs. Aaron Stone, astride a snowmachine with a Gray Wolf decal on the side, appeared in one of the shots. George Clinton didn't show up in any of them.

"Officer Active?" said a voice from behind him. He turned to find a lean fit-looking man with short graying hair extending his hand. Active shook it. "Michael Jermain, chief engineer of the Gray Wolf," the man said. "Sorry about the empty desk. Marie's at lunch."

"No problem," Active said. "I hope my call didn't interrupt anything important."

"Nah, just going over some production logs from the mine. Come on in."

Jermain led the way to a corner office two doors down the hall from the lobby. One window of the office looked south, over the west end of the airport. The other looked west, out over the bay. The walls were decorated with animal heads: a moose, a caribou, a grizzly, a black bear, a wolf, even a wolverine. The only trophy animal from around Chukchi that Active didn't see was a Dall sheep.

Jermain's desk stood under the south window. He dropped into a big executive-style chair behind the desk and motioned toward a smaller one in front of it.

Active took the chair and placed his notebook in front of him on a corner of the

144

desk. A bright afternoon cloudscape filled the window behind Jermain. Active could barely make out the engineer's features in the backlight.

"Didn't we meet before?" Jermain asked.

"I think so. It was when the governor came up for the opening of the Gray Wolf. He couldn't bring his regular bodyguard for some reason, so I filled in at the reception."

"Right, right, I remember. Nathan — OK if I call you Nathan?" Jermain said. Active nodded. "Well, Nathan, you must have done a good job. He got out of town alive."

"I was really careful. You wouldn't believe the paperwork if somebody shoots the governor on your shift." His eyes strayed again to the heads staring down from the walls.

"You hunt, Nathan?"

"A little. Not as much as my relatives around here, though. I was raised in Anchorage."

"Yeah, I think I heard that," Jermain said. "Well, I love it. Mining's a good dodge for a guy like me. I don't actually run a mine very long. My specialty is getting them built and cranked up and running right, then I move on. I've launched mines all over the world. Canada, Africa, Malaysia, South America, even Russia. Wherever I go, I hunt. By the time I leave, I've normally got every one of the major local heads. You look in *Boone and Crockett*, you'll see my name all over the place. And you should see my trophy room back home in Colorado."

Active looked from the animals back to the engineer. "You don't get any grief from Chukchi Region? That's kind of a touchy subject around here, white outsiders coming in and shooting trophies."

"Yeah, that's why we tell our white employees to live in Anchorage and let us fly them back and forth to their shifts," Jermain said.

"But you get away with it?"

"Tom Werner has dropped a couple hints, but that's about it." Jermain shrugged, but his jaw looked tight.

"A lot of people in Chukchi would take a hint from Tom Werner as a commandment from God."

"He wants the Gray Wolf to go right a lot more than he wants to run off one white guy who's not going to be around much longer anyway," Jermain said. "Besides, I'm careful. I've got a Cessna 185 over at the airport and I keep away from

146

the villages when I hunt. That way, nobody sees me and I don't take animals somebody on a snowmachine or in a riverboat can get at. Plus, I usually give the meat to one of the *aanas* around town or to the Senior Center."

"Whatever works." Now Active shrugged.

"Local politics is about the same everywhere," Jermain said. "I make sure the mine ticks like a Swiss watch, I hire lots of Tom Werner's shareholders, not to mention his board members, and he stays out of my face."

"Have you been out lately?"

"As a matter of fact, I was out Wednes— no, Tuesday," Jermain said. "I'm planning a caribou hunt pretty soon so I want to find the main herd and figure out when it'll be far enough from the villages that I can take a couple."

"Have any luck?"

"Any luck?"

"With the caribou? Did you get any?"

"Of course not. Like I said, I was only scouting," Jermain said. "I'm well aware of the law against hunting the same day you're airborne."

Active wrote "airborne" in his notebook and smiled. "Too bad. My buddies in fish and game would love to have another 185

147

in their fleet. They tell me it's the number one choice of poachers. Not to mention game cops."

"My insurance doesn't cover impoundments, Nathan," Jermain said. "So I'm a careful man."

"Yeah, you said that."

"I'm a busy man too. How can I help you? I gather you think somebody might be bumping off our employees?"

Active pulled his Pearlcorder from a coat pocket and laid it on the desk between himself and Jermain. "OK if I start this?"

A muscle in Jermain's jaw twitched slightly, but he nodded. Active clicked the Record and Play buttons.

"What can you tell me about George Clinton and Aaron Stone?"

"Not much," Jermain said, eyes on the tape recorder. "Aaron had been with us a couple years, since before the mine actually opened. He was a mechanic. Self-taught, but better at fixing things in cold weather than anybody else we've got. I can have somebody copy his personnel file and send it over, if you want." He wrote something on his desk blotter.

"Was he having trouble at work?"

"Not that I know of. He finished his two

weeks Monday and headed back to town on his snowmachine. That was the last thing anybody at the mine knew until we heard on the radio he was dead."

"And George Clinton?"

"Him I barely knew," Jermain said. "We only hired him about six months ago. Tom Werner called me one day, said George was a cousin of his, and asked me to get him a job. I called my personnel director and told her to find something for him, and she put him on as a janitor."

"Was he having problems at the mine?"

"None that I heard about but we can pull his file, too." Jermain wrote on the blotter again. "Like I said, I didn't know George Clinton at all. I'm not sure we ever even spoke."

"You never spoke to him?" Active asked.

"Not that I can recall, no," Jermain said. "Though I guess it's possible."

"It's possible?"

"Of course," Jermain said. "I have a million conversations, but I don't remember them all. Do you?"

"Do you think he could have come here at some point to talk to you about some problem he could have been having at work?"

"I guess he could have," Jermain said. "But nothing like that jogs my memory right at the moment."

"It's just that his father told me he might have come here to talk to you on Monday," Active said. "About some problem at work. That wouldn't be your recollection?"

Jermain cleared his throat, pulled an appointment book from a drawer, and flipped through the pages. He stopped at one and bent over it for a moment, tapping a pencil on his desk blotter.

The salt-and-pepper hair was thinning on top, Active noticed. He looked out the south window, out the west window, and at the wolf head on the wall.

He looked at Jermain's Chief Engineer nameplate and back at his bald spot. "So that wouldn't be your recollection," he said again. "That George Clinton came here Monday? To talk to you about some problem at the Gray Wolf?"

"No, he's not in my schedule here." Jermain looked up from the page and pushed the book across the desk.

Active studied it. Nothing on the Monday page looked like an appointment with George Clinton.

"So I'm sure I didn't meet with him Monday." Jermain closed the book. "What problem was he supposed to have talked to me about anyway?"

"If he never talked to you, I guess it doesn't matter." Active stared at Jermain and Jermain stared at his blotter. "Does it?"

"I guess not," the engineer said. "I was just wondering."

Active wrote "I guess not" in his notebook and pretended to study it thoughtfully. He counted to thirty, to let Jermain stew a little. "Did you happen to pass through the Katy Creek area when you were out in your plane not shooting caribou?" he asked finally. "Tuesday would be about when Aaron Stone died. Perhaps you noticed something."

Jermain took a few seconds to answer. "Ah, no, I went southeast. Down toward the Dog River and the Kuchiliuk Hills."

Active flipped to a new page in his notebook, looked out the south window, studied the tip of his pen with a frown, pulled a fresh one out of an inside coat pocket.

"You didn't go north at all?"

"No, I didn't. Check with the FAA. They should still have my flight plan on file."

Active wrote "FAA" on the new page.

"How about Tuesday night, Wednesday morning?"

Jermain frowned, looking confused. "No, I got back around dark. So I wasn't in the Katy Creek area Tuesday night, either. Or Wednesday morning."

"I'm not talking about Aaron Stone. I'm talking about George Clinton. That's when he died."

The muscle in Jermain's jaw twitched again. He was obviously worried, Nathan thought. Maybe he had something to hide. Or maybe he didn't know what was going on either and was afraid that he would be fired if the problem turned out to be at the Gray Wolf.

"Are you suggesting I killed him?" Jermain asked.

"Of course not." Active doodled in his notebook, letting the silence work. A pattern of intertwined vines sprouted on the page. When it began to appear they would spell "Lucy," he stopped doodling and stared at the engineer.

Jermain fidgeted with his pencil and stared back. Finally he said, "Well, what's your point then?"

"I was just wondering if you might have been in the Dreamland that night and seen something. Obviously, if we had an actual witness to George's suicide, that would pretty much lay things to rest."

"I didn't go anywhere that night," Jermain said. "I was here till about eight, then I went back to my room at the Arctic Inn, watched some TV, and went to bed."

Active wrote "Arctic Inn" in his notebook. "Anything else you'd like to tell me, Mr. Jermain?"

"No, I've told you all I know," he said. "I'd like to talk some more, but I've got a mine to run. Are we about done?"

"We're done." Active clicked off the tape recorder and put it back in his pocket. "Go ahead and send me those personnel files, if you would."

Jermain nodded wordlessly.

They shook hands and Active left the office. As he crossed the lobby, a button on the phone at the vacant receptionist's desk lit up. He reached for the phone, then hesitated, staring at the tiny pinprick of light.

Without a wiretap order, anything he heard would be inadmissible. But at least he'd hear it with his own ears, whatever it was. He picked up the receiver and unscrewed the mouthpiece, then lifted out the round, waferlike microphone and pushed the lighted button.

". . . get up here as fast as you can,"

Jermain's voice said. "A state trooper was just here."

"What did he want?" said a second voice.

"Damned if I know," Jermain said. "He practically accused me of poaching caribou, then he asked me if I killed George Clinton and Aaron Stone. He was all over the map."

"You didn't tell him anything, did you?"

"I told him I was out looking for caribou when Stone died and asleep when Clinton died. I said he could have their personnel files."

The other man was silent, which Jermain seemed to take as an accusation. "Well, I had to do something. I didn't want to make him any more suspicious than he already is."

"OK, but I am advising you not to talk to him again," the second voice said. "Does Tom Werner know about this visit yet?"

"I don't think so. He's up at the mine. How soon can you get here?"

"Hang on, let me check my schedule," the second voice said. "Let's see . . . I've got a hearing tomorrow afternoon, I can get out tomorrow night. That should put me in Chukchi Sunday morning at the

154

latest. You'll be okay till then if you stay away from that trooper."

"I don't know. I'll try."

"Just tell him the company is referring inquiries to me if he tries to contact you again."

Active hung up the receptionist's phone and waited until the lighted button went dark. Then he reassembled the mouthpiece and let himself out of the GeoNord offices.

He stood on the steps and thought about the conversation he had just heard. Jermain apparently had a lawyer on tap. Why? The chief engineer was a balding white executive worried his mine would be blamed for a couple of Native suicides. He could even be another trigger-happy caribou poacher. But could he be a murderer?

Active's eyes were tearing in the same cold west wind that had raked George Clinton's funeral. He wiped them with the back of a glove, got into the Suburban, and bounced south, across the west end of the runway to the FAA Flight Service Station. Inside, a woman was on duty at a console of microphones, instruments, indicator lights, and switches.

A speaker on the console spat a burst of static, then a raspy voice said, "Chukchi

155

radio, six-three alpha, twelve north for landing."

The woman at the console pulled a boom microphone to her lips and said, "Roger, six-three alpha," followed by some aviation jargon Active didn't understand.

Through a glass door, he saw the station chief, a Nome Inupiaq named Ben Akoochuk, hunched over a manual type-writer in a tiny office next to the control room. He spotted Active and came out, hand extended.

"In theory, I can't show you anybody's flight plan without a search warrant," he said when Active asked if Jermain's Cessna had been out of its tie-downs on Monday, Tuesday, or Wednesday.

Active frowned.

Akoochuk smiled. "But, in practice, I could let you look at it and then you could come back with a search warrant if you think you need it." He led Active into the little office, then rummaged in a file drawer and came up with a cardboard slip an inch high and six inches wide. "You ever see one of these?"

Active shook his head.

"Well, it's a flight strip. The controllers, like Donna out there, write down their radio contacts with the pilots on them.

Jermain's plane was only out once in the past week, on Tuesday, and this is the strip from that flight."

Active leaned over Akoochuk's shoulder and looked at the strip. It was full of numbers and symbols that looked like shorthand. "What does it say?"

"It says he filed a flight plan about eleven o'clock Tuesday morning." Akoochuk pointed to the first line on the strip. "He told us he was going down by the Dog River and the Kuchiliuk Hills and he would be back by seven P.M. He actually got back about five, according to this."

"He was out six hours? Can his plane carry that much gas?"

"Not without a belly tank, which Jermain doesn't have," Akoochuk said. "But that doesn't mean anything. He could have landed out in the country for a while."

"Can a Cessna 185 haul a snowmachine?"

"Sure, if it's not a real big one and you take out everything but the pilot's seat. In fact, Jermain's got one. Look."

Akoochuk handed Active a pair of binoculars and pointed at a sleek blue-and-silver plane tied down thirty yards from the FAA station. Active raised the binoculars to his eyes and saw a set of handlebars just visible through a rear window of the plane.

"I guess if he can't land where he wants to, he puts her down as close as he can and takes the snowgo the rest of the way," Akoochuk said.

Active looked back at the flight strip. "If I understand this right, you heard from him when he was leaving and then again when he got back and wanted to land. What about in between? Did he call you from the Dog or the Kuchiliuk Hills?"

"Nope. See here? We never heard from him till he was twelve miles south of the airport, inbound." Akoochuk pointed to a line on the strip.

"So is there any way to know where he really was all day?"

"Not really," Akoochuk said. "Once they get out of sight of the airport, they can turn off their radios and pretend to be Charles Lindbergh if they want to. Jermain could have flown to Kotzebue and had a couple of shots at the Ponderosa, for all I know."

"Don't pilots have to report in regularly or something?"

"Only the airlines. With these little guys, it's all voluntary. They don't even have to file flight plans if they don't want to."

Akoochuk put the flight strip back in its folder. "How come you're so interested in Jermain, anyway? He been shooting caribou the same day he was airborne?"

"Unofficially, I can tell you, could be."

"How about officially?"

"Officially? Officially we troopers never discuss an investigation. If there is an investigation."

Active returned to the trooper office, called the Gray Wolf, identified himself to the operator, and asked to speak with Tom Werner.

"I'll page him," the operator said. She put Active on hold and he listened to a feed of an Anchorage country-and-western station for perhaps five minutes. Then the receptionist came back on.

"You're still blinking," she said. "Mr. Werner didn't pick up?"

"Not yet."

"He must have his pager turned off. Can I take a message?"

"Tell him I'm coming up to the Gray Wolf tomorrow and I'd like to talk with him."

"OK," the receptionist said. "Can I tell him what it's about?"

"No, just that I'd like to speak with

him. If he wants to call me back tonight, the Chukchi police dispatchers can find me."

"OK," she said, and hung up.

Next he called Cowboy Decker to set up a charter to the Gray Wolf for the following morning. Decker said he was busy and the shuttle was going up anyway and would be cheaper. Active called Lienhofer's and made a reservation.

He added a summary of his interview with Jermain to his report and dropped the tape into the folder.

It was quitting time and Friday to boot, so he drove to the Northern Dragon and ordered Number Twelve, the sinus-clearing Szechuan Beef, from a Korean girl who spoke almost no English. Probably another of the innumerable daughters, sisters, cousins, and nieces of Kyung Kim, the Northern Dragon's proprietor.

Kim moved a steady stream of Korean immigrants through the restaurant. Active assumed they worked for nearly nothing or perhaps even paid Kim to get a green card and into America. Where they went after their few months in Chukchi, he had no idea, but he assumed it was someplace warmer.

Active supposed also that there was a

high probability that much was illegal about Kim's operation. But the Northern Dragon was a federal problem. He had resolved to enjoy the occasional Number Twelve with a clear conscience until such time as the Immigration and Naturalization Service decided to pay the Northern Dragon another visit and deport most of the staff, as had happened shortly after his arrival in Chukchi.

When he had finished the Number Twelve, he drove to Pauline Generous's house and turned on his siren for a couple of hoots. No one came out, so he walked through the *kunnichuk* and knocked on the inner door. He waited a couple minutes and knocked again.

Finally, Lucy answered it. "Oh, hi, Nathan," she said. "Pauline went to the store. She said you could wait. Or if you can't wait she can take a taxi to bingo."

Lucy was holding a blue bathrobe closed and had a pink towel wrapped around her head. "Don't mind me," she said when she saw him looking. "My water's frozen, so I came over to use Pauline's shower. I just have to dry my hair, then I'm leaving for my accounting class at the community college. You could watch TV. There's pop in the refrigerator."

"Muktuk and seal oil too, *nalauqmiiyaaq*," she added. She tossed him a remote control and disappeared into the bathroom.

He took a Diet Coke from the refrigerator. A hair dryer whined to life as he sat down and clicked on the state satellite channel. A basketball game was on. He half-drowsed as ten very tall millionaires raced up and down the floor of a stadium in Texas.

Gradually, he realized that the noise of Lucy's hair dryer had become louder. He glanced at the bathroom. The door was open a foot or so.

Lucy had released her grasp on the bathrobe as she worked on her hair, and it had swung open. He could see a smooth sweep of brown curves from thigh to belly to throat, interrupted once where a small, perfect breast jutted from the blue folds. He knew he should clear his throat or scrape his chair or just get up and leave. But he didn't.

The cord of the hair dryer tangled in the collar of the bathrobe. Lucy shrugged it off and let it slide to the floor, now baring a lush swell of hip and concave arch of back. She reached forward and adjusted a mirror for a side view of her hair, in the process giving Active a better view.

His eyes went to her pubic thatch, then back to her breasts, flexing tautly as she ran the brush through her gleaming black hair and followed it with the dryer. He was mesmerized by her areolas, such a deep, intense brown against the lighter brown of her skin that they seemed to glow with their own dark inner light. They were like two eyes staring back into his own.

Lucy clicked off the dryer. He jumped, and realized that two very real black eyes had been staring into his for some time. She turned from the mirror and faced him and for the first time he saw all of her, straight on.

"Would you like me to close the door?" she asked.

He tried to speak, couldn't, and shook his head numbly.

She walked toward him, hands at her sides, and stopped before him. He put his arms around her hips and buried his face in the triangle of hair. He smelled bath oil, a salt marsh under a hot sun, a cool, moss-grown spring.

"What if Pauline comes back?" he asked suddenly.

"She won't," Lucy answered. "She promised."

"And your class?"

"I'm already getting an A. I can miss one."

She led him into Pauline's bedroom and then her boldness deserted her. She scooted under the covers and looked away as he undressed.

As he sank into her honeyed flesh, he thought again of the jade coils of the Katonak and the laughing raven, and, despairingly, of Aaron Stone and George Clinton smiling sympathetically as they drifted away in the ice floes.

Pauline was waiting across the street when he left the house. She came over and climbed into an uncomfortable silence in the Suburban.

"You smell like Lucy's shampoo," she said finally, with an air of satisfaction.

"That wasn't right, what you did," Active said.

"Not good for young man go too long without woman."

"It still wasn't right. I don't think I have the same feeling for Lucy that she has for me. You shouldn't have told her to do this."

"Not good for young man to be without a woman," she said stubbornly. "Go mental, start messing with old ladies or even dogs. Early days ago, nobody make such a big deal about it. Young man and woman want to get together, they go in tent, start baby, that's that. Nowadays, everybody think too much, talk too much, go mental. That's what I tell your *aaka* when I talk to her today. Now turn on your flasher."

"You told Martha about . . . about . . . about your plot with Lucy? My God, what did she say?"

"I never tell her nothing about that," Pauline said. "I don't think she like Lucy."

"How can you tell?"

"Woman always know what other woman think," Pauline said. "So I just ask Martha if she think you're mental because you take old lady to bingo all the time. She say, no, she think you just learn different way to do things at Anchorage." She turned and looked at him. The lenses of her glasses were like two radar dishes aimed at him.

"Then I say, maybe you're mental from going too long without woman and I ask your *aaka* if you have girlfriend down there. She laugh, but she say you don't. You like boys better, maybe?"

"Of course not," Active said. "I'm just

too busy with my trooper work to take care of a woman right now."

"Maybe you need woman to take care of you."

"Maybe someday," Active said. "Not now."

"Hmmph," Pauline said. "Turn on your flasher. Bingo start already."

"Oh, yeah," Active said, remembering why he had come to the old lady's house to begin with. He started the Suburban and headed down Beach Street for the Lions Club.

But he left the flasher off. "First, what about Tillie Miller? Does she have a granddaughter like Lucy who can talk to her?"

"No one," Pauline said. "No one. You heard about that tuberculosis, come through long time ago, kill us Natives?"

He nodded.

"Kill my uncle, kill my first husband, kill everybody in Tillie's family but her, and she's in hospital long time with it herself. Since she get out, she never talk to nobody hardly. She just make mukluks and mittens to sell, walk around town and drink and fight, like now."

He turned on the flasher.

Chapter 9
Saturday Morning, Gray Wolf Mine

Saturday dawned under a high film of opalescent cloud, a ruthless white sky that leached all contour and distinction from the snowy landscape. When Active came out of the trooper office, electric snow eels jittered across his retinas before he could get his sunglasses on. Even with the smoked glass for protection, he squinted as he steered the Suburban down Third Street toward the airport to board the Gray Wolf shuttle.

It was five days since George Clinton and Aaron Stone had gotten off shift at the mine. Three days since George's body had turned up across from the Dreamland. Two days since he and Cowboy had found Aaron's body under the spruces at Qaqsrauq Lake.

But Aaron had almost certainly died first, since his body was frozen solid when they found it. Assuming, as the rumpled pillow and unrolled sleeping bag suggested, that he had slept at least one night at Katy Creek, he could have been killed as early as Tuesday — four days ago.

Murders not solved quickly were usually not solved at all and he wasn't even sure this was a murder case. What did he have, really? Statistical anomalies. Crazy talk from a drunken bereaved *aana*. A jumpy mining engineer who had apparently hired a lawyer, which proved only that he was jumpy.

Active parked, walked into the terminal, gave an Inupiat girl at the counter his travel request, got a ticket, and went out onto the tarmac.

The Gray Wolf shuttle was a Twin Otter, an ugly, stubby Bush workhorse with no bathroom or flight attendants. Just two turboprop engines and two young pilots wearing mirror sunglasses and Lienhofer Aviation shirts with epaulets on the shoulders. They were on a career track that had long since passed Cowboy Decker by, building hours until they had enough time in their logbooks to get out of Chukchi and into the cockpit of an Alaska Airlines jet. Somewhat like Nathan Active. Or so he hoped.

He found a seat beside a middle-aged Inupiat woman in a black Arctic Cat snowmachine suit and Sorel boots. On her lap a yellow Walkman lay atop a folded green parka with a Gray Wolf patch sewn onto a shoulder.

"You're that Eskimo trooper, ah?" she said as he snapped his seat belt. "I heard about you."

"Nathan Active, at your service."

"Lillian Ross." She extended her hand.

He shook it and studied her face. Ross was a Chukchi surname, but he didn't remember having seen her around town. "You live out in one of the villages?"

"No, Anchorage," she said. "Soon as my husband and I get jobs at the Gray Wolf, we get our kids out of Chukchi fast as we can. It's not good for them here. Bad schools, too much drinking and fighting. Too much west wind too."

She dug into a parka pocket and pulled out a package of Juicy Fruit. "You want one? It's good for your ears when you fly."

He shook his head. She unwrapped a stick from the pack and began chewing.

"How do you like Anchorage?"

"It's OK," Ross said. "We have nice house in Muldoon area, kids go to good schools. But it's hard to get Eskimo food. And the kids miss their *aana*. Maybe if the liquor ban pass, we will move back."

"Yeah, sometimes I'm not sure An-

169

chorage is really in Alaska," he said. "I lived in Muldoon myself when I was a kid."

"That was when you was with your *nalauqmiut* parents, right?"

He nodded. "Who takes care of the kids while you're up here?"

"My sister live in Anchorage too," she said. "She watch them when my Lennie and I are both away. But our shifts are staggered, so one of us is usually there."

"Doesn't it cost a lot to fly back and forth to Chukchi all the time?"

"No, the Gray Wolf pay for us to commute."

"Really? I thought the Gray Wolf was supposed to help the economy in Chukchi, not Anchorage." The pilots started the Otter's right engine. Then the propeller on the left whined to life.

"Well, that's kind of what Tom Werner say when we ask him about it," Ross said, her voice rising to be heard over the engines. "But we tell him, if white engineers and bosses can live in Anchorage, commute to mine, how come Eskimos can't? Then the Gray Wolf have to let us."

She finished in a shout, then shook her head, slipped on her earphones, and started the Walkman.

Active put foam plugs in his ears, leaned back, and went to sleep.

He awoke when the pilots throttled back over the Gray Wolf, the whine of the turbine engines collapsing to a burble. From the air, the mine looked so sterile that, except for the snow on the ground, it might have been a moon colony. A landing strip scratched across the floor of a rocky treeless mountain bowl; a cluster of blocky industrial buildings with pickups and snowmachines scattered around; a dirt-walled settling pond, iced over in the cold. And the scar of the mine pit itself, with earth movers scraping out the ore and dumping it into huge trucks that hauled it to the plant.

The pilots dropped the Otter onto the gravel runway, pulled onto an apron where a pickup and a van waited, and shut down the engines.

"Look, it's Tom Werner himself," Ross said as they left the plane. She pointed at the pickup. She got in the van, and Active walked toward the truck, a cold wind plucking at his parka.

Tom Werner was smoking a cigarette, presumably from the pack of Marlboros on the dash. He was wearing the blue sunglasses from the funeral, but this time he had on a shiny Gray Wolf windbreaker.

He stuck his hand out the window of the truck. "Nathan," he said. "Welcome to the Gray Wolf. Ever been here before?"

Active shook his head.

"Get in and I'll give you the grand tour."

Active walked around the front of the truck and climbed into the passenger seat. "You got my message?"

"Not till after I already heard you were coming from my kid sister." Werner grinned at Active's look of mystification. "She works for Lienhofer. She booked your flight last night and took your ticket this morning. Then she called me and told me to find out if a certain state trooper has a regular girlfriend."

Active shook his head. "I'm surrounded."

"Yep," Werner said. "A young man with prospects and no wife . . . well, he's a challenge to all of Inupiat womankind."

Werner started the truck and drove them up a gravel road that paralleled the runway, then climbed toward the rim of the bowl. He stopped at a pullout on the crest. To the left the mine lay snow-covered in its bowl, the sharp-edged manmade things seeming to float on a white ocean under the white sky.

To the right, the road descended the slope, crossed Gray Wolf Creek, and ran, a thread of gray-brown etched on a sea of white, along the Nuliakuk River toward the port on the coast. It was a scar on the purity of the Arctic desert, Active supposed, but such a tiny scar, and the only one in millions of acres of tundra. Further proof of the Arctic's near-total imperviousness to man's efforts to make it anything other than the beautiful frozen barren it had always been.

"You know how we got this mine, Nathan?"

He had heard most of the story, but it was obvious Werner wanted to tell it. He shook his head.

"Brains, timing, and luck. The usual things you need to get anything out of the white man. When we were trying to put the mine together, copper prices were low and interest rates were high, like now. GeoNord said it didn't pencil out. They were going to pull out unless somebody else paid for the road down to Nuliakuk and the port there too."

Werner stopped talking and pointed out the window of the pickup. "Look at that."

Active squinted into the glare. "What? I don't see anything."

"Snowy owl," Werner said. "It's a good day for him. He's invisible against this sky."

Finally, Active caught a flicker of white as the bird passed in front of a rocky outcrop scraped free of snow by the wind. "What will he find to eat out here?"

"Not much," Werner said. "But he's keeping an eye on the brush along the creek bed down there. If a rabbit shows his nose, our friend will feast."

"You were telling me how GeoNord was ready to pull out."

"Right," Werner said. "Right. I was in the state senate then, so I put in a bill for a hundred and eighty million dollars to have the state build the road and port, just like it builds roads and ports for the white people in Anchorage and Fairbanks." He took some Dentyne gum from inside his windbreaker, unwrapped two pieces, and put them in his mouth. He saw Active watching. "Want some?"

"No, thanks."

"Anyway, I worked the Gray Wolf bill through the senate, but Governor Turner said it was special-interest legislation and he got it bottled up in the House. The legislature adjourned for the summer and I thought we were dead. Then Turner almost got impeached. You remember the Ship Creek prison scandal?"

Active had been at the university in Fairbanks the summer a grand jury accused Governor Dale Turner of throwing the prison contract to a gang of Anchorage construction executives who had put more than a hundred thousand dollars into his election campaign. The legislature had called itself into special session and tried to impeach Turner. He had survived by two votes in the senate but lost the next election by twenty thousand.

"I remember," Active said. "The governor fired the attorney general and the head prosecutor, but got distracted before he worked his way down to the trooper investigators. Everyone was very relieved."

Werner chuckled, then continued. "So, the impeachment hearings were going full tilt and the governor's lobbyist came around to see how the Bush Caucus was leaning. I told him the Bush Caucus was leaning in favor of the Gray Wolf Infrastructure Project. He called back a couple hours later to say the governor had been doing a lot of soul-searching and had decided the Gray Wolf was in the public interest, after all. The Bush Caucus voted against impeachment and the Gray Wolf bill passed on the first day of the next regular session."

"So Governor Turner was a man of his word," Active said.

Werner smiled, started the pickup, and headed back down into the bowl.

"Anyway, the Gray Wolf's been generating jobs three, four years now, ever since construction started," he said. "Unemployment's dropping in Chukchi, the social workers tell me wife-beating is down sixty percent, and child abuse is lower too. When we get the liquor ban, I think it will get even better. There's a chance here that we Inupiat can deal with Western culture on our own terms for once, instead of getting run over by it."

Werner took him through the plant, pointing out the ball mills that crushed the ore and the flotation tanks and furnaces that extracted the copper from it. They went through the Gray Wolf's warehouses, then to a cavernous shop filled with pickups, dump trucks, earth movers, and snowmachines in various stages of repair by men and women in Gray Wolf coveralls.

"This is where Aaron worked mainly," Werner said.

"So these people worked with him?" Active motioned at the rumps of two mechanics whose heads were buried under the hood of a Ford pickup.

"No, his crew went off shift the same time he did last week," Werner said. "I can probably have somebody dig up their names and home addresses. You want them?"

Active shrugged. "Sure."

"We'll fax it to the trooper offices this afternoon or tomorrow. You want a list of the janitors who worked with George Clinton too?"

Active nodded, and Werner pulled a little notebook from a hip pocket, wrote in it, and put it away.

Werner took him quickly through the cafeteria and the recreation area, then to the hive of Atco trailers where the workers slept.

"This was George's during his last shift." Werner opened a door to one of the cell-like sleeping rooms. "Looks like it's empty this shift, though."

It contained a single bed, a desk and lamp, a television and a closet, but no sign of a sink, shower, or toilet. Evidently, the bathroom facilities were communal at the Gray Wolf.

Active looked in the desk drawers and the closet, but found nothing to show that George Clinton had ever lived there.

"We have lockers they can leave their

stuff in between shifts," Werner said. "George's was empty. I'll show you what was in Aaron's in a minute."

He led the way to a door that said Chukchi Region Inc.

"We have our own little setup here, separate from Geo-Nord." Werner opened the door and motioned Active into the empty office. "It's mainly so the Native workers will have some place to go if they have problems with GeoNord. I'm usually up here at least once a week, and, when I'm not, someone else from the Chukchi office is. We even have an eight hundred number in case there's a problem when we're not around."

He sat at one end of a green vinyl couch in the little suite's waiting room and motioned for Active to sit at the other. The only other furnishings in the room were an old gray metal desk with a telephone and lamp on it and a filing cabinet, also gray and metal. An Alaska Airlines calendar hung on a wall, but the page hadn't been turned in two months.

"So what are you finding out about George and Aaron?" Werner started to take off the blue sunglasses, then seemed to think better of it. He slid them back up the bridge of his nose. "I hear you think maybe they didn't kill themselves?"

178

"I haven't reached any conclusions yet," Active said. "I just want to be thorough. Were they having any problems at work? Either one of them ever use your eight hundred number?"

"George Clinton had a little trouble, but not serious," Werner said. "He came into the Chukchi office to see me about it, oh, maybe three weeks ago."

"What was the problem?"

"One of the white guys here was giving him a hard time, and he thought the guy hated Eskimos."

"Was it Michael Jermain?"

Werner frowned. "Jermain? No, why would you think of him?"

"He was pretty jumpy when I talked to him yesterday. And I hear he's bringing in a lawyer."

"Really? Any idea who?"

Active shook his head.

"I wouldn't make too much of it," Werner said. "Jermain's the nervous type. Probably just wants to make sure he and the company don't get blamed for over-stressing the help or something."

"Yeah, probably," Active said. "So what about the guy who was hassling George?"

"I told George I could probably get the guy fired but I thought he should work it out himself, like I had to do when I was younger. Some of these old guys have worked remote so long, all you have to be is human and they hate you. George said he would think about it a while, try to take care of it himself, and come see me again if he couldn't. That was the last I heard about it."

"What's the man's name?" Active asked, pulling out his notebook. "I'll see if George seemed upset enough about him to kill himself. Or if the guy acts mean enough to have killed George."

Werner dragged silently on a Marlboro and looked out the window at the white hills around the mine. "I'm trying to remember. I'm not sure George ever told me the name."

"You didn't get his name? Couldn't somebody like that disrupt things at the mine?"

"Sure, he could," Werner said. "But George wanted to handle it himself and I decided to let him. You can ask around if you want, but the Gray Wolf has something like four hundred employees. And about half of them are off shift any given day. They're scattered from Seattle to Barter Island."

"How about Aaron Stone? Do you know why he might kill himself?"

"No idea," Werner said. "He started

here before the mine opened, did his job, never caused trouble. I heard he might hit the Dreamland sometimes when he was off shift, but I never heard of him having a drinking problem at work."

Werner stood up and went to the filing cabinet. "We did find this when we cleaned out his locker, though." He pulled a shopping bag from a drawer and handed it to Active.

The trooper looked in. Two pairs of white socks, one clean and one dirty. One Louis L'Amour novel. A copy of the Alaska hunting and trapping regulations. And four Jack Daniel's miniatures, the kind stewardesses sold on airliners.

"Aaron would have been suspended for a month if he got caught with those," Werner said. "Since the Gray Wolf isn't a democracy, we don't need an election to ban liquor up here. But, like I said, I never heard of it causing problems for him on the job. He seemed fine."

Active closed the shopping bag and set it beside him on the couch. "That's what puzzles me about these two deaths. Two of them so close together, neither with much reason to do it, one guy well past suicide age, and they both worked here. Were they friends?"

"Not that I know of," Werner said. "But I wouldn't expect it. Different ages, the families weren't related."

Active wrote in his notebook for a moment, then looked out the window.

"What did you find in George Clinton's locker?"

"Nothing. Looks like he took everything with him when he rotated off shift. Most of our workers do."

"So do you think they killed themselves?"

"How can anyone know?" Werner said. "But if they didn't, that means somebody murdered them and made it look like suicide. Who would do that? You think some outsider is shooting Eskimos?"

Active shrugged.

"They don't need to, Nathan. They just send in liquor and we kill ourselves."

They were silent. Werner got up and walked over to the window. He smoked as a dump truck thudded past with a load of concentrate, headed for the coast.

"I have a theory," he said at last. "Not really a theory, more of a feeling. You know, the old-time Inupiat weren't much afraid of death. They thought of it more as another phase of life, and one that would probably be easier than hunting seals in a blizzard. At least, that's what they told the white anthropologists."

"You're saying suicide is more natural for the Inupiat?"

"I think it's possible," Werner said. "I think I'm too westernized to really grasp the idea. I speak hardly any Inupiaq, you know. When I was growing up, the government still sent Native kids to those Outside high schools where we weren't allowed to speak anything but English. But sometimes I think I catch a glimpse of how the old-timers thought, like how you could barely see that snowy owl up on the ridge just now."

He left the window and returned to the couch.

"We Inupiat used to have to leave our old ones out on the ice to die when times were hard," he said. "Or sometimes the elders would decide on their own when they couldn't contribute any more. I read one book about the early days where an old man ordered his family to help him hang himself, and they did it. I think maybe it wasn't so hard for them, because they all thought he was just moving on to the next phase of life."

"But George Clinton and Aaron Stone were still contributing."

183

"Maybe they just got curious or impatient. Who knows what they were thinking?" Werner shook his head. "Whatever it was, I hope this liquor vote Tuesday will make suicide less common." He looked as forlorn as he had on the bluff the day before.

"Yeah, I heard you at the funeral," Active said.

"I've been to so many, I can hardly drag myself anymore." Werner was silent for a long time. "Well, do you need anything else from me?"

"I guess not," Active said. "When will the next shuttle be up? Or should I call Chukchi for a charter?"

"The plane you came in on is still here." Werner pointed out the window at the runway. "They held it for some guys who had to finish work on the ball mills."

They left the office and climbed into Werner's truck. "So how are things with the troopers?" he asked as they bounced toward the airstrip.

"Oh, not bad," Active said. "I think the honchos are just relieved we're between political scandals at the moment, so we can chase regular crooks."

"I'm sure," Werner said. "How's your boss, Carnaby, doing, anyway?"

"He professes great happiness at being in the Bush again, where the real work of the troopers is done."

Werner chuckled. "Too bad about that mess with Howell. I knew Carnaby when he was starting out in the Nome detachment. He seemed like a pretty straight shooter. Liked Eskimos too, as far as I could see."

"He's a good man," Active said. "He was teaching at the trooper academy when I was there. I think a lot of the village guys would have dropped out if he hadn't been around. They used to call him Super Trooper."

"What does he think of your suicide investigation?"

"Actually, he's on leave," Active said. "Personal business in Anchorage."

"In other words, Senator Howell's problems are far from over?"

Active turned and stared at him. Werner kept his eyes on the road.

"I wouldn't know about that," Active said. "We're barred by court order from investigating the good senator. It's now a federal matter. If it's any matter at all."

"So I hear. But I also hear this: If Carnaby *was* investigating Howell, on his own time, say, he'd be looking for a woman named Bobbi Jean Jenkins. Stripper, party girl, little bit of a cocaine whore? Key witness in the Howell matter, but hard to find?"

Active froze. How would Werner know what Carnaby was up to? Who else knew?

"Don't worry, I want to help Carnaby and you too," Werner said. "It's just that our present senator, who happens to be my cousin Darryl Beaver, hears things in Juneau now and again and he passes them along to me. This was one of the things he heard."

"It's on the street in Juneau that Carnaby's still after Howell? My God."

"Not on the street, exactly," Werner said. "But Darryl's very gnawingly inquisitive. And since Senator Howell opposes us on the Native hunting-rights bill, I suggested Darryl ask around some more to see if there's any way we could help in this investigation that Carnaby *isn't* conducting." He looked at Active and winked.

Active shook his head and stared out the side window of the pickup.

"So Darryl talked to some lobbyists," Werner said. "He talked to some of Bobbi Jean's girlfriends, and, sure enough, somebody knew something. She's dancing in Las Vegas."

Werner slid a strip of yellow lined paper across the seat toward Active. "Helen Ready — Lodestar Lounge" was scrawled on it, along with a telephone number in the 702 area code.

"Take it. You give it to Carnaby, he gives it to the FBI, and Howell's out of our way on the hunting-rights bill. Carnaby gets his career back and maybe he recommends you to run the Chukchi detachment when he heads back to headquarters."

Werner turned the pickup onto the apron and stopped beside the airstrip. "And maybe about the same time, Cousin Darryl calls the director of Public Safety up before the Rural Affairs Committee to testify on the trooper program to get more Natives into management. We Inupiat have to take care of each other, like the whites do."

Active stared at the paper. Werner stared at Active and dragged on his Marlboro. Active pushed the paper back to Werner. "Thanks, but I just can't take it."

"Whatever." Werner shrugged and put the paper in a pocket of his windbreaker. "I just hope Carnaby finds Bobbi Jean before too many more people hear he's looking."

Active got out of the pickup and walked

onto the shuttle. Before he buckled his seat belt, he pulled out his notebook and wrote down the number of the Lodestar Lounge in Las Vegas, Nevada.

Chapter 10
Saturday Night, Chukchi

Active slipped into the Dreamland and stood quietly beside the double doors as his eyes adjusted to the gloom and his ears to the roar.

A bar covered with linoleum floor tiles ran down the right side of the long room and tables ran down the left. Neon signs high on the walls beamed out Heineken and Budweiser and Arctic Gold through the thick haze that always hung near the ceiling. And there was that Dreamland smell: sweat, beer, cigarettes, and dust.

It was only nine o'clock, but already most of the bar stools and chairs were filled. Glasses, bottles, and cans rattled on tabletops. People laughed and swore, and shouted to make themselves heard over all the voices and the heavy metal band screaming from the little dance floor at the end of the room. A poster stapled to the wall beside the door said they were the Catastronauts, "direct from Anchorage."

Some of the serious drunks were already head-down over the tables. Active watched as Hector Martinez grabbed one by the collar and belt and frog-marched him toward the double doors. You had to be sober enough to sit up and drink if you wanted to take up space at the Dreamland.

Active squeezed in at the bar and caught the bartender's eye as he returned from his ejection duties.

"What do you want?" Martinez asked sourly. "I got no problems tonight and if I did they'd be city cop problems, not yours."

"A Diet Coke and some information," Active said.

Martinez moved down the bar, towards the cooler. He was Chukchi's unlikeliest citizen, in Active's opinion. As dark as the Inupiat he lived among, but taller, Martinez always looked as if he had just stepped off the set of a Western: cowboy boots, cowboy shirt, bolo tie, and, except in the coldest weather, a Stetson.

He was bartending and waiting tables in Nome, the story went, when two of the Okolona sisters hit town with the Chukchi High School girls' basketball team for a tournament. Martinez had been in the north long enough to know the Okolona family was the closest thing to old money in Chukchi. When the basketball team flew home a week later, Susie Okolona, the rare homely daughter in a bloodline fabled for beauties, was Susie Martinez. And Hector was on the first rung of the American opportunity ladder.

Now, three little Martinezes were making their way through the Chukchi school system and Hector ran the Okolona empire: general stores in two of the outlying villages, a grocery and snowmachine dealership in Chukchi, and the Dreamland money machine.

The mystery was, why was Hector Martinez in Nome in the first place? The gossip river had it that he had fled north — far north — after shooting his wife and her boyfriend in Guadalajara.

Active doubted it. For one thing, similar stories trailed half the outsiders in the Arctic, especially those who, like Martinez, never spoke of their pasts. For another thing, Active had checked Martinez out in the national crime computer and found nothing. Of course, the computer wasn't reliable when it came to aliens and Hector Martinez could be the Hispanic equivalent of John Smith. Still, Martinez had been around the Arctic for fifteen years without shooting anybody, so Active had not pushed it.

Martinez set a Diet Coke on the linoleum bar top and took Active's money. "Information, huh? About what?"

"About George Clinton. Did you talk to him when he was in here that night?"

"Just to take his order. I already told all this to the city cops. Why don't you ask them? I got work to do."

"Did he talk to anybody except the guys he was with?"

"How would I know?" Martinez opened the cash register, fished out three quarters, and put them on the bar in front of Active. "I didn't see him talk to anybody, but how do I know what he did in the john or if he went outside for a smoke?"

"Did he come here a lot?"

"Nah, not much. That night was the first time he been in for maybe a couple of months. I think one of his buddies said it was George's bachelor party. I guess he was going to marry Emily Hoffman."

"Yeah, I heard," Active said. "I guess she's taking it pretty hard. Know where I could find her?"

"She's right over there." Martinez pointed to where a bearded *nalauqmiut* with a ponytail was drinking beer with a slender, delicate-featured Inupiaq girl who looked about seventeen. "She's been coming in a lot since he shot himself."

Active felt relieved — first, that Emily was alive, and second, that her baby wasn't showing yet. Then he realized he had no idea whether liquor was worse for a baby early in pregnancy or late. He picked up his Diet Coke and scooped up the quarters from the bar.

"Maybe I should charge for my information," Martinez said. "The liquor ban passes, that's all I'll be able to sell. Goddamn, it's un-American. I come here, work hard, build this place up, now the do-gooders and the government want to take it all away."

"Tell the Okolonas to open a Chinese restaurant, like the Koreans."

"Goddamn Koreans are taking over everything," Martinez said. "You watch, pretty soon you Eskimos and the *nalauqmiuts* too will all be working for the Koreans. Me too, if the liquor ban passes. We should close the borders."

Active turned from the bar and walked to Emily Hoffman's table. Her drinking partner wore a down vest over white coveralls and had a daub of white paint on his beard. He also had a diamond stud in his right ear. Probably a construction worker from the new National Guard armory going up at the north end of town, Active decided.

"Mind if I join you?" he asked. "I'm Trooper Nathan Active."

The girl nodded in recognition, though he didn't recall having met her before. The painter turned in his chair and looked up at Active. "Sure," he said cautiously.

"I didn't catch your name."

"Oh, sorry," the painter said, putting out his hand. "Travis Taylor, Local 618."

"How long have you known Emily, Mr. Taylor?"

"Since Thursday," Taylor said. "In fact, she's been staying with me at the Arctic Inn. You gonna sit down?"

Active stayed on his feet and looked down at the painter. At least he knew now why Emily had been so hard to find. "Been keeping her liquored up, have you?"

"She claims she's twenty-one. The Mexican carded her when she came in. Gimme a break."

"I am twenty-one!" the girl said.

"You aware she's expecting a child?" Active asked. "You know you're pouring those Olys into an unborn baby? You ever hear of fetal alcohol syndrome?"

"You shut up, Nathan," Emily said, slurring her words slightly. "Stay out of my business."

"Jesus," Taylor said. "All I wanted was a little . . . company. Spare me the cultural genocide rap, there, Officer Nanook."

"Fuck you, Travis," the girl said. She began to sob.

"Jesus," Taylor said again. He picked up his beer, stalked away, and glared at them from a stool at the bar.

Active sat down, shrugged out of his parka, and hung it on the back of his chair. Emily grabbed his arm and buried her face in his neck, bawling into his uniform shirt.

He stiffened, detached her hand from his elbow, and gently pushed her back into her seat. He wiped his collar with a handkerchief, then handed it to her and sipped his Diet Coke while she mopped at her eyes and blew her nose.

"You shouldn't be here, Emily."

"Why did George do it?" she asked. "Now he never see his baby. Am I too ugly? Too mean with him?"

"You're very pretty. But you'll be ugly if you spend much time in this place. And you'll hurt your baby. George's baby."

"Fuck him. If he don't care about his

195

baby, why should I?" She took a drink from her Oly. "Got a cigarette?"

Active sighed. "No, and you shouldn't smoke, either."

"Fuck you, Nathan." She took another drink from the Oly.

"Look, I need to talk to you. Can we leave this place?"

"No, we could talk here," she said.

"Did George tell you anything special when he came back from the Gray Wolf on Monday? I heard the *nalauqmiuts* up there were giving him a hard time. Was he mad at the *nalauqmiuts?*"

"He tell me he love me, take me to Hawaii for honeymoon." She started to cry again.

Active waited until the sobs subsided. "Did he tell you anything about work?"

"He say something about a problem up there, but not about the *nalauqmiuts*. I think he like the *nalauqmiuts* at the mine OK. He go hunting with them couple times."

"What was the problem at the mine?"

The girl's mouth moved, but Active couldn't hear the words. The Catastronauts' drummer was finishing off a song in a barrage of rim shots. Active waited until the drummer bashed his way to silence.

"I couldn't hear you," Active said. "What was the problem at the mine?"

"Something about leashes," the girl said.

"Leashes? At the Gray Wolf? You mean like for dogs? Do they have guard dogs there?"

"No, not leashes. LEASHES. You deaf?"

"Leases? You mean like leases for the land the mine is on?"

"No, like suck your blood, Nathan. LEE-CHES." She said it slowly and loudly, with great concentration. "You mental?"

"Leeches? At the Gray Wolf?"

"That's what George say. Leeches killing fish at the Gray Wolf, something like that. I can't remember for sure, we barely talk about it. He don't seem very worried." She blew her nose into his handkerchief again, then offered it to him in a sodden lump.

"No, thanks, you keep it." He pushed her hand back. "You say George wasn't worried about the leeches?"

"No, he say GeoNord will take care of it. I guess he talk to somebody about it when he get off shift last week."

"Who did he talk to?"

"Somebody at GeoNord, I guess."

"Was it Michael Jermain?"

"I dunno. He never say." She put the Oly to her lips and turned it up.

197

He looked away as it gurgled down her throat. What on earth was she talking about? It made so little sense, he could hardly think of another question.

Finally, Emily set the can on the table, then looked at him dreamily. "You think Travis would adopt George's baby? Maybe we could call him George Taylor."

Active studied the painter, still eyeing them from the bar. "I doubt it. He doesn't look like the marrying kind."

"You never know," the girl said. "He seem nice."

"He's just —" Active started to explain exactly what it was that Travis Taylor saw in Emily Hoffman, then gave it up as hopeless. "Look, how did George find out about these leeches?"

Emily lowered the can and twirled it, studying the shiny aluminum as if it were a crystal ball, full of answers. "Let's see, what he say? I think he say he find pick —" Emily's eyes widened and Active heard a commotion behind him. "Look out, Nathan!" she screamed, shoving herself back from the table.

He was halfway out of his chair when something thudded into his back. He staggered forward a few steps, right hand going for the .357 on his hip, caught his balance, and turned to see he wouldn't need the gun.

Two men were wheeling slowly in a drunken minuet, grasping each other's arms, shoving and occasionally throwing clumsy, ineffectual punches. "Goddamn you shit, you stay away from her," one said.

"If you can't keep her happy —" They went down and the second drunk's advice on satisfying a woman was lost in the crash.

Active reached the dogpile simultaneously with Hector Martinez. They pulled the combatants apart and hauled them to their feet.

Martinez had ended up with his hands on the collar and belt of the second drunk. "All right, you get out of here, Jonathan. I told you before not to mess with anybody's wife in my place." He headed for the door with Jonathan staggering ahead of him, arms and legs flapping loosely like a marionette's. The crowd that had ringed the gladiators drifted away.

"What about this one?" Nathan shouted.

"Ah, Simeon's harmless except when somebody dances with his wife," Martinez yelled back over his shoulder. "Let him go."

Active released Simeon and he staggered

toward the men's room, his fingers pressed to a cut on his lip that was leaking blood down his chin and onto a white sweatshirt that said Point Hope Harpooners.

Active righted his chair and pulled it back to the table, which somehow had stayed on its legs through the scuffle. He looked around for Emily and finally spotted her on the dance floor with Travis. It looked like they were in a contest to see which one could swallow the other's tongue first.

He pulled on his parka and shoved his way to the deck outside the Dreamland's doors. He paused, trying to push the image of pretty pregnant drunk Emily out of his mind and concentrate on her words. Leeches killing fish? What did it mean, if anything?

Suddenly the double doors banged open behind him. A woman flew out, staggered across the deck, and landed on her back in the gravel and snow. As the drunks around the front of the bar scattered, Simeon leapt through the open door, dived off the deck, straddled the woman, and began pounding her face with his fists. The drunks closed in again to watch.

"Goddamn you shit," Simeon screamed.

Active plunged in, knocked Simeon off,

planted a knee in his chest, and realized the nearest handcuffs were in the Suburban. Just then, the city police van pulled up.

Mason, the cop, trotted over and took Active's place on Simeon's chest. Mason was pulling out a set of handcuffs when a bystander walked over and said in a high voice, "It's OK, man, she's his wife."

Mason looked closely at the brawler's face, then at the woman, then at the bystander, and said, "Oh, yeah, you're right, Kinnuk." He helped the man up, then shook him. "Don't let this happen again, Simeon."

"Go ahead, arrest him," Active said. "I witnessed the whole thing. This is an easy assault conviction."

"Sorry, Nathan. The D.A. says no domestic violence prosecutions without a complaint from the victim. And this victim won't complain." Mason turned to the woman and helped her up.

"You should arrest him," she said, blowing bubbles in the blood and mucus coming from her nose. "He always beat me up."

"Mary, if you'd quit drinking and fooling around, this wouldn't happen," Mason told her. "Besides, if I do arrest Simeon, you'll just drop the charges when you sober up, same as always. Now you go on home to your kids."

He turned back to Simeon and shook him again. "And you go to your mom's house for the night, or I will arrest you, Simeon."

Instead, Simeon jerked his head toward the bar. Mary nodded, and they walked back into the Dreamland, arm in arm.

"This is what the D.A. calls a dodney," Mason said.

"A dodney?"

"D-O-D-N-H-I. Drunk On Drunk, No Human Involvement. The new D.A.'s supposedly gonna be a woman. Maybe she'll see it different, but right now all we can do is scold 'em."

Active was putting his key in the Suburban's ignition when it hit him. His adoptive parents' home in Muldoon, the first few years they lived there. No public water or sewer yet, so they had a well in a corner of the front yard and a septic tank at the downhill end of the back yard. In summer, the area just below the septic tank was always the greenest, lushest part of the lawn. That was where wastes from the tank seeped into the soil. The leach field, Ed Wilhite had called it. But in Muldoon, the leach field only meant more mowing for young Nathan Active. It had never killed any fish. Poor dim little Emily Hoffman hadn't understood what George Clinton was telling her, but at least she had remembered it.

He started the engine and put the Suburban in gear, but something about the crowd around the front of the Dreamland made him jam on the brakes. He studied the faces for a moment, then rolled down his window as a familiar female figure started for the double doors.

"Lucy!" he shouted. "You don't really want to go in there, do you?"

Slowly, she turned and faced him. Slowly, she crossed the deck, descended the steps, and walked to the window of the Suburban.

"I never wanted to before, but tonight I do," she told him. "I can't do anything right."

She felt his eyes on her, but she didn't look up.

"Get in," he said. "I'll take you home."

"Oh, you're not afraid I'll trap you again?" She looked into his eyes, then away. "No thanks."

"Is that what Pauline told you? That I said you trapped me?"

She clenched her teeth to keep her chin from trembling and squeezed her eyes shut against the tears. She felt them trickle down her cheeks anyway and stood in silent helpless fury by the Suburban. *Just like a woman,* he was probably thinking.

She saw him fumble in the glove compartment. Then he handed her something. *Oh, no, a packet of Kleenex!*

"Get in," he said again. "We'll get some coffee at the Korean's place if you don't want to go home yet. We need to talk."

"I don't want anybody to see my eyes like this," she said. She opened the packet and wiped them with a wad of tissue.

"All right, I'll get the coffee to go and we can drink it in the Suburban," he said. "That way it'll be official business. OK? Will you get in?"

"Hmpph," she said.

"You're a lot like your grandmother, you know."

"Hmmph," she said again. But she found herself walking around to the passenger door and climbing in.

Nathan drove them to the Northern Dragon and went in for the coffee. The moment the door closed behind him, she flipped open her purse and made emergency repairs to her face. When he came

204

out and handed her coffee in a Styrofoam cup, she inhaled deeply, then took a big gulp. It cleared out her sinuses some, but not as much as she had hoped. She would probably still snuffle like a kid with a runny nose if she tried to talk.

He drove the Suburban across the bridge over the lagoon, past the trail to the cemetery, and a little way toward the tundra lakes that supplied Chukchi's drinking water. He stopped where the road topped a rise and turned the Suburban to face the village.

The night was cloudy. No moon, stars, or aurora in sight. Just the lights of the village, spread from left to right like a beaded bracelet.

"Kind of pretty from this distance," he said. "Who knows, if the liquor ban passes, it might even be pretty from close up someday."

She said nothing, but took another slug of coffee for her sinuses. He turned on the radio and tuned in KSNO. The news was on. The announcer said something about the balance of trade. A snowmachine buzzed past, its headlight illuminating the interior of the Suburban.

She studied him from the corner of her eye. His eyes were so careful and wary, they made his face seem as cold and far-off as the northern lights. But then the lips, unexpectedly full and vulnerable, turned those wary eyes into pools of loneliness so deep that, as always, she felt herself drowning.

The snowmachine passed and his face receded into shadow. She took a final sip of coffee and a deep breath.

"I'm sorry about last night." Her voice sounded fairly normal, at least to her. And her sinuses felt fine. "Pauline is just so old-fashioned."

"Old-fashioned?"

"You know. If two people like each other, they should just get together and let everything take care of itself."

"She gave me the same lecture about going in the tent and starting a baby," he said. "But I don't think things are so simple now."

"You didn't enjoy it?" She put a hand on his thigh. "You acted like you did." She thought she felt him stir, then he put her hand back in her lap. Politely but firmly.

"You kidding?" he asked. "Your body, it's like that warm place the old-timers thought we would go in the afterlife. Inupiat heaven. Of course, I enjoyed it. I'm a man, after all."

"I noticed," she said. "I'm still tender. And so?"

"And so I'd like to drop the rear seat and invite you back there this minute."

"OK," she said softly.

"No, that wouldn't be right," he said in that sober way of his. "It would be OK if we were both serious . . . or even if we were both just fooling around. But I don't think you want to fool around and I don't want . . . I can't be serious about anything but my work right now. I have to make my way in the troopers." He turned the Suburban's heater down a notch and unzipped his parka.

"You're not serious?" she said. "What about at work? You hang around Dispatch all the time because you like telephones?"

"That was a mistake. I'm sorry. I wasn't thinking."

"Maybe you think too much, Nathan!" She stopped herself from saying more, alarmed at the complaining tone in her voice. Where did that come from? She had to sound less reproachful. "Don't you ever just jump in?" she asked softly.

"I think I'm an example of what happens when people just jump in," he said. "My mother jumped in bed with my father when they were both too young. Now I have to buy twice as many presents on Mother's Day as a normal person."

She unzipped her parka and shrugged out of it. From the corner of her eye, she saw him studying her. She put her hands behind her neck and leaned her head back. She felt his eyes drop from her face and slide down her throat, then over her breasts. When other men did that, she was angry. But with Nathan it was like a caress. She felt herself flush, first at the throat, then lower and lower. She waited for him to kiss her or at least speak. But he turned his eyes back toward the lights of Chukchi and said nothing.

She pulled the coat over her shoulders again and tried to think how to get the conversation back to the two of them, but no ideas came. "What happened to your father anyway?" she asked. She had to fill the silence with something. "Your real one, I mean. Is he still around?"

"He was a Nome man named Charles Penn. A couple years after I came along, I guess he joined the army to get out of the Bush and learn to fly helicopters. He was shot down in Vietnam. Once, when the traveling version of the Vietnam Wall came to Anchorage, I went down and found his name and made a rubbing of it."

Nathan's voice was flat, like a kid giving a book report in school. There should be something in it — anger, sadness, something — she thought. "What did you feel?"

"Not much," he said in the same flat voice. "A little regret that I never met him, a little curiosity about what he was like. But by then I knew who I was. The adopted-out son of an Inupiat woman, the adopted son of two white people."

"Your *nalauqmiut* parents weren't good to you?"

"Of course they were. But there was always something missing . . . like they were full-time baby-sitters instead of real parents. I don't know."

Another snowmachine buzzed by, this one headed into town and pulling a dogsled, a rider on the runners. She couldn't think of anything to say now. The silence built up and up until he broke it.

"What about your parents?"

"They live upriver, in Ebrulik," she said. "My dad runs the village store there."

The engine of the Suburban rumbled and the heater droned. Now neither of them said anything for a long time. She thought Nathan must have run out of ideas too.

"So where are we?" he asked finally.

"About a mile from town, I guess."

"You know what I mean. Are you all right now?"

She sensed he was wrapping things up, trying to close her like one of his case files, but she couldn't think of anything to do about it. His resistance to intimacy was a wall she couldn't climb.

"No, I'm not all right," she said. "But I'll live. I won't go into the Dreamland if that's what you mean. At least not tonight." That tone of reproach she hated was back in her voice, but she couldn't help herself.

"Look, if you want to get out of Chukchi, I might be able to help you find a dispatch job with the troopers in Anchorage," he said.

So now he was trying to send her away. What a mess she had made. "Just take me home!" She heard the tremor in her voice and felt her eyes starting to go again. She fought to keep from bawling.

"What? What's . . . Just tell me what I missed."

"Shut up, damn you. Take me home." She gave up and started sobbing.

She saw him shake his head and put the Suburban in gear. He switched on KSNO as they started back to town.

"To Rodney in Chukchi from Dad in

Nuliakuk," the announcer said. "Sending a seal down by Lienhofer's tomorrow. Bring your snowgo to the airport."

Chapter 11
Sunday Morning, Chukchi

It was a few minutes before eight and a Sunday morning to boot, but the lights were on when Active arrived at the log cabin that served as the Chukchi outpost and living quarters of the Alaska Department of Environmental Protection. An Arctic Cat with a small dogsled hitched to the back stood at the *kunnichuk* door, which was propped open with the shell of an old Macintosh computer.

He shut off the Suburban and walked around the tail of the sled into the *kunnichuk,* then backed out as a big cardboard box barged toward him at chest level. The box was labeled "Childs, ADEP, Bethel." Two smallish hands were its only visible support.

"Do you mind?" said a woman's voice from behind the box. "I gotta get this shit to the fucking airport. You'd fucking think they'd fucking pay somebody to do this since it was their fucking idea, but, no, I gotta do it my own fucking self."

"Hey, let me get it." He took the box, dropped it into the basket of the sled, and turned to face Kathy Childs, the environmental department's only biologist in Chukchi. In fact, as far as he knew, she was the department's only employee north of Nome.

Childs had a lean, sinewy body, brown hair in a long thick braid, and blue eyes that blazed startlingly from a face tanned nut brown by near-constant exposure to wind and sky. This morning, she was outfitted in a pair of rust-colored Carhartt bib overalls with a set of thermal underwear beneath, and Sorel boots. Her foul mouth, he had concluded on the basis of a nodding acquaintance and a few quick conversations, was attached to a fine mind and a good heart.

"Oh, thanks, Nathan. Didn't recognize you from behind the box there." She plopped down on the sled.

"Day off to a bad start?"

"Yeah, you could say that. I'm being transferred to Bethel."

"Not Bethel! My God, why?"

"It's probably the only place they could find with more drunks and mosquitoes than fucking Chukchi."

213

"No, I mean why are you being transferred?"

"Beats the shit out of me. Ask Juneau."

"Yeah, like Juneau talks to me," he said. "When's your replacement coming? Who is it?"

"There isn't going to be one. This office is being mothballed indefinitely." She stood up and started back into the house. "They'll service Chukchi out of Nome. Like a bull services a cow, would be my guess."

"Hang on a minute. How much stuff you got?"

"Tons. Two sled loads, maybe three. And I gotta get it on the morning flight." She looked at her wristwatch. "Which, fuck, leaves in forty-eight minutes. Shit."

"Let's use the Suburban. We can get it in one trip and that'll give me a chance to pump you a little bit."

"In your dreams, Macho Man," she said. But she grinned and hoisted the box out of the sled. He opened the Suburban's rear doors and she slid it in.

"Shut that trash mouth a minute and listen," he said. "I need some information about the Gray Wolf."

"The Gray Wolf and Bethel in one day. Jesus fuck."

"Well, we don't have much time if you're leaving on the morning plane."

"My stuff is, but I'm not. I'm taking the dogs up the Isignaq for a few days and knocking down some caribou. At least my mutts will eat well in Bethel. We can come back here and talk after we're done at the airport."

He helped her load the other boxes from the office into the Suburban. Some were addressed to her in Bethel. Others were marked for the environmental protection district office in Nome. When the boxes were all loaded, she kicked the dead Macintosh out of the way and slammed the *kunnichuk* door. He closed the Suburban, drove the two blocks to the airport, and heaved the boxes up onto the Alaska Airlines freight dock as she signed papers for the agent.

The pressure off now, they drove back to what had been her office. He sat on the dead Macintosh and she slumped on a tattered brown couch held up by a can of Spam where a leg was missing. Unlike the boxes on the way to Bethel and Nome, she explained, the couch belonged to the landlord.

"I'd offer you some coffee but the machine's on its way to Bethel too. So what do you want to know about the Gray Wolf? It's a copper mine, it's big, and everybody loves it."

"I was just wondering about those fish kills on the Nuliakuk. Is the Gray Wolf causing them?"

"Of course not. Haven't you heard what GeoNord says? They're the result of natural mineral seeps in the area. Nothing whatever to do with by-products from the mine."

She leaned forward, unsnapped the shoulder straps of the Carhartts, and rolled the front and rear bibs down to her waist. Then she pulled the cuffs of the thermal undershirt up past her elbows. "Fucking hot in here."

The house's inner door and the *kunnichuk* door were both partly open and the temperature was about zero outside. He was feeling a little cold, despite his parka. Not for the first time, he marveled at the raw physical vigor Kathy Childs exuded and wondered what she would be like in bed.

Also not for the first time, he realized he didn't have the slightest desire to find out. Was she a lesbian? Or was he just intimidated by this woman who talked and seemed to think like a man? He looked away from her and tried to get back to business. "Is that what you think? The fish kills are natural?"

"Fuck, it could be. There's always been mineral seeps into Gray Wolf Creek. That's how they figured out there might be copper there in the first place." She picked at a rip in one of the couch cushions. A little clump of white stuffing squeezed out.

"But what does the Alaska Department of Environmental Protection say? Officially?"

"The DEP doesn't say shit. All we know is what GeoNord tells us and their data don't show any impact from the mine."

"You don't do your own monitoring?"

"Fuck, no. Why would we want to do that? You think GeoNord can't be trusted to monitor itself?"

"Well . . ."

"Don't look at me like that, fuckhead." She balled up the stuffing and threw it at him. "Of course I know we should be doing our own tests. But every time I push for a monitoring program the district director in Nome says we don't have the money, so we go with what GeoNord gives us."

He shook his head and stretched out his

legs. The Macintosh was too low to make a good seat. "Sweet deal for GeoNord."

"That's what I thought too. So I snuck up to the Nuliakuk on my trusty Arctic Cat and collected a few of those dead fish and sent them to a friend at the DEP lab down in Juneau." She unlaced her Sorels and pulled them off, then propped her stockinged feet up on the boots and sighed. "That's better. Jesus, I knew I was dressing too warm today."

"And what did your friend find out?"

"Not shit. Somehow Shotwell — that's the district director in Nome — heard about it and called and told me to lay off. Said he didn't want any half-assed measures when it came to the Gray Wolf. Either we'd do full-scale monitoring or we wouldn't do any. And since we couldn't afford a real monitoring program . . ."

". . . you're not doing any monitoring at all."

"You got that right. Then he told me the money had run out for the Chukchi office and he was moving me to Bethel."

"You think the office here is closing because of your dead fish?"

"Fuck, who knows what goes on up there in the ionosphere? Guys at Shotwell's level don't even breathe oxygen like you and me. All I know is, the Gray Wolf is somebody else's baby now." She drew back her right foot and kicked a Sorel across the floor at him. "And I start looking for a federal job the minute I get to Bethel. I'm tired of this chicken-shit outfit."

He caught the boot with his foot and slid it back to the couch. "What kind of by-products do they get at the Gray Wolf anyway?"

"Well, copper ore has a bunch of minerals in it. Some of them are fairly nasty."

"Such as?"

"Antimony, arsenic, sulfur. Actually, the antimony's not much of a problem. But arsenic and sulfur you have to . . ."

"Sulfur as in sulfuric acid? And arsenic as in . . . arsenic?"

"Sure, bad stuff. But the pollution controls up there should take care of it." She started pulling the Sorels on again. "GeoNord takes it out during processing and ships it south. I guess they sell it on the West Coast and get back some of the cost of handling it."

"Couldn't they just put it back in the ground where it came from? Like with some kind of leach field or something?" He watched carefully as he said it, but she gave no sign she had ever heard of a leach

219

field at the Gray Wolf. The state of perpetual fury in which she seemed to exist made it hard to be sure, though.

"Fuck, no. That mountain's like a giant sponge. You put that stuff back in the ground after it's separated from the copper, it'll flush right through. No telling where it's gonna end up." She pulled up the bibs of the Carhartts, flipped the straps back over her shoulders, and snapped them.

"Why you interested, Nathan?" She said it casually, but the amazing blue eyes were like searchlights in her dark face. "You thinking there's some kind of fish and game violation?"

"Not really," he said, avoiding the beams of the blue searchlights. "My stepfather likes to go up there for trout and he was complaining about the fish kills the other night. I just thought I'd check around a little."

"I didn't think a state agency would get serious about the Gray Wolf," she said. "Anyway, I don't think even GeoNord would try something as stupid as a leach field. They'd be looking at a fine the size of the national debt. From the Feds if not us."

She pulled on the Sorels and walked to

the door, then turned and looked back at him. Her hands were inside her front bib and she was rocking back and forth on the balls of her feet. "So, you wanna go get some caribou with me, Macho Man? I hear they're crossing at Jade Portage now. It'll be like swatting mosquitoes."

He tried not to let his mouth fall open at the invitation. What was she proposing?

It could be several nights of nonstop gymnastics in a double sleeping bag, or it could be a simple caribou hunt. She had a hungry dog team to feed for the winter and the bag limit for the western Arctic herd was five animals a day. With two people hunting, that was ten animals a day. They could slaughter caribou until they were crusted in blood up to their elbows.

Whichever it was, he doubted he could keep up with her. Besides, whenever he tried to picture her without the Carhartts, Lucy Generous's face came into his mind. Wearing that look she got when she was hurt and trying not to show it.

"Nah, I don't hunt much," he said finally.

"Didn't think so," she said. She walked out into the *kunnichuk*, then stuck her head back inside the cabin proper.

"Close the door when you leave," she

said. "Or not, your choice. Fuck 'em." Her head disappeared and, a moment later, he heard the snowmachine cough to life and pull away.

Back in the Sunday hush of the deserted trooper office, he laid his notebook on the desk and flipped through his Rolodex, then his file drawers. He locked his fingers behind his head and frowned at the ceiling. Where was it? Suddenly he remembered, took a slip of paper from his wallet, and dialed the Anchorage number on it.

"It's Nathan," he said after a few seconds. "Did you find her?"

"Nope," Patrick Carnaby said. "Not a trace."

"I heard something."

"You heard something?"

"I heard she's at the Lo . . ."

"Don't touch this," Carnaby interrupted. "You've still got a career left."

"I came by this information accidentally."

"In other words, you didn't hear it from whoever you heard it from, that kind of thing?"

"Something like that."

Carnaby was quiet for several seconds. Active heard a radio in the background. Pots and pans rattled. A teenage boy called, "Dad, breakfast is ready."

"Just a minute," Dad yelled back. Life as usual at the Carnaby household in Anchorage, except Dad's career was shot and his office was now six hundred miles away in Chukchi.

"All right," Carnaby said into the phone finally. "What is it?"

"She's dancing at the Lodestar Lounge in Las Vegas." Active opened his notebook and read the telephone number.

"What name is she using?"

"Helen Ready."

"Helen Reddy?" Carnaby said. "You mean like the singer Helen Reddy? Won't she get sued?"

"No, Helen R-E-A-D-Y. As in ready for action, I think. But you didn't hear any of this from me."

"I feel like I'm in one of those conversations my undercover guys used to tape."

"Let's hope not," Active said.

"I'll say. Anyway, thanks. If this works out and I . . . well, if you ever need anything . . ."

"Some things don't need saying."

"Then I won't say it," Carnaby said. "So how are things in Chukchi?" He didn't sound very interested.

"Oh, the same," Active said. "Couple more apparent suicides, not much else." He held his breath. The old Super Trooper from the academy would catch the "apparent" in a second.

"Maybe Tom Werner's liquor ban will help, if he gets it," Carnaby said. Active relaxed. Evidently the new Carnaby was too preoccupied with Helen Ready to analyze sentence structure. He didn't even ask who had died. "How's the vote looking?"

"It's anybody's guess," Active said. "I think it'll be close."

They hung up. Active went to the window and frowned across the lagoon for several minutes. What was going on at the Gray Wolf? George Clinton thought he had found out something about a leach field. Was it possible that GeoNord *would* have been that stupid? At any rate, George had decided it was somehow causing the fish kills and had gone to the GeoNord offices, then turned up dead across from the Dreamland. Then Active and Cowboy Decker had found Aaron Stone in the spruce grove at Loon Lake. What was the connection? Was there one? Who had the know-how and the means to kill two men under such different conditions? Jermain was the only name that came to mind.

It wasn't much of a hand, but it was all he had. He walked back to his desk and dialed GeoNord's number, hoping the engineer was still in Chukchi.

"It's Nathan Active," he said, feeling relieved, when Jermain answered on the fourth ring. "I'd like to talk to you again about the murders of Aaron Stone and George Clinton."

"The what?"

"The murders of Aaron Stone and George Clinton."

"Jesus," Jermain said. "Hang on."

The engineer put him on hold and he listened to a syrupy instrumental. Why did it seem familiar? Suddenly he smiled. "I Am Woman," Helen Reddy's greatest hit. Maybe her only hit. If there was a God, he was obviously in the mood for jokes today. Or maybe God was she, considering the song. Either way, God was a better comic than music programmer.

Helen Reddy stopped with a click. "Alex Fortune," a voice said. Why did it sound familiar? "How can I help you?"

"I was holding for Michael Jermain," Active said. "Can you put him back on?"

"I'm Mr. Jermain's attorney," Fortune said. "How can I help you?"

Of course. It was the voice Active had heard when he listened in on Jermain's conversation at GeoNord headquarters — the voice whose owner had said he would be in Chukchi by Sunday.

"His attorney?" Active wrote the name in his notebook and stared at it. It was familiar too, but why?

"What is it you wanted with my client?"

Active hesitated. Interviewing Jermain alone was one thing. He had been jumpy the first time and now Active had more information. With a little luck, this time the engineer might crack. But with his attorney present?

On the other hand, Active reminded himself, what was there to lose? Even if Jermain didn't crack, perhaps he would disclose something that would pump life back into this moribund investigation.

He swallowed, took a deep breath, and said it fast, his voice half an octave higher than usual. "I want to interview your client about the murders of George Clinton and Aaron Stone."

Fortune was silent. Then there was a click and the hold music came back on. Active waited through two songs, neither

226

of which he recognized. With another click Fortune returned.

"Murders? That's absurd. Everyone knows they were suicides. What basis do you have for your allegation?"

"I've located a witness to one of the homicides," Active said.

"What witness?"

"A witness who might be safer if his or her name doesn't get around," Active said.

"You won't even disclose the gender of this alleged witness? Isn't that a little melodramatic, Trooper Active?"

Active pictured Tillie Miller with a hole in her leathery, hairy old throat. "Not necessarily."

"And this witness identified the killer?"

"Partially." So Tillie hadn't exactly said a chief engineer killed George Clinton. She had said a *qauqlik,* a head man, a chief, killed a boy. Close enough.

Fortune clicked off again and Active listened to the end of one instrumental and the start of another. Then the lawyer came back on. "Can you come to Mr. Jermain's office? About three?"

Chapter 12
Sunday Afternoon, Chukchi

Active tried not to stare as he shook Fortune's hand. The lawyer was the first utterly hairless person he had ever seen. Nothing on the scalp, no mustache or beard, not even eyebrows or eyelashes. The only thing on his head was a pair of gold-rimmed glasses.

"A pleasure to meet you, Trooper Active," Fortune said with a wide grin, big ears jutting from the gleaming skull. Was he ill? No, his grip was strong. Perhaps the goblin look was part of his uniform, like the sand-colored suit he wore. Active didn't know clothes, but Fortune's outfit looked as if it cost as much as a snowmachine.

Active nodded at Jermain, who gave a tight jerk of his head and said nothing. The engineer stood behind Fortune as if for shelter. "I don't think I've ever seen a three-piece suit in Chukchi, Mr. Fortune."

"I'm afraid I didn't have time to run by Eddie Bauer before I left San Francisco," Fortune said with another smile.

"San Francisco?" Finally, Active remembered. "You're the Alex Fortune who defended Clayton Howell." GeoNord hadn't sent up a mere staff lawyer; Fortune was one of the highest-priced criminal defense attorneys on the West Coast.

"The same," Fortune said with a little bow. "GeoNord hires only the best. But speaking of the Howell affair, how is our mutual friend Captain Carnaby?"

"He's a sergeant now."

"So he is," Fortune said. "My mistake. How is *Sergeant* Carnaby these days?"

"He's fine."

"I'm glad to hear it," Fortune said. "I understand he's a good man. And of course it's always regrettable when bad things happen to good people."

"There's a lot of that going around."

"It's always a risk when someone . . . overreaches, however laudable his intentions." Fortune nodded at a chair on one side of Jermain's conference table. "Won't you sit?"

Active walked over and stood behind the chair. "After you." He stared at Fortune. Fortune stared back.

Jermain started to sit across from Active. He looked at Fortune and froze halfway down, then stood again.

Finally, Fortune smiled and sat down. So did Jermain, looking disgusted. Fortune opened a briefcase, took out a yellow legal pad and a gold ball-point pen, and laid them on the table.

Active sat, pulled out his Pearlcorder, clicked it on, and set it down in front of him. "Shall we start Mr. Jermain's statement now? Today is . . ."

Fortune held up a perfectly manicured hand and Active stopped. With the same hand, Fortune reached down and clicked off the recorder. He opened the little plastic door, removed the microcassette, and placed it on the table beside the recorder.

"There won't be any statement," Fortune said. "Not today. Probably not ever. Certainly not until you give us some reason why Mr. Jermain should say anything whatever. A *partial* identification, you said?"

The lawyer's confidence was unnerving, but of course lawyers like Alex Fortune were paid extremely well to look confident.

"That's not all."

"Not all?" Fortune looked from Active to Jermain and back again. Jermain looked at his hands.

"I've located another witness who says George Clinton and Aaron Stone were investigating an illegal leach field at the Gray Wolf when they were killed." Perhaps Emily Hoffman hadn't actually mentioned Aaron Stone or used the word "investigating" at the Dreamland last night. But it was close enough.

Jermain's head jerked up. He glanced from Active to Fortune. Fortune's bland smile didn't change. But when he reached for his gold ballpoint, Active noted with satisfaction, he missed and knocked it two inches to the left.

He picked it up and tapped it lightly on the yellow pad. "Would that be a partial ID or a full ID on the leach field, Trooper Active?" He looked down and wrote something with the ballpoint.

"I would characterize it as a sufficient ID, Mr. Fortune." Active mustered a smile of his own, hoping it approached the serene confidence radiating from Fortune. "Put the two witnesses together, and Mr. Jermain is the logical suspect. He obviously has the hunting skills to kill the two men." Active waved at the trophies staring down from the walls of Jermain's office.

Jermain looked at the heads. Fortune was still writing. His eyes didn't leave the yellow pad.

"Mr. Jermain's plane and his snow-machine give him the mobility that would have been needed to kill Aaron Stone at Katy Creek," Active said. "Because of the thaw last week, no one from Chukchi could have crossed the bay on the ice.

"And Mr. Jermain had the motive, to put it mildly. According to my witness, that leach field is the cause of the fish kills on the Nuliakuk. I would think keeping something like that secret would be absolutely crucial to the Gray Wolf's chief engineer." Active nodded at Jermain, then looked at Fortune. "Not to mention his employer."

He switched his gaze back to the engineer, who was now watching Fortune intently. "Murdering two people to cover up the willful poisoning of an important subsistence stream — I'd say a jury of *aanas* and caribou hunters and berry pickers is highly likely to grant Mr. Jermain here a lifetime of state hospitality at the Anvil Mountain Correctional Center."

Active stopped, feeling a mild optimism

that faded in the long silence that ensued. Fortune continued writing for a time, then paused and looked up quizzically. Active realized the lawyer was waiting to see if he had finished. He tried to find something else to say, but couldn't.

At last Fortune laid his pen on the legal pad, his smile broader than ever and now somewhat incredulous. "That's your case? Fragmentary oral evidence, supposition, and hypothesis?"

Active met the lawyer's gaze for a moment, then looked down at the Pearlcorder on the table.

"You're wasting our time, Trooper Active." Fortune put the pen in his pocket, dropped the legal pad into his briefcase, and snapped it shut. "If you had real evidence for any of this nonsense, you'd be here with an arrest warrant instead of your little recorder."

The lawyer stood up and extended his hand. "Good day, now."

Active shook the hand and gazed into Fortune's eyes, where he saw something that looked like pity. Jermain just stared, wordless.

Numbly, Active put the Pearlcorder and cassette in his pocket, fumbled with his notebook, dropped it, picked it up, pocketed it too, and left the GeoNord offices. They had learned most of what he knew, plus all that he surmised, and he was leaving no smarter than when he arrived.

Chapter 13
Monday Morning, Chukchi

Active's eyelids felt as if they were lined with river gravel when he arrived at the office the next morning. He had spent the night wide-eyed in the dark, trying to stop his mental VCR from rewinding and replaying the showdown with Jermain and Fortune. Every time, it ended the same: with Nathan Active being chased out of the office, Pearlcorder and all.

Well, what should he have expected? The lawyer was right. If you held the case up to the light, it barely cast a shadow. Where did he go from here?

"Lucy Generous asked me to give you this," Evelyn O'Brien said as he headed for the coffeepot. She handed him a packet of Kleenex. She kept her eyes on the telephone bill she was checking against the office logs.

"What did she say?"

"She said, 'Give this to Nathan.' " He thought the corners of the secretary's mouth twitched. But he couldn't be sure because she didn't raise her head.

"That's it? She didn't say anything else?"

"Like what?"

He went into his office, slammed the door, and put the coffee on his desk. How had Lucy gotten inside his head like this? He hung his coat and hat on the hooks by the door and looked out the east window at the lagoon, frozen now from shore to shore. Snowmachines buzzed back and forth between the village and the rolling swells of tundra back of the lagoon. What would she say about Saturday night on the bluff if he walked downstairs to talk to her right now? What would *he* say? Finally, he shook his head and dropped into the chair at his desk.

He closed his eyes and massaged them with a thumb and forefinger. Instantly, the mental VCR clicked on again and he was back in the GeoNord office with Fortune and Jermain. The VCR kept rewinding to the moment he had said the words "leach field." Jermain had jumped as if kicked in the shins. Fortune had been cooler, but there was that tiny fumble with the gold ballpoint.

After that, Fortune had paid careful attention to everything Active had said, writing it all down on his legal pad. Finally, he had waited for more. When it didn't come, he had ridiculed Active's "oral evidence" and sent him away.

Clearly, the words *leach field* had meant something to the pair. Almost certainly, the Gray Wolf had one, necessarily a secret. But where? There had been no surface evidence when he had flown in and out for his talk with Tom Werner, but that was only to be expected. In the first place, leach fields were underground. In the second, no one would put an illegal leach field where it was easy to spot. It could be under one of the buildings, under any one of the hundreds of acres of snow-covered gravel at the mine site, anywhere. And the only two people he could think of who might know where it was and be willing to tell him were dead.

His phone chirruped, but Evelyn O'Brien picked it up in the outer office as he paused his mental VCR. He looked at her through his window, eyebrows raised inquiringly. She spoke into the phone, then listened. Then she looked at Active, pointed at Carnaby's office, then down at the phone.

He was instantly uneasy. Carnaby rarely

called in now that he was on personal leave, and never this early in the day.

Active scooped up the receiver. "Hi, boss, how's the great white hunter? You find Helen Ready yet?"

"As a matter of fact, the FBI picked her up in Las Vegas last night and put her straight on a plane for Anchorage," Carnaby said. "I'm told she has a date with the grand jury later today."

"Excellent. Congratulations."

"Well, I owe it to you, Nathan. Thanks again. Who told you about the Lodestar Lounge anyway?"

Active hesitated. Tom Werner hadn't actually asked him to keep quiet. Still, naming the source of the Helen Ready tip seemed to push against the edges of the court order banning trooper investigation of Senator Howell.

"You really want to know that?"

"Sure, why not?" Carnaby asked. "The state court will have to mind its own business now that the feds are rolling."

"It was Tom Werner. He said he knew you from the old days in Nome and he wanted to help."

"I guess I owe Tom Werner too."

"I'll let him know."

There was a silence that went on long

enough to become uncomfortable. Finally Carnaby cleared his throat. "But that's not why I called."

"I had a feeling." Active switched the phone to his right ear from his left, which was starting to sweat.

"Bill Felix called me here at home this morning. I imagine you know what it was about."

"I have an idea." Active's stomach cramped. Bill Felix was the Alaska commissioner of Public Safety. He wasn't the head of the troopers — he was the man who hired the head of the troopers. For Bill Felix to bypass the chain of command and contact a detachment commander like Carnaby was . . . well, Active had never heard of it before.

"It seems that Alex Fortune called him and complained you've been making wild charges."

"They know each other?"

"They worked together in the Anchorage D.A.'s office when they were starting out," Carnaby said. "Anyway, Fortune says you're claiming the Gray Wolf is killing fish in the Nuliakuk, accusing Michael Jermain of shooting Aaron Stone and — who was it? — one of Daniel Clinton's boys?"

"Yes, George Clinton."

"Well, have you?"

"What?"

"Been making these charges."

"I guess I did."

"So tell me about it," Carnaby said tightly. "What have you got?"

Active took Carnaby through the evidence and then sketched the case he had built on it. He felt himself flushing as he realized how it must sound to a veteran like his boss, how Carnaby must be feeling at the thought of having to explain it to Commissioner Felix. Not to mention all the other bosses between him and Felix in the trooper food chain.

Carnaby was quiet for a long time after Active finished. Then he cleared his throat again. "Your witnesses are Tillie Miller and Emily Hoffman?"

"Yessir," Active said. It was all he could think of.

"And they were both drunk when you interviewed them?"

"Well, with Tillie you can never be sure . . ."

"Jesus Christ, Nathan!" Carnaby was shouting now. Active had never heard him do that. "You've got to know how thin this is!"

"Yessir."

Carnaby paused, evidently to collect himself. "I'm sorry I shouted. I try not to do that."

"I know," Active said.

Carnaby paused again. Then, "Fortune said you were a loose cannon. He suggested to Felix that both of us be counseled on the perils of overreaching."

"He gave me a little briefing on the same subject."

"Christ, you mean . . ." Carnaby caught himself and spoke in a normal tone. "You say Bill Felix called *you* directly about this?"

"No, I mean Fortune talked to me about the perils of overreaching. He, ah, he mentioned you as an example."

Carnaby exhaled gustily, as if he had been punched in the gut. Active heard him draw a deep, shaky breath before speaking again.

"This guy Fortune is as dangerous as black ice."

"Yessir, I know that."

"Then I assume your gut is telling you you're onto something?"

"Yessir. Ever since I saw they were both shot in the Adam's apple."

"That's pretty unusual, all right. And a cop should always trust his gut."

"Yessir."

"But if this blows up on you, on us . . . well, I don't need another . . ." Carnaby faltered to a stop.

"Nossir."

"Especially now, with Bobbi Jean . . ."

"Nossir."

"And, believe me, you don't need your first one."

Active felt pity for the older man, mingled with the fear of ending up like the Super Trooper. "I'll drop the case."

"You sure?"

"Yeah, it's OK." Now Active's right ear was sweating, so he switched back to the left. "It's turned into nothing but a world-class collection of dead ends, anyway. I'll type up my notes and file them and forget it."

"You sure?"

"I'm sure."

"All right, look," Carnaby said. "Fax me the report when you're done. That way I can tell Felix I've got it in my hands and it says the case is closed."

"OK."

They hung up and Active put his fingers to his eyelids again. What did it matter? Every cop had a case in his files that he took to bed at night and woke up with in the morning. At least if the feds nailed

Howell, Carnaby would get his career back.

And maybe Nathan Active would become commander of the Chukchi detachment, like Tom Werner had said. And *then* maybe he would reopen the Gray Wolf murders.

Or maybe not. Maybe he would be promoted to Anchorage first. And then maybe Chukchi with all its drunks and *aanas* and mayhem, Chukchi with its Kay-Snow and "Mukluk Messenger," the Chukchi of his mother and Leroy and Sonny, of Kinnuk Wilson, of Pauline Generous and even Lucy, would be someone else's problem and he could think straight again.

He pulled out his notebook and began typing the interviews into the computer. When he came to the summary he had scrawled after his talk with Emily Hoffman at the Dreamland, he frowned in concentration. In his notes, the conversation ended with Simeon and Jonathan crashing into their table.

That was accurate enough, but something was missing. What were they talking about just before the battle erupted? Ah, now he remembered. He had asked Emily how George found out about the "leeches" at the Gray Wolf.

And she had said what? Nothing?

No, she had started to answer. What was it, something about a pick? That was it. "He find pick," she had said. What did that mean? A pick to dig the leach field? A pick to locate it?

Should he talk to her again? The case was closed, of course, but this wouldn't be a new interview, or even a reinterview. It would just be a matter of completing the original interview so he could complete his notes, which would allow him to complete his file and close the case. Just like Patrick Carnaby was probably telling Bill Felix that Nathan Active was doing at this very moment.

One more question couldn't hurt.

Active parked the Suburban on the ocean side of Beach Street in front of the Arctic Inn, a three-story wooden structure that looked west over Chukchi Bay. The Arctic Inn's main architectural statement was its greenish brown wood siding called T-111. The stuff was just one step up from ordinary plywood, but it passed for stylish in Chukchi, especially fifteen years earlier when Chukchi Region Inc. had built the Arctic Inn on the theory that tourists would flock to the Arctic to admire the tundra and the Inupiat. Instead, the place had become home to traveling businessmen and bureaucrats, construction hands like Travis Taylor, and folks in from the surrounding villages for a night or two in the big town.

Odd-looking steel pipes with cooling fins on the tips stuck out diagonally from the soil under the Arctic Inn. They were part of a high-tech system designed to keep the permafrost from thawing and slowly lowering the Plywood Palace, as it was known, into the muck.

The Arctic Inn had no door onto Beach Street, so Active walked down the alley past the permafrost pipes and turned into the side door that led into the lobby.

The front desk was staffed by a teen-age Inupiat girl who was chattering into a telephone and watching MTV on a miniature set on the counter when Active walked up. He asked what room Travis Taylor was in and she scribbled "329" on a yellow stickie without missing a beat in her conversation. Active took the slip of paper and climbed the stairs to the third floor.

Room 329 was at the end of the hall, next to an emergency exit with a sign warning Alarm Will Sound. He knocked, waited, and knocked again. Finally, he tried the knob and the door slid open.

The room smelled of pizza, beer, sweat, and sex, and was dark except for a little light leaking in around the window blinds and through the open door from the dimly lit hallway behind him.

A naked girl, just recognizable in the dusk as Emily Hoffman, lay curled on her left side on a double bed, facing him. Without clothes, she looked even younger than she had in the Dreamland, almost genderless, with her thin childlike limbs. There was just the slightest hint of a belly, rising and falling with her breathing, proof that Mother Nature, at least, deemed her an adult female, ready for the work of propagating the race.

Beside her on the bed, he saw what looked like the remains of a pizza and a twelve-pack of Oly. There was no sign of Travis Taylor, who presumably was off painting the new armory.

Active crossed to the bed and drew a sheet over the girl's nakedness. Then he returned to the doorway and knocked loudly on the frame.

"Emily. Wake up. It's Nathan Active."

She stirred, mumbled, "Mmmf fway oma fleep," rolled over to face the window, and was still again.

"Emily. Wake up. I need to talk to you."

No response. He walked to the bed, leaned over her, and raised the blind on the window in front of her. Then he pushed her shoulder.

"Emily. It's Nathan."

Still no response. He noticed a TV controller on the bed next to the pizza box. He picked it up, clicked on the set in the corner, and surfed till he found the MTV channel. A band identified at the bottom of the screen as Lung blasted into the room. Active turned the volume up as high as he could bear, then sat on the corner of the bed and waited.

Finally the girl rolled over and opened her eyes enough to peer, first at the television, then at him.

"*Arii*, Nathan! I've got a headache." Her face was oily and the left side of her chin was silvery with saliva.

He muted the set and the girl relaxed.

"Can you wake up now? We have to talk."

She rolled back to the window. He clicked the controller and Lung howled from the set again.

"All right, turn it off," she said, her back still toward him. "We could talk." He clicked the set into silence and she rolled to face him. She started grabbing Oly cans and shaking them. "I'm thirsty. You got anything to drink?"

He went into the bathroom and returned with a glass of water. She sat up, letting the sheet drop to her waist, drained the glass, and dropped it beside her on the bed. She wiped her mouth and looked at him.

"You should put something on." He nodded vaguely at the fallen sheet and looked away.

"*Arii*," he heard her say, with a groan. "I never notice. You turn your back and I'll go in the bathroom."

He felt her move off the bed, then heard the bathroom door close. He waited until it opened again and Emily came out wearing a man's bathrobe several sizes too large for her. Her face was clean and her hair was brushed now, but she was carrying an Oly in one hand. She sat down on the bed, took a sip from the beer, pulled a pack of cigarettes from under the pillow, and lit one with a Bic she fished from a pocket of the robe.

She took a long drag and said, "OK, what?"

"Do you remember what we were talking about at the Dreamland Saturday night?"

"When?"

"Saturday. You were there with Travis? Remember?"

"I think my head hurts too much."

He sighed. "You were telling me about leeches killing fish at the Gray Wolf. You said . . ."

"Oh, yeah, now I remember. Simeon and that guy bumped into us, then while I was dancing with Travis you left." She squeezed her eyes shut, circled her arms around a remembered partner, and swayed to remembered music, a tear sliding down each cheek. "George liked to dance. You like to dance with me sometime, Nathan?"

He put his hand on her shoulders and shook her lightly. "Emily. I need you to think about what we said Saturday night. You said George told you about the leeches and how he found a pick."

She opened her eyes, looked at him, wrinkled her nose, and squinted in the Inupiat frown of negation. "He never say nothing about a pick."

"But you said he found one."

"I never say nothing like that." She wiped her eyes on a sleeve of the bath-robe.

"Never mind, then. How did George find out about the leeches?"

"Like I tell you at Dreamland, he find picture." She put the cigarette to her lips and drew in, gazing over his shoulder at the soundless images on the television screen. Then she looked at him. "You forget?"

"A picture? Not a pick? George found a picture of the leeches? Like a photograph?"

"No, a picture like you draw, I guess." She frowned and watched the smoke curl up from her cigarette. "He call it a screenomatic, something like that."

Active let the word roll around his head for a second. Then his brain made the connection. "A schematic? Did George say he found a schematic of the leeches?"

"That sound right," Emily said. "A schemomatic."

"Did he say where he found it?"

"In the head man's office, I think. He find it while he's cleaning up."

"Did he show it to anybody? Do you have it?"

"I don't know what he do with it." Her eyes strayed to the television again. "George say GeoNord will have to take care of it."

250

Active stood up, walked to the corner, and switched the television off. He turned and faced the girl. "Look, if I had that schematic, I might be able to help GeoNord stop the leeches from killing fish in the Nuliakuk. Do you think George brought it back with him?"

"I dunno. He leave his stuff at my mom's when he stay with us, but I don't know what's in it."

"We could go look."

Emily squeezed her eyes shut and tears trickled down again. "I don't want my mom to see me like this."

"Maybe she's not home."

Emily was silent, thinking it over. "Could be. Sometimes she go to store on Monday. I guess I could call."

She picked up the phone from the nightstand and dialed. "If she answer, I'll hang up. I don't want to talk to her now."

Active nodded and waited.

Finally, Emily hung up. "I guess she's not home. We could go over there."

She stood up and started for the bathroom. "You could watch MTV while I get ready."

Chapter 14

Monday Afternoon, Chukchi

The ride to Emily Hoffman's mother's house was uneventful, except for when the girl shouted, "Stop, Nathan!" as they passed the Lions Club.

He slammed on the brakes and Emily jumped out. She lurched over to the club, leaned against the orange T-111 wall, and vomited. A clear liquid that could have been this morning's beer came up, followed by what looked like the remains of last night's pizza. He thought about going over to offer aid, but decided he could in good conscience stay in the Suburban as long as Emily remained standing. So he watched from a safe distance as her stomach emptied and she progressed to dry heaves.

Finally they stopped too, and she tottered back to the Suburban and climbed in. She leaned her head against the padded dashboard and sighed.

"Maybe George's baby doesn't like beer for breakfast," he said.

"Fuck you, Nathan." She wiped her mouth and nose on her parka sleeve, leaving a glistening stripe of pizza fragments and mucus on the green nylon.

"There's some Kleenex in the glove compartment." He put the Suburban in gear and pulled away, following her somewhat belligerent directions to her mother's place.

"Good," Emily said as they stopped in front. "Mom's four-wheeler's not here. She's still at the store, I guess."

Emily's mother — he didn't ask if there was a father in the picture — lived in what people in Chukchi called a BIA house: twenty-four feet wide by thirty-six feet long, plywood sides, aluminum roof, and a little *kunnichuk* in front. They were sprinkled all over town, the fruit of some forgotten program from the Bureau of Indian Affairs.

This one was run-down, but not as badly as some Active had seen. The paint was an ambiguous gray that might once have been red, and one corner of the *kunnichuk* sagged slightly where a supporting post was sinking into the tundra. But all the windows had glass and the place was free of the scorch marks that would indicate it had ever caught fire, the fate that seemed to befall most BIA houses sooner or later.

They climbed out of the Suburban and

Emily led him into the house. It was much nicer inside than out, reasonably clean, done in bright colors, with framed Bible scenes hung on the walls.

Emily took him to a door near the back. A sign on it said Emily's, without explaining Emily's what. She let him in and he looked around.

It was a teenage girl's room, with posters of rock stars on the walls, and one dresser top entirely covered by makeup and the tools for applying it.

The bedspread was fringed and covered with a pattern of big bright flowers. It was a single bed, and Active wondered how Emily and George had managed to share it and get any sleep, assuming they wanted to. He also wondered why the mother consented to the sleepovers, but decided it was, like the whereabouts of Emily's father, a subject best left unexplored.

He looked around the rest of the room. The top of a chest of drawers beside the bed was filled with pictures in department-store frames. Many were of Emily with various combinations of girlfriends — at school, in an aluminum riverboat pulled up on a gravel bar on a sunny summer day, at slumber parties. But several showed George Clinton, alone or with Emily.

In one corner, a pyramid of stuffed animals rose nearly to waist level.

In another corner he saw a duffel bag and a backpack. Both were open, the contents spilling out onto the floor. Active pointed at the mess. "Is that George's stuff?"

At Emily's nod, he knelt, picked up a wrinkled pair of Levi's, and went through the pockets. Nothing. Next, a red plaid wool shirt. Nothing there either.

As he worked through George Clinton's possessions, he was vaguely aware of Emily moving around the room, then he heard the bedsprings squeak.

When he finished the search, he turned and saw that she was sitting on a corner of the bed watching him. She held George's red plaid shirt against her chest.

"The schematic's not here," he said, studying the girl. He decided to try a long shot. "Did he say anything about showing it to Aaron Stone?"

"He never say, but he might do it." Emily sniffed the shirt, then lay back on the bed and hugged it. "They were kind of friends. Aaron was teaching George how to work on the machines. George wanted to get mechanic's job, make more money now that we were getting married and having baby."

Emily took a picture of George, grinning in sunglasses from the saddle of a snow-machine, off the chest beside the bed and studied it, resting the frame on the little potbelly caused by her pregnancy. "Why he leave me, Nathan?"

"Maybe he didn't do it on purpose. Maybe it was some kind of accident."

She brightened, but then the smile faded. "Nah, it don't seem like accident to me, out on the tundra by himself in the middle of the night like that." She closed her eyes and now hugged both the shirt and the picture.

"You never can tell." A yellow blanket was folded at the foot of the bed. He pulled it up over her. "Sometimes it happens when people carry guns while they're drinking."

"I guess," Emily said drowsily, snuggling under the blanket. "I don't want my mom to see me like this," she said. But her breathing soon slowed and he realized she was asleep.

Active tiptoed out and closed the door with the Emily's sign on it. As he came out of the *kunnichuk*, an Inupiat woman pulled up on a Honda four-wheeler towing a little trailer filled with groceries in boxes. She killed the engine, glanced at the Suburban, studied him in his uniform, and said sharply, "Is it something with Emily?"

"She's fine," he said. "She's in her bedroom asleep. I brought her home."

"You get her away from that *nalauqmiut* painter? That's good. Will she stay now?"

"I don't know," he said. The woman lifted one of the boxes from the four-wheeler trailer and hurried past him into the house.

He climbed into the Suburban, picturing Aaron Stone's cabin in his mind. Could the schematic be there? He doubted it. He had searched it carefully. On Stone's body or his snowmachine? He doubted that too. He had gone through the Yamaha and Stone's clothing before shipping the corpse off to Anchorage for autopsy.

He started the engine and drove to Clara Stone's house. She was just coming out when he pulled up. She wore a flowered parka with a wolf ruff and a handsome pair of caribou mukluks that Active supposed were the product of Aaron Stone's hunting prowess.

He rolled down his window. "Good morning. Can I give you a lift?"

She walked across the gravel street to talk to him. "I'm going to Arctic Mercantile," she said.

"Well, get in and I'll take you. I wanted to ask you something else for my report anyway."

She came around the nose of the Suburban and climbed into the passenger seat.

"How you doing?"

"Not too bad," she said. "Little better since my daughter come down from Nuliakuk with her kids."

"Yeah, I remember you said she was coming."

They bounced along Beach Street until Active broke the silence. "Can you talk about it a little bit if I ask some questions?"

"I guess," she said. "What is it?"

"I was just wondering if Aaron said anything about having a picture or a drawing when he called you from the Gray Wolf." He turned the Suburban east on Lake Street, towards the lagoon and Arctic Mercantile.

"No, he just say he's going caribou hunting, so he'll send his paycheck, some other stuff, home by mail, same as always. He don't like to bring it on his snowgo, might get lost or wet or something."

"Was there anything unusual with his paycheck when it came?"

258

Her eyes widened and she clapped a hand over her mouth. "You know, I never check the mail since last week. I'm too upset to remember, I guess. We could go get it now."

Active made two more right turns to get them back to Beach Street, then a left to take them to the old wooden post office overlooking Chukchi Bay. Clara went in and he watched through the big front window as she opened a mailbox, pulled out an armload of mail, and returned to the Suburban.

She flipped through the stack to a thick manila envelope hand addressed to her at Box 114 from "Aaron, Gray Wolf."

"That's funny," she said. "Usually he put his check in regular envelope. Wonder what's in here." She put a finger under the flap, ripped it along the top, and pulled out the contents. There was a small window envelope that apparently contained a pay-check and a big sheet of paper that had been folded to fit in the manila envelope. Clipped to it was a sheet of typing paper with a hand-written note.

Clara read the note, then handed it, still clipped to the big paper, to Active.

"My Sweetie," Active read. "Please keep this for me till I'm home with you again.

Might be very important! — Your loving Aaron."

He unfolded the sheet enough to see a complicated technical drawing, then refolded it and looked at the woman. "Can I have this?"

"Maybe I could just keep his note?" Tears glistened on her round brown cheeks.

He handed her the note. She read it again, put it back in the manila envelope, folded that in quarters, and put it into her purse. "What he send?"

"I'm not sure," Active said. "But I think it might help us stop the fish kills on the Nuliakuk."

"Yeah, I know Aaron worry about that." Clara took a tissue from her purse and wiped her eyes and cheeks. "He say if the river's going bad, it will poison the water at Nuliakuk village, hurt our daughter and her family. He sure love those grandkids." She blew her nose and looked straight ahead.

"You want me to take you back home?"

"No, it's OK. You can take me to Arctic Mercantile. I need chocolate chips to make cookies for those grandkids."

Active dropped her at the big store by the lagoon, then went to his office in the public safety building, closed the door with the briefest of nods to Evelyn O'Brien, and spread the schematic out on his desk.

It was about eleven by seventeen inches. The label at the top identified it only as Sewer System. Most of the sheet was filled with a tangle of lines and boxes that could have been pumps and pipes.

One of the lines — the biggest one — led out of the tangle toward a stippled area in the lower right corner of the page. But parallel jagged marks slashed through it about halfway there.

If he remembered correctly the little he had learned about mechanical drawing, those jagged marks represented a break in the diagram, meaning the stippled area was farther from the tangle of machinery than the drawing suggested.

Not that it mattered much. No scale or compass rose was printed on the drawing, so it wouldn't have been possible to figure the distance or direction to the leach field anyway, if that was what the stippled area represented.

Active studied the drawing more closely. It wasn't dated either, nor did it bear any clue to the identity of the company that had prepared it.

Perhaps the drawing showed a leach

field, perhaps not. One thing was certain, though: It was as much a puzzle as a drawing, and he couldn't decipher it.

But he knew someone who could, someone who knew a lot about the Gray Wolf and sewer systems and dead fish on the Nuliakuk. Someone whose amazing blue eyes were probably at this very moment training the crosshairs of a hunting rifle on the kill spot at the base of a caribou's neck.

He dialed Lienhofer Aviation and was gratified to hear the smoky scrape of Cowboy Decker's voice on the other end of the line.

"Your Super Cub running? I need to go to Jade Portage right now."

"Right now? It's almost lunchtime."

Active looked at his watch and was shocked to see that Decker was correct. Where had the morning gone? "I'll get some hamburgers at the Korean's and we can eat on the way."

"Make it two double cheeses with fries and you're in business," Decker said. "I'll go gas 'er up."

Active made two copies of the schematic and locked the original in his desk. Twenty-eight minutes later, he pulled the Suburban up beside the red-and-white

Super Cub. Cowboy squatted at the tail of the plane, smoking a cigarette and doing something underneath of the tail. A roll of gray tape rested on top of the tail.

Active grabbed the paper bag, translucent with grease, from the seat beside him, walked over, and dropped it onto the front seat of the Super Cub. Then he squatted beside the pilot. "Something wrong?"

"Ah, I put a little rip in the fabric when we landed at Stone's camp the other day," Cowboy said. "Tail must have caught some brush. But I can't fix it today. Damned duct tape won't stick in the cold."

He stood up, a strip of the insufficiently sticky tape clinging to the fingers of his right hand. He flipped his hand up and down until the tape spun off into the snow.

"Don't worry," he said at Active's look of alarm. "We flew around with it like this half that day when we were looking for Aaron. Takes more than a little rip in the tail to bring down a Super Cub."

Active shrugged, climbed in, put the food bag between his feet, and waited as Decker went through the preflight ritual. He pulled off the engine cover, took out the preheater, snuffed the heater out, and stowed both in the little cargo bay behind

Active's seat. Then he checked the oil, climbed in, and started the engine.

He taxied out to the runway and shoved the throttle forward. The engine roared and then they were in the sky again.

Chapter 15
Monday Afternoon, Jade Portage

As they climbed out to the east, Active realized something he had been too preoccupied to notice until now: the Arctic was at its shameless best again today. Clear and sunny, the snowy ridges etched so sharply against the fierce blue of the sky they felt like knife blades on his eye. It wasn't even that cold — maybe five or ten below, low enough to interfere with duct-tape stickum, but with the sun shining like it was, not bad for humans.

They left the Chukchi Peninsula and crossed Isignaq Inlet to the mouth of the Isignaq River. It was the next major drainage south of the Katonak, and slightly larger. It also drained slightly gentler country. While the mountains along the Katonak tended to be bare jagged crags, the summits along the Isignaq were rounded, with more spruce on the lower slopes and even stands of birch and poplar in the riverbottom. The valley opened out before them, a white embrace.

"What about those burgers?" Decker said through the intercom.

"Oh, yeah." Active wrenched his attention from the scenery, took a Diet Coke and cheeseburger from the bag for himself, and passed the rest up to Cowboy.

They chewed in silence as the valley glided beneath them, Active feeling slightly ashamed to be eating a cheeseburger here in the middle of this white wilderness. They should be eating frozen fish dipped in seal oil.

"What's at Jade Portage?" Cowboy said in a muffled voice, presumably because his mouth was full of the Korean's cheeseburger.

"Kathy Childs," Active said. "She's up here with her dog team. I have to talk to her about something."

"Like what?"

"Like police business."

"Uh-huh." Decker sounded skeptical. Perhaps he too had noticed Kathy Childs's blue eyes.

Active didn't say anything.

"Will I be waiting till you finish your, ah, business or would you like me to come back tomorrow?" Decker asked with a snicker. "Or maybe you'll be mushing back with Kathy?"

"Maybe I'll fly the plane back and you'll stay," Active said.

"Maybe I'll just do that," Decker said.

"And maybe your wife will just strip you naked in divorce court," Active said. "You'll be out in the snow in your underwear."

"Good point," Decker said. "I'd probably best leave the sport hunting to young marksmen like yourself."

As they got farther up the Isignaq, they saw more and more caribou moving across the tundra south of the river.

Finally Jade Portage itself came into sight, the famous spot that the western Arctic caribou had chosen as the only suitable crossing of the Isignaq on their annual pilgrimage to the wintering grounds in the valleys to the south.

Now they saw caribou on the tundra north of the river too, moving along tramped-down trails through the snow toward the two-mile-long sandbar that marked the portage. A big band, maybe two or three thousand, Active estimated, milled on the tundra a mile or so off the river, and a few roamed the willow and alder thickets on the higher ground at the back of the sandbar, but Active didn't see any at the water's edge. No doubt the caribou, in their inscrutable fashion, would all decide to cross at once.

Though they had seen open water at the fastest riffles on their way upstream, the river was frozen at the portage, except for a trail of broken refreezing ice that led from one side to the other. The caribou, driven by their ancient urges, couldn't wait for thick ice. They would cross the river, even if it meant breaking through and swimming.

There were a dozen tent camps along the sandbar, villagers from up and down the river also converging on Jade Portage to lay in meat for the winter.

Decker dropped the Super Cub to a few feet above the river ice and buzzed the camps on the bank. Most had snow-machines drawn up in front but one, at the downstream end, had a dog team staked out in the willows higher up the bank. Five caribou carcasses were scattered around the tent, and a figure with a long-bladed knife in its hand knelt beside one.

The figure looked up as they passed over. Active thought he recognized Kathy Childs but it was hard to be sure because sunglasses covered the eyes. The Carhartts definitely looked right, though.

"That's gotta be her, huh?" Decker asked through the intercom.

"Must be," Active said. "Let's go check."

Decker brought the Super Cub around again and dropped the fat tundra tires onto the snow in front of the white wall tent with the dog team. They bounced to a stop, Decker cut the engine, and Kathy Childs bounded over as they climbed out.

"Macho Man!" she said delightedly. "You change your mind? How long can you stay?"

Active was sure he glimpsed a knowing smile on Decker's lips as the pilot turned away to cover the Super Cub's engine.

"Not long." He hoped she'd take off the sunglasses so he could see the blue eyes again. "I'm here on business, believe it or not."

"Shit, that would explain the uniform," she said. "I'm trying my damnedest not to think about anything even close to business up here. Can't it wait? Like till next year maybe?"

"No, it's pretty urgent. Can we go in the tent?"

She shrugged and started up the sandbar. Then she turned and looked at Decker, who was just tying down the last lace of the engine cover.

"Hey, Cowboy," she said. "That's some of the best caribou stew you ever ate on the Coleman there." She motioned at a little field kitchen set up in front of the tent. "Why don't you crank it up and we'll have some after Macho Man finishes his business?"

Cowboy shook his head. "We ate on the way. I'm full."

"Me too," Active said.

"What, Lienhofer's has food service now?"

"We brought some of the Korean's hamburgers," Decker said.

"You're passing up fresh caribou stew for those grease bombs?"

Decker looked glum, but shrugged and said nothing.

She looked accusingly at Active, who shrugged too. She shook her head, pulled off the sunglasses, and motioned him into the tent.

The only furniture was a wooden folding cot with an air mattress and sleeping bag on it, so he spread a copy of the schematic on the sleeping bag. "This look familiar? I think maybe it's from the Gray Wolf."

Kathy Childs bent over the drawing. "The label doesn't mention the Gray Wolf. What's the connection?"

He was silent until she twisted to look at him. He turned his eyes away and said, "I can't tell you."

She turned back to the drawing. "Well, it says 'Sewer System' but . . ." She traced a finger through the jumble of symbols on the paper, and along the line with the break in it.

"But what?"

"But we have drawings of their sewer system and I never saw this one before. And I got pretty familiar with the file after the fish started dying up there." She moved her finger to the stippled area, studied it briefly, then turned the blue X-rays on him again, somewhat accusingly.

"This the leach field you were asking about the other day?"

"Could be. What do you think?"

"Could be almost anything, since it's not labeled." She studied the diagram again, then shook her head. "I don't know."

"What?"

"Something's not right here. This looks like a piece of the Gray Wolf, but not really. The layout is different. Like maybe it's the sewer system of some other mine and they were using it as a model for the Gray Wolf system."

He looked down at the diagram. It didn't make any more sense than before. "Well, thanks for taking a look."

"Sorry."

"No problem. It was just a hunch I had, that you might be able to figure it out."

She led the way out of the tent and blinked in the sunlight for a moment, then put on the sunglasses again. Cowboy had fired up the Coleman camp stove after all, and was perched on a five-gallon Blazo can, eating out of the stew pot with a big wooden spoon.

"Nathan, you gotta try this," the pilot mumbled around a mouthful of stew.

"No, thanks," Active said. "We need to get back."

"Sure you don't want to stay a while and shoot some caribou?" she said. "You knock down five apiece, I'll be all set. I can leave tonight, and I'll give you a couple hind-quarters each."

Active shook his head. "We do have to get back. And I don't even have a hunting license."

"Fucking A," she said. It was plain Kathy Childs could not imagine a grown healthy man in the Arctic without one.

She turned to the pilot, still dipping stew from the pot on the camp stove.

"Cowboy, you want to pop a few before you go? I can only shoot five a day myself, and there's all kinds of wolves following the herd. I think they might drag the meat off faster than I can shoot it, unless I can figure a way to stay awake all night."

Decker looked as if he might be figuring a way to stay awake all night with Kathy Childs. "It's Nathan's charter," he said. They both looked at Active.

"Sorry, guys. Business is business."

Decker sucked in a last spoonful of stew, pushed a piece of pilot bread in after it, then stood up and they walked down to the plane. Kathy Childs watched as Decker pulled off the engine cover and stowed it, then she returned to the tent as they climbed in.

As Decker started the plane, Active saw her come out of the tent, the schematic in her hand. He thought of stopping the pilot so he could retrieve it, but decided it didn't matter much if she kept a copy. He watched as she held it up to the sky and studied it.

Decker pushed the throttle forward and the Super Cub rolled in a wide turn, the blast from the propeller kicking up a small snowstorm. "I'm going to taxi back up the bar and take off the same way we landed," he said through the intercom. "She'll roll better if we use the tracks we made before."

Decker backtracked about a hundred

yards, pivoted the plane around the left wheel, and roared towards Childs's camp. They lifted off a few yards before the camp and were just abreast of it, perhaps ten feet in the air, when Active saw Kathy Childs sprint down the slope towards the plane, waving the schematic over her head, her mouth moving in what was obviously a shout.

Active slapped the pilot's right shoulder. "Hey, Cowboy, put her down again. I think Kathy wants to talk to us."

Decker shook his head, but he dutifully brought the plane around for another landing on the now well-worn path on the snowy sandbar. Kathy Childs was waiting when he pulled up beside her camp and cut the engine.

"Macho Man, look at this." She held the schematic up to the sky, the back side of the sheet facing her, as they flipped open the Super Cub's two little half-doors. "The damned thing . . ."

She stopped talking as Active frowned and jerked his head toward the pilot in the front seat. "Let's go to the tent."

"All right then, come on; fuck, what are you waiting for?" She rolled the schematic into a tube and swatted him when he was too slow climbing out of the plane.

She galloped toward the tent and waited in the doorway as he walked up the sandbar. Once they were both inside, she unrolled the drawing and handed it to him. "Hold that up to the south wall of the tent there, where the sun's hitting it."

He shrugged, knelt, and placed the drawing along the top of the tent's low side wall, then looked up at her questioningly. She grimaced. "No, not that way. Turn it over and look at it from the back."

He flipped the schematic over and spread it against the luminous canvas again. The drawing on the other side showed through clearly.

"See?" she said triumphantly.

"See what? It's even more confusing backwards, if that's what you mean."

"That's the point." She squatted beside him, grabbed the drawing, and held it against the wall of the tent. "They reversed the damned thing. I knew there was something funny about it, so I turned it over and held it up to the sun and, voila! I'm back home at the Gray Wolf!"

"You mean it's the Gray Wolf sewer system after all?"

"It's the Gray Wolf all right, but it's not the sewer system." She jabbed a finger against the jumble of symbols where the pipeline originated. "This is the Gray Wolf water-treatment plant, where they clean out the junk that comes out of the ore."

He studied the symbols again. "I thought they just dumped the water in their settling pond."

"Yeah, but when the solids settle out, then they pump it into the treatment plant, clean it up, and pump it into Gray Wolf Creek. At least that's what they're supposed to do." She ran her finger along the pipeline. "Looks like some of the water is bypassing the treatment plant and going through here, toxics and all."

Her finger stopped at the stippled area, where the pipeline ended. "And if this is a leach field, it's flushing those toxics into that Swiss cheese of a mountain."

"Why would they bypass their own system?"

She straightened up and looked down at him. "Maybe the treatment plant can't handle all the crud they're getting. So they have to get rid of it some other way."

He rose to his feet again too. "Couldn't they just expand the treatment plant?"

"Maybe they're too cheap. This is a multinational corporation we're talking about here, Macho Man." She sat on the cot, spread the schematic on her lap, right side up, and poked the stippled area. "Anyway, if this is a leach field, it's gotta explain the kills, huh?"

He jumped a little and swiveled to stare at her. "What do you know about . . ." He cut himself off when he realized she meant the fish kills. He started to turn back to the schematic but the blue eyes had already locked on to his.

"This isn't about fish kills at all, is it?" She grasped his wrist, tightly enough that it hurt a little. "The troopers don't investigate pollution. You think somebody killed Aaron Stone and George Clinton, don't you? And this leach field had something to do with it."

"I can't talk about it."

"I knew it! Fucking GeoNord."

He wrenched his gaze from hers and his wrist from her grasp and turned to the drawing. He pointed to the line leading to the leach field. "The wastes in here, that would be the stuff you were talking about before — arsenic, sulfur, what was the other one?"

"Antimony."

"That's it, antimony." He felt her eyes on him as he studied the drawing. He tapped the stippled area. "Where would they put a leach field?"

She squatted and ran her finger along the line to the stipples again. "Let's see, this runs off to the southwest. You got the road running by there, then you're pretty much on the airport, and past that it's tundra."

"Would it make sense to put it under the airport?"

"It might." He watched over her shoulder as she studied the schematic backwards. "There's always some kind of work going on at the airport, so nobody would notice if they did put in a leach field. And if they got some subsidence once it was in, it would automatically get filled in with gravel without anybody having to give an order because it was at the airport. They're always getting sink-holes up there from all the disturbance to the natural ground cover, anyway. Yeah, one of the parking areas at the airport would be a pretty good place."

Active took the diagram and folded it in quarters. "Thanks. You really came through."

"We at the Department of Environmental Protection live to serve." Kathy Childs rose from the cot and made a mock bow, then looked serious. "What now?"

He shrugged, still avoiding the blue probes.

She shrugged too. "Good luck, then. You get the bastards."

He reached for the door, then turned, forcing himself to look into the blue eyes finally. "Maybe it would be better not to mention this to . . ."

"To Shotwell and that crowd? Fat fucking chance. But if you need me for a witness, just whistle. I'll put on a business suit and carry a briefcase and wave my Ph.D. at the jury and they'll fucking fry those GeoNord assholes."

On the way back to Chukchi in the rear seat of Cowboy Decker's Super Cub, Active thought long and hard about what he would say to Fortune when he got the lawyer on the phone. He finally decided four words would do the trick.

It was after dark when Decker pulled the plane into its tie-down. Active jumped out, started the chilly Suburban, and drove to his office.

First, he called the Arctic Inn, where the desk clerk told him Fortune had just checked out to catch the evening Alaska Airlines flight to Anchorage. Then he called the Alaska Airlines terminal and had the lawyer paged.

Finally, the languid, confident voice was in his ear. "This is Alex Fortune."

He said the four words. "I have the schematic."

"What? Who is this?" The voice sounded less confident.

"It's Nathan Active. I have the schematic of the leach field."

There was a long silence. In the background, Active heard the "now boarding" announcement over the terminal's public address system, first in English, next in Inupiaq. Then, from Fortune, "Where did you get it?"

"Never mind that. I want to interview your client again."

"I understood you had, ah, terminated your investigation."

"Now that I have the schematic, it's open again. And I want to talk to Jermain."

Fortune was silent again. "And if we decline?"

"I'll arrest him for the murders of Aaron Stone and George Clinton."

"We can see you at three o'clock tomorrow."

"No, tonight."

"It'll have to be tomorrow," the lawyer

said. "Michael Jermain went up to the mine this afternoon. I'll have to arrange a charter to get him back."

"That won't take till three P.M."

"Sorry, that's the best I can do."

Jermain and Fortune would no doubt spend the whole day plotting strategy, perhaps even on the phone to Europe, Active knew. But he couldn't think of a way to budge the lawyer.

"All right, three o'clock then."

"Three o'clock. And Trooper Active? Don't waste our time again, or I'll make another call to my friend Bill Felix. And you'll end up playing rent-a-cop at a mall in Anchorage."

Chapter 16
Tuesday Afternoon, Chukchi

Active slid a copy of the schematic across the conference table. Jermain stared at it as if it were an animal trap that would snap off his fingers if he touched it. Fortune put on his gold rims and bent over the drawing, exuding the same relaxed assurance as always.

"I don't see anything here about the Gray Wolf," he said finally, straightening to look at Active. "Or a leach field."

He took off the glasses and dropped them onto the drawing. "I'm starting to wonder why we're here."

"Turn it over."

"What?"

Active made a flipping motion with his hand. "Turn it over." The evening before, he had taped the drawing to the window of his office door, trained a gooseneck lamp on it, and traced the diagram onto the back. Now it showed the water-treatment plant, pipeline, and leach field in their normal relationships, not reversed.

Fortune put the glasses on again, turned the drawing over, and looked at the back. Did he pale slightly? "Backwards, forwards, what's the difference? At most, you have a drawing of what may be a sewer system connected to what may be a leach field. If it is at the Gray Wolf, so what? Putting in a sewer system is hardly a crime."

"I have a witness who will testify this area here" — he traced it out on the schematic — "is the water-treatment plant, and this is the pipeline carrying off the wastes, and this is the leach field where you're flushing it into the ground so it can kill fish in the Nuliakuk."

"A witness?"

"A government employee."

"Your witness has seen this pipeline and leach field, I take it?"

"No, but she's seen enough to get me a search warrant and a court order to dig up your airport till we find it."

"She?"

"He, she, what's the difference?"

Fortune tilted his head back and closed his eyes, as if searching a mental filing cabinet for the name of a female government employee who might know something about the Gray Wolf. He opened his eyes and looked at Jermain. "Michael?"

Jermain shook his head.

"Maybe you'll get your search warrant, maybe you won't," Fortune said. "Maybe you'll find something, maybe you won't. But you'll have a fight on your hands."

"Fine, then. I'm arresting Michael Jermain for murder right now." Active stood up and pulled a set of handcuffs from his belt. "You have the right to remain silent . . ."

"Really, Trooper Active, you're being melodramatic again."

"Put out your arms, please, Mr. Jermain. Anything you say can and will . . ."

"Trooper Active, you hardly need handcuff a man of . . ."

Jermain cut the lawyer off. "Fuck this, I'm going to talk to him."

"Michael, shut up," Fortune said. "I'll do the talking."

"Fuck you too, then," the engineer said. "I never liked this from the start and I'm not facing murder charges for anybody. You're fired as my lawyer. You and GeoNord go your way, I'll go mine."

"Will you excuse us for a moment, Trooper Active?" Without waiting for an answer, the lawyer motioned for Jermain to get up and they walked to the office door. "Marie, will you give us a moment of privacy?" Active heard Fortune say as the door closed. Distantly, he heard the outer door to the suite open and shut, presumably as the receptionist left.

Active heard muffled voices in conversation. Once he heard Jermain shout, "I told you I hate this shit. I'm through with it. I don't care . . ." and then the voices became unintelligible again.

In less than five minutes, the office door opened and the two came back in and took their seats at the table. They stared at him as if they didn't know how to begin.

"Shall we start Mr. Jermain's statement now?" Active asked.

"There'll be no statement," Fortune said in a strained voice. "But, very much against my advice, Mr. Jermain is willing to have an off-the-record conversation about what he might say if he ever does make a statement. An offer of proof, you might say." Fortune glanced at Jermain, who grimaced in disgust but nodded.

Fortune turned the browless eyes and radar-dish ears back toward Active. "And, of course, we need to agree on the conditions under which Mr. Jermain might make a statement. If he ever does."

"What conditions?"

"Immunity from criminal prosecution

for GeoNord and Michael Jermain in any matter relating to the deaths of George Clinton and Aaron Stone."

"That's ridiculous. You know I think he killed them both. Why should he get immunity?"

"You don't have to give him anything till you've heard what he has to say. Why not just listen?"

"You know I can't give immunity," Active said after a long pause. "I'm not a prosecutor."

"We know that," Fortune said. "But unless your district attorney has far more time and investigators on his hands than any Bush D.A. I ever knew, he's likely to follow your advice."

Active turned the offer over in his mind. If he said no, the case would turn into a slow, slogging search-warrant duel. What would a judge say if he asked for a warrant to search the soil under the Gray Wolf for a secret leach field? *And what's your probable cause, Trooper Active?* "Well, Your Honor, I heard it from a drunk woman at the Dreamland. Also, a Department of Environmental Protection employee who just got demoted thinks there might be something to it."

And if they did get a warrant, what would it cost to search the airfield? And what would they use, now that the ground was frozen hard for the winter? An oil-drilling rig? Dynamite? God, where would the troopers get the money? What would Patrick Carnaby and Bill Felix say, assuming they said anything other than "You're fired"?

"Naturally, any promise of confidentiality I make is off if you lie to me," he said.

"Naturally," Fortune said

Active was silent again. "And what if I hear you out and then decide to recommend prosecution anyway?"

"Once you listen to Mr. Jermain's story, I'm confident you'll see you can't crack this case without his help," Fortune said. "You know Mr. Jermain can't be compelled to testify if he's under indictment."

"Then why talk to me at all?"

"Because Mr. Jermain has become convinced you won't give up," Fortune said. "I'm less certain of that, but I have to acknowledge a substantial likelihood that Mr. Jermain, not to mention GeoNord, will needlessly and unfairly incur substantial damage if you continue under your present mistaken theory of the case."

Active stood up, walked to Jermain's west window, and looked out over the ice of Chukchi Bay. Fortune spoke from be-

287

hind him. "And, unlikely as it may seem to you, GeoNord would prefer to do the right thing, financial considerations permitting."

A snowmachine droned past the window a few yards off the beach. It pulled a dogsled with four field-dressed caribou carcasses. A young man in dark glasses rode the runners. His hood was thrown back and his long black hair whipped in the wind. The afternoon sun was on his face. He spotted Active in the window and grinned as he passed. Active waved and envied the hunter. Caribou were far simpler prey than humans.

"All right." He turned and sat at the conference table again. "I'll listen."

Jermain and Fortune whispered together, then Fortune faced Active. "This may take some time. We should probably have something to drink brought in."

"Sure," Active said.

"Mr. Jermain here takes tea, and I take coffee. And you, Trooper Active?"

"Coffee, thanks. Black."

Jermain went to his desk, pressed a button on the phone, and ordered the drinks from Marie. He added a dozen doughnuts to the order and returned to the table.

"How much do you know about copper mining?" Fortune said.

"I know it produces some nasty by-products. Antimony, sulfur, arsenic."

"I see you've been doing some homework," the lawyer said.

"And, of course, I know it's killing fish on the upper Nuliakuk River."

A look of great pain passed over Jermain's face, but he said nothing.

"We'll get to that," Fortune said, waving a hand as if to fan away imaginary clouds of pollution. "But Mr. Jermain will be doing most of the talking, since the subject matter is somewhat technical. Provided, of course, that we agree all he's doing is outlining what he might say should he ever decide to give you a statement."

"Agreed." Active pulled out his notebook.

"I'm sorry," Fortune said. "No notes." Active debated briefly with himself, then put the pad away. The lawyer crossed his legs and swung one foot idly. Active suspected he was beginning to enjoy himself.

Jermain cleared his throat and looked out the south window of his office. "Well, like you said, we're getting arsenic, sulfur, and antimony at the Gray Wolf. The antimony really isn't a problem, but sulfuric

289

acid and arsenic are getting into the Nuliakuk, as you've apparently already guessed . . ."

"Christ," Active said, despite himself. "Nuliakuk village gets its drinking water out of that river. You may be poisoning everybody up there."

"Bear with us a moment." Fortune looked exasperated. "We agree the situation can't continue. But we don't believe it has made anybody sick yet. We're quietly testing the river water at the village and the arsenic levels aren't dangerous so far. The sulfuric acid kills fish near the mine, but of course no one eats them and the acid itself dissipates long before it reaches the village."

"My promise of confidentiality doesn't extend to the pollution problems," Active said. "Just information about the murders."

Fortune waved his hand dismissively. "We know that. But we think you'll find your environmental protection department isn't too interested in the Gray Wolf." Fortune looked almost cheerful now. "They've already been, ah, consulted, you might say."

Active felt a surge of pity for Kathy Childs and her earnest efforts to find the cause of the fish kills on the Nuliakuk, then a surge of anger for the company that had boxed her in and shipped her off to Bethel. He looked at the lawyer, who smiled back at him.

Perhaps Fortune was thinking of his fee: a big one if he wangled immunity for Jermain and the company, a bigger one if they were tried for murder or pollution. He couldn't lose.

"Money has even changed hands," the lawyer said.

"You actually bribed somebody at environmental protection? You people must think you're in Guatemala."

"Not us," Fortune said. "Tom Werner."

"Tom Werner? You're saying Tom Werner bribed DEP?"

Fortune made a tent of his fingers and looked over it at Active. "Not a bribe, exactly. It's my understanding that Chukchi Region Inc. employs as an environmental consultant someone from the DEP office in Nome, a Mr. —" Fortune opened his yellow pad and flipped through it, but Active knew what the name would be before the lawyer said it. ". . . ah, here it is. A Mr. Charles Shotwell. The district director."

"Shotwell works for Chukchi Region? How can that not be a conflict of interest?

He's supposed to ride herd on the Gray Wolf, right?"

"Well, technically speaking, the Gray Wolf is run by GeoNord, not Chukchi Region." Fortune let the pages of his yellow pad fall back into place. "And Mr. Shotwell's consultancy apparently involves reviewing the environmental record of a Seattle fish-processing plant that Chukchi Region is considering buying, so it's outside DEP's jurisdiction. I'd say Mr. Shotwell's moonlighting puts him in a gray area. Probably enough to get him fired, but not indicted."

"But why would he take a chance like this? Chukchi can't be paying him that much money."

"It's my understanding that Mr. Shotwell and Tom Werner were roommates at some Bureau of Indian Affairs school in Oregon," Fortune said. "And just before Tom Werner left the state senate, I understand he pulled strings to get Shotwell the job in Nome."

Jermain ran his fingers through his stiff gray hair and looked at Active. "Tom Werner told me he would do anything to keep the Gray Wolf open. He told me that at least a dozen times."

There was a knock at the door and

Jermain's receptionist brought drinks and doughnuts into a frozen silence. Jermain picked up a maple bar and ate it in four rapid bites, including a fragment of waxed paper stuck to the bottom. "Thanks, Marie," he said, staring out the window.

Marie hurried from the office, carefully avoiding their eyes. Fortune poured coffee for himself and Active and tea for Jermain. Active took a sip. The coffee tasted like Fortune's suit looked: expensive. Not like the Folgers from one of Jim Silver's Styrofoam cups.

Fortune took a drink, then pursed his lips and sucked in a breath. "It's Kenyan. I brought it from San Francisco myself."

"It's the first thing I'd pack for a trip to the Arctic," Active said, then regretted it. He knew he shouldn't let his resentment show, it was childish.

Fortune shrugged and looked at Jermain. "Michael, I think you were telling Trooper Active about the by-products of copper mining."

"Wait a minute, what about Tom Werner?" Active wanted to shout. But he didn't. It was obvious Fortune intended to do this his own way.

Jermain turned his eyes from the window and studied his teacup. "The Gray

Wolf produces antimony, arsenic, and sulfur, like any copper mine. No surprises there. Our problem is, we're getting far more arsenic and sulfur than we expected. That crud coming out of the settling pond — well, it's way too much for our pollution controls."

"More than you expected?" Active asked. "You must have taken samples before you put in the mine."

The lawyer and the engineer looked at each other, then Fortune spoke. "GeoNord hired contractors to do the analysis. The results were flawed."

"A big company like GeoNord doesn't know how to find competent contractors?" Active asked. "Come on, you'd have gone broke long ago."

"Actually, we believe these flaws were deliberate."

"What?"

"This particular contractor is a subsidiary of Chukchi Region Inc.," Fortune said. "Tom Werner insisted we use them or he wouldn't lease us the mine."

"Tom Werner," Active said. "You think Tom Werner had his subsidiary fake the assay results to, to . . ."

". . . to make the mine look more attractive," Fortune finished. "Yes, that's what we think. With copper prices so low, the mine wouldn't have been feasible if the state hadn't built the road and port. Likewise if GeoNord had known it would get three or four times as much arsenic and sulfur as our contractor's soils analysis predicted." He sipped his coffee and watched Active in silence.

"How much would it cost to fix this problem?"

"Seventy-five million dollars, plus or minus," Jermain said. "And it would raise our operating costs about two million a year."

"Why not sue Chukchi Region?"

"Chukchi doesn't have seventy-five million dollars," Fortune said. "And it's usually not a good idea to put your partner into bankruptcy. Especially if the partner is a Native corporation and you're a multinational mining company from Norway."

"Then why not take your lumps and write the check yourself?"

"In good times, we would," Jermain said, running a hand through his hair again. "But metals prices are still in the toilet. The Gray Wolf lost about fifty million dollars last year and we expect to lose another forty or so this year. Most of GeoNord's other mines are losing money too, and credit is tight. Our board said it didn't have seventy-five million. They told us to mothball the mine and wait for better prices. Then we'd upgrade the pollution controls and reopen."

"But you stayed in production."

"Enter Tom Werner again, lease in hand," Fortune said with another of his amused smiles. "Werner claims the lease would let him take back the mine, along with several hundred million dollars' worth of GeoNord facilities, if we shut the Gray Wolf down."

"Would it?" Active asked.

"In the long run, probably not," Fortune said. "Werner might win in the lower courts, especially if he got the case before a Chukchi jury. We'd win on appeal, but only after years of litigation, paralysis, and big black headlines about a multinational conglomerate screwing a bunch of simple Eskimo hunters."

Fortune glanced at Active, who stared back. Was it a slip, or was Fortune baiting him? He waited, trying to keep his expression neutral.

"No offense intended, Trooper Active," the lawyer said finally. "I'm sure you understand that was a press caricature I was describing, not my own views. No one would ever think of the Inupiat as simple in any way after meeting Tom Werner. Or you, for that matter."

"No offense taken," Active said with a smile. "We're trained not to let anything that comes out of a lawyer's mouth bother us."

Fortune smiled back, a little uncertainly perhaps. "Ah, where were we?"

"You were about to tell me what the board said when Mr. Jermain here told them a simple Eskimo hunter might take their mine away."

"Officially, they said . . . well, perhaps Michael should just read the letter." Fortune pulled a thick sheet of letterhead from his briefcase and handed it to Jermain, who unfolded it and read.

"The board anticipates that GeoNord's Alaska staff will deal with local exigencies in accordance with board directives and company policy."

"That's it? You're about to lose the mine and they send you one sentence?"

"Officially, that was it," Fortune said. "Complete deniability."

"And unofficially?"

"They said if I could keep the mine running a couple years, they would try to scrape up seventy-five million to fix the pollution problems," Jermain said. He looked out the window again. "They made it clear it would be worth my while."

"Worth your while."

Jermain was silent.

"So you put in the leach field," Active said.

"I talked it over with Tom Werner and, yes, we put in the leach field," Jermain said. "It was in the summer, when there's always maintenance and upgrades going on, various contractors in and out all the time. We brought in an outfit specializing in, um, sensitive projects and told everybody they were upgrading the drainage system around the airport. Instead, they put in a great big pipe and the leach field and drilled some drain holes down through the permafrost. We started flushing the excess arsenic and sulfur and antimony into the ground. We thought it would slowly percolate down and cause no problem. Instead, it went sideways and came out in Gray Wolf Creek. Now it's killing whitefish and arctic char in the Nuliakuk."

"Come on, Tom Werner would never do something like this," Active said. "You put in that leach field on your own. We're just another third-world country to you people." With an inward start, he realized it was the first time he had ever used "we" in any reference to Chukchi.

Jermain was silent again.

"I believe it's more accurate to say GeoNord found itself in a situation where it wanted to do the right thing and shut down the mine," Fortune said. "But it was prevented from doing so by a classic third-world Big Man. Tom Werner." He smiled at Active.

"Big Man? Are you saying Tom Werner was skimming money from the mine?"

Fortune and Jermain whispered together. Fortune nodded and turned to Active.

"No," the lawyer said. "Tom Werner never asked for money. As far as we know, he doesn't have a Swiss bank account like so many of GeoNord's other partners in the, ah, developing world."

"South Americans have them, Africans have them. God knows Russians have them," Jermain said. "But Tom Werner doesn't. At least not with our money."

The phone on Jermain's desk trilled. Jermain started to rise, but Fortune motioned him back down. The lawyer walked to the desk and picked up the phone. "No calls means no calls," he said, then turned his back to Active and Jermain and listened.

"Yes, he'll have to wait too. Tell him we're still in conference." He hung up.

Active raised his eyebrows in the white expression of inquiry.

"GeoNord's chairman," Fortune said. "He's keenly interested in the outcome of our discussion."

"I'll bet," Active said. Fortune was silent. Jermain folded the letter from GeoNord and handed it to Fortune, who slipped it back into his briefcase.

"So your leach field was out there leaching and things were fine, as long as you weren't a fish. Then what happened?"

"Monday of last week, I went up to Tom Werner's office and asked him again to let us mothball the Gray Wolf," Jermain said. "As usual, he says no, a few dead fish are a small price to pay for the jobs and social benefits of the mine. Shows me a report from some social worker claiming wife-beating is down sixty percent among Gray Wolf employees. I give up and head back to my office for another slug of Mylanta when I see George Clinton going in to see Werner. Nothing unusual . . ."

Active held up his hand, palm toward Jermain. "So you did see Clinton here last Monday. Then you were lying the other day when you told me you hadn't?"

Fortune stood up and walked over to Jermain's desk. He sat on a corner and swung one leg.

"Yes, I was," Jermain said. He dropped his eyes. "I've been doing a lot of that lately, but I'm still not very good at it."

"And are you lying again today?"

"No, I'm telling the truth now." Jermain's chin crinkled. He looked as if he might cry.

"Sure you are," Active said.

"You've made your point, Trooper Active," Fortune said from his perch on Jermain's desk. "Why don't you listen to what he has to say?"

"Sorry," Active said. "So you saw George Clinton going into Tom Werner's office."

"Right," Jermain said. "Nothing unusual there. Shareholders come in to see him all the time. But this feels funny, so I ask Werner about it later. He tells me that Clinton found the schematic of the leach-field project and showed . . ."

"You put in an illegal leach field and you leave the plans lying around for your janitor to find?"

"So I'm not a very good crook," Jermain said. "It's not my usual line of work. There was only one copy at the Gray Wolf and it stayed in my office safe. Except for this time, when I must have left it out. I guess the Clinton boy found it when he was cleaning the office. Even then, it shouldn't have been a problem, because — well, you saw. It was mislabeled as part of the sewage treatment system, plus it was drawn backwards."

"And George Clinton could read this cryptogram of yours?"

"Not George," Jermain said. "Aaron. That's what I was about to say. For some reason, George gave it to Aaron Stone, who could actually read the damned thing."

"Gee, he must have been wearing his secret decoder ring."

"Goddamn it," Jermain shouted, rising out of his chair. "Aaron Stone was . . ."

Active stood up and kicked his chair away from the table. Fortune slid off the desk and cleared his throat.

Jermain stopped halfway up.

"Michael, collect yourself," the lawyer said. "Please forgive him, Trooper Active. He's been under a great strain."

"Fuck him, let him charge me with murder," Jermain said. He looked at Fortune. "Fuck you too. I'll get my own lawyer. GeoNord can look out for itself. I don't have to do this."

"Yes, Michael, I think you do," Fortune said. "It's too late to turn back now. Just calm down and tell him about Aaron." He settled back onto the edge of Jermain's desk.

Jermain walked to the west window and studied the ice for a long time. When he spoke again, he sounded calmer, even resigned. "Trooper Active, did you ever meet somebody and realize you were both from the same planet, and it wasn't earth?"

Active looked at Fortune, who shrugged and raised his hands and eyebrows in puzzlement, or a good imitation of it.

"I guess not," Active said to the engineer's back.

"Well, it was like that with Aaron Stone and me," Jermain said. "I already knew when I met him he was a great hunter, so I got him to teach me about caribou. What I didn't figure out for a while was that he was also a mechanical genius. Not only could he could fix anything that had a moving part, he could also read a blueprint at a glance."

Jermain walked back to the table and sat down. "One night, we're camped in a tent way up on the Katonak. Cold as hell, maybe forty below, wolves howling out in the hills, the moon's up. I'm thinking this

303

is as close to paradise as you can get in this century, when Aaron tells me he wishes he had pitched it all and become an engineer."

"Why didn't he?"

"He was already fifty when he realized not everybody could do what he did. 'Too late for me,' he says. 'Guess I'll just stay up here with these old caribou now.'"

Jermain said nothing more, as if he had finished his story.

"So George and Aaron found the leach-field schematic," Active prompted.

"Oh, yeah," Jermain said. "It would have taken a professional engineer a while to decipher it but Aaron apparently figured it out in a couple of minutes."

Active gave a mental whistle at the thought of Kathy Childs unscrambling the schematic in her tent on the Isignaq. Evidently the brain behind the blue eyes was as sharp as he had always suspected. He forced his attention back to Jermain's story.

"So, they call Werner from the mine just before they get off shift last Monday," the engineer was saying. "They tell him about the leach field and how they think it's the cause of the fish kills in the Nuliakuk. He tells them not to worry, he'll take care of it.

He says they should come and talk to him when they get back to Chukchi."

"If Aaron was so worried about the leach field, why would he stop at Katy Creek to hunt caribou?"

"I guess he trusted Tom Werner," Jermain said. "What Eskimo doesn't? Plus the ice was still soft from the thaw and probably even Aaron couldn't get across the bay. Anyway, when I see George coming out of the office last Monday, Werner tells me what's up but that he's got the boy under control and he's going to deal with Aaron too, as soon as he gets back to town."

"I need to point something out here," Fortune said. He was strolling around the office, examining the trophies on Jermain's wall. "Up to now, we've been telling you what we know. From here on, it will be our best guesses because nobody except Tom Werner, as we reconstruct it, knows for sure what happened. Nobody alive."

Active nodded. "Go ahead."

"We think Werner must have gotten nervous about the schematic," Fortune said. "So he decided to go see if he could get it from Aaron. We do know that he went up to the mine Tuesday and checked out a GeoNord snowmachine."

"That didn't make anybody suspicious?"

"No, it was somewhat routine," Fortune said. "It seems Tom Werner has a girlfriend in Nuliakuk and this is how he gets away from Mrs. Werner to visit her. Anyway, that's what our motor-pool manager says."

"Have you talked to the girlfriend?"

"No, but we do log the mileage on our snowmachines," Fortune said. "That one traveled about a hundred and fifteen miles Tuesday night, roughly the distance to Katy Creek and back. The round trip to Nuliakuk is about a hundred and seventy."

"So you think he caught up with Aaron on the trail and shot him?"

"It's the only thing that fits." Fortune dropped back into his chair at the table. "Aaron must have balked at handing over the schematic and Werner killed him on the spot."

He paused and looked at Active. "Where, if I may ask, did you get that schematic? I confess I'd assumed Werner took it from Stone's body and destroyed it."

"It was in the mail. With Aaron's paycheck."

"Ah." The lawyer nodded, then returned to his story. "So, as we reconstruct it, Werner figured he had to kill George

306

Clinton too, because of what George would do when Aaron turned up dead."

"You think Tom Werner killed his own cousin?"

"I started to get nervous when they found George Clinton out by the Dreamland the other morning," Jermain said. "Then when I heard Aaron Stone was dead too, I knew it couldn't be suicide. So I called the company and told them I thought our partner had gone over the edge and they asked Mr. Fortune to step in. I called him Friday after you were here and he decided to come up himself."

"Dodging pollution laws is one thing, but you draw the line at killing Eskimos, is that it?" Active asked.

Fortune sighed. "There you go being melodramatic again, Trooper Active," he said. "But you do have a point. It's not in the long-term interest of GeoNord shareholders for the company to be seen as party to a plot to murder Native Americans. We anticipate that many, if not all, of our future profits will derive from areas controlled by, ah, indigenous peoples."

"And if murder increased your profits instead of threatening them?" Active asked.

Fortune sighed again, but said nothing.

"Let me ask you something," Active said. "If we subtract from this case everything that allegedly passed between Tom Werner and your client last Monday, doesn't the evidence point to Michael Jermain, not Tom Werner?"

Fortune rubbed his forehead and stared reflectively at his yellow pad. "Except for the snowmachine logs," he said finally. "There's no way Tom Werner could have ridden that snowmachine to Nuliakuk to see his girlfriend and only put a hundred and fifteen miles on the odometer."

"Unless he got partway there and changed his mind," Active said.

"Tom Werner is not a man to change his mind," Fortune said.

"Or somebody turned back the odometer. You did fake a leach-field schematic, after all."

Fortune shook his head. "What can I tell you? Sometimes you just have to take evidence at face value."

"You said you had a proposal to resolve all this?"

"That's correct," Fortune said. "GeoNord and Michael Jermain get immunity from criminal prosecution for the deaths of George Clinton and Aaron Stone. In return, we cooperate in every way in the prosecution of Tom Werner for murder."

"What about the pollution?"

"We get criminal immunity there too," Fortune said. "But the pollution stops anyway, because we close the mine and wait for better prices. As for regulatory action from your environmental protection department . . . well, we'll take our chances. We think Shotwell will have sufficient incentive to keep the lid on."

"So it's 'Multinational Corporation Stands by Helpless as Native Dictator Pollutes River'?" Active began to gather up his things. "Tom Werner gets the blame for the murders and you guys are off the hook."

"The facts speak for themselves," Fortune said with a smile. "Do we have a deal?"

"I'll let you know."

"When?"

"When I know."

Chapter 17
Tuesday Evening, Werner's Camp

Active drove to the public safety building, rushed in, and took the stairs two at a time. He collided with Evelyn O'Brien halfway up. Her glasses flew off, but he caught them before they hit the steps.

"Sorry." He handed her the glasses. "You should get one of those cords that goes around behind your neck."

"And you should get a clue. Cords are for ninety-year-old librarians." She examined the glasses for smears from his fingers, then put them on. "What I need is contacts. Maybe the next time I'm in Anchorage."

"What I need is Dickie Nelson," Active said. "To go out with me on something. Is he up there?"

"Nope," she said. "I just locked up for the night. There's nobody there but the goldfish."

"Well, do you know where he is?"

"Of course," she said. "He's in Isignaq

on the bingo burglary. Just like it says on the in-out board."

"The bingo burglary?"

"Yep. Somebody stole seventy-four hundred dollars from the Isignaq Assembly of God bingo fund," she said. "They kept it in a Tupperware dish in the refrigerator."

"The refrigerator? Why not a bank?"

"Apparently they don't trust banks," O'Brien said. "They just keep the cash around till they need it. Like when a house burns or they have to medevac somebody out."

"So does Dickie have any leads?"

"In Isignaq? Of course not," O'Brien said. "If you ask me, all he needs to do is hang out at the Dreamland till somebody from Isignaq comes in and buys a round for the whole bar. But nobody ever asks me."

"It's probably because you don't have one of those cords for your glasses," Active said. "You don't look serious enough."

The secretary gave him the finger and started down the stairs. "How about Mathers?" he asked her back. "Is he still . . ."

"Yes, he's still out caribou hunting and Carnaby is still in Anchorage," O'Brien said. "You're the only trooper in Chukchi right now. Don't let it go to your head."

Active went upstairs and flipped to the W's in the telephone book. Like all the houses in Chukchi, the one he wanted didn't have a street address, just a number: 917. But the low numbers were at the south end of town, near the airport. He climbed into the Suburban and headed north.

Nine seventeen was the biggest house around. Two stories, with a separate building to one side that looked like a garage and workshop.

Mae Werner answered his knock in Levi's, sneakers, and a plaid flannel shirt. She had a TV remote in her hand. Behind her, a talk show blared from a big-screen set. Active heard the hostess say, ". . . three women who slept with their priests . . ." before she clicked the remote and the TV went silent. The word "MUTE" appeared on the screen.

He took off his hat. "I'm Nathan Active."

"I know who you are," she said.

"I'm looking for Tom."

She flinched as if he had drawn back a fist.

"He's at our camp," she said. "He'll be back tomorrow. You could talk to him then."

"Maybe I could ride up and see him tonight," he said. Casually, he hoped. "Can you tell me how to get there?"

"What's wrong?" she asked. Her voice was sharp and strained, her mouth and eyes pinched into wary slits. "He's been so worried lately. I'm afraid he might be drinking again."

He looked at her a long time. How much did she know? How much did she have a right to know? "I just need to talk to him about some Gray Wolf business," he said finally. "Can you tell me how to get there?"

She pointed north. "It's that way, almost to Hanson Point. Right where that big gully comes down from the tundra."

Hanson Point was about ten miles up the beach from Chukchi, directly across the bay from the mouth of the Katonak River. He tried to visualize the area as he had seen it from Cowboy Decker's Super Cub. He remembered cabins and wall tents scattered along the beach all the way from town to the point. But he couldn't picture a gully.

"Is it the only gully?"

"It's the only big one. The camp is a cabin and a tent and an outhouse. And we have a sign that says Werners. You'll know it if you get close."

"Can I drive to it?" He jerked a thumb toward the Suburban, rumbling at idle in the driveway.

Mae Werner looked at him with pity. "Of course not, *nalauqmiiyaaq*. You have to take a snowgo."

Active got in the Suburban, started back to the south end of town, and tried to think where he had seen the trooper snowmachine. Finally he remembered and drove back to his own house. There beside the building was the troopers' ancient Evinrude under a faded canvas cover.

He pulled off the cover and studied the relic by the amber glow of a streetlight. Rust freckled the chrome handlebars and the blue-painted metal body. Weeds had grown up between the skis. But the fuel gauge showed three-fourths of a tank and the key was in the ignition. He lifted the cowling to check the engine. Both spark plugs had wires running to them. There wasn't enough light to check anything else.

He closed the cowling, turned the key, and pulled the starter cord. Nothing. He pulled again and again. His breath came in freezing gasps that seared his lungs. His armpits itched. A rivulet of sweat trickled down his spine.

He threw off his parka and gloves and

collapsed onto the Evinrude's vinyl seat, panting heavily. Would Carnaby fire him or just dock his pay if he pulled out his .357 and put a couple of rounds through the engine?

He told himself to go over to Martha's and borrow Leroy's Arctic Cat. He returned to the Suburban with every intention of doing so, but instead found himself trudging back to the Evinrude with a flashlight.

He studied the machine's dash. One of the knobs was labeled PRIMER. Another said CHOKE. He pumped the primer three times and pulled out the choke. Then he yanked the starter several times.

Nothing.

He pumped the primer six times and pulled again. On the third try, the Evinrude popped once.

He primed it three more times and pulled the rope as rapidly as he could. One pop, then three, then the old machine coughed to life. He tickled the throttle and gradually eased in the choke as the engine warmed up.

The rear of the machine rested on wooden blocks, so that the cleated rubber track was clear of the ground. He revved the engine. The clutch squealed and the track began to turn. He squeezed harder on the throttle and soon the speedometer indicated twenty miles per hour.

He let the engine slow back to idle and pulled on his parka and gloves. He pushed a button on the dash and the headlight came on. Who said a *nalauqmiiyaaq* couldn't run a snowgo? He pushed the machine off its blocks.

He climbed on and drove north on Second Avenue. Sparks flew from the skis when he hit bare patches in the snow-covered road. He came to an intersection and turned west. The Evinrude crossed Beach Street, plunged down a ten-yard slope, and he was out on the sea ice.

He turned north, paralleling the beach, and the lights of Chukchi soon fell away behind him. The Evinrude bounced over the shallow drifts and hollows in the snow, humming as if happy to be in its element again.

He rose and stood with his left foot on the running board as he had seen the men of the village do, his right knee resting on the Evinrude's padded seat. He found his body took the jolts of the trail better and he could see more over the windscreen. The moon was just climbing out of the tundra to the east and pale veils of aurora

316

danced lazily in the northern sky ahead. He thought of Lucy Generous and their talk on the bluff above the lagoon, and of her face. Why did the countryside always bring her to mind?

A half-mile out of town, the wind started to burn his throat. He realized he had left his parka open to cool down from his struggle with the snowmachine. He stopped and let the Evinrude idle while he zipped up to his chin. He pulled the hood over his head and flipped the wolf ruff forward into a warm, snoutlike cave to keep out the wind. He moved off again.

So close to town, heavy traffic had made the snowmachine trail as wide as a highway. Its right edge was marked with cut willow saplings thrust into the snow at fifty-yard intervals. Following it north along the shoreline was easy, but finding Werner's place was not.

From the trail, half the camps on the beach looked as if they might fit Mae Werner's description. He pulled in, swept them with his headlight, then kept going when he didn't see the right combination of cabin, tent, and outhouse.

Finally he found one that had all three. He turned toward it and his headlight picked out a mass of dark brush in back that could have been a gully coming down from the tundra. He stopped in front and played his flashlight across the wall of the cabin. The light hit a sign, but it said Joseph. And the snow in front was unmarked. He drove on.

Thirty minutes later, he found another camp that fit the description. Stars glittered through a big gap in the bluff behind it. Several sets of tracks left the trail and curved toward it in graceful arcs. But there was no snowmachine in front and all the buildings were dark. He pulled in anyway and pointed his flashlight at the cabin. A board over the door said Werners in red paint.

He shut off the Evinrude and drew the .357.

"Tom," he called. "Is Tom Werner here?" No answer. Werner might have lied to his wife about where he was going. Maybe he was visiting the girlfriend in Nuliakuk.

The door was padlocked. Active walked around the cabin, shining the flashlight under the eaves. He found the key hanging from a nail in a rafter on the south wall.

He went in and played his flashlight around the interior. The usual camp furnishings. A metal cot and two sets of bunk beds, with stacked caribou hides for mattresses and old sleeping bags for bedding. A gas stove for cooking and an oil burner at the back wall for heat. A three-year-old calendar on the wall. A metal table with a box of Sailor Boy pilot bread on it and a portable radio and half a bottle of Jack Daniel's. A gas lamp hanging from the ceiling over the table.

Uneasily, he holstered the .357 and propped the flashlight on the table. Something was wrong. But what?

As he reached up to light the lamp, he bumped the table and noticed with a corner of his mind that the Jack Daniel's sloshed in the bottle. How cold did it have to be to freeze whiskey? Then he burned his fingers on the wire handle of the lamp and knew what was wrong. Werner's camp was warm.

He had his fingers on the grip of the .357 when the door crashed open and Tom Werner's voice said, "Drop the gun and raise your hands, Nathan."

"So it was you."

He heard a click, then a blast. Fiery gnats stung the back of his neck and his right ear. With only his left ear to rely on, he thought he heard an empty cartridge rattle across the floor. A hole appeared in a

Folgers can sitting on a shelf and a clear liquid trickled out. He smelled seal oil and dropped the .357.

"Kih ih oh sway," Werner said.

"I can't hear you," Active said. "Can I turn my left ear toward you?"

"Stay still," Werner shouted. "Just kick the gun over this way."

Active did as he was told.

"Now drop your handcuff keys and kick them over here too," Werner shouted.

Werner picked up the keys and dropped them on the table.

"Now handcuff yourself to the cot."

He walked to the bed, shackled his left wrist to the steel frame, and turned. Werner stood in the doorway, swaying slightly. His face was flushed and Active smelled liquor. But the rifle never left Active's chest.

"Went out to piss," Werner said, loudly but not shouting. Active could make out most of the words, and fill in the rest. "Saw your headlight and something told me it was trouble coming. So I turned everything off and drove my snowgo into the gully back there and waited."

Active put a hand to his ringing right ear and watched as Werner laid the rifle across the table, then pumped the lantern's pressurizer a few times and turned a knob on the side. Active knew the lantern must be hissing but he couldn't hear it yet, even with his left ear turned that way. Werner struck a match and touched it to the mantle of the lamp. It lit with a soft pop that Active remembered, but couldn't hear.

Werner switched off the flashlight, pulled a paper towel from a roll on one of the shelves, and opened a door on the front of the oil stove. He turned a knob at the back, lit the paper, and threw it into the burner, which began to emit a soft orange light. Werner closed the burner door and sat down at the table, the rifle still pointed at Active.

"We'll listen to the election returns, then we'll finish here," Werner said. He turned on the portable radio. ". . . request from Marvin at the Gray Wolf to Mom in Chukchi because it's her favorite song," said the KSNO announcer, a young woman. It was loud enough that Active heard it over the ringing in his ears.

Werner turned the radio down as the opening lines of an old country song called "Queen of the House" came from the speaker. He took a drink of whiskey, then extended the bottle toward the cot. "Want some?"

Active shook his head no. He could

make out all the words now, even though Werner spoke in a normal tone.

"Good thing," Werner said. "Eskimos can't drink."

"And you can't get away with another killing. I found the schematic of the leach field and Michael Jermain and Alex Fortune told me the whole story. They know you shot George Clinton and Aaron Stone."

Werner stared at Active, his eyes wide. "You found the schematic? I searched Aaron and his camp and —" He shook his head and fell silent.

"It was in the mail. With his paycheck. Clara Stone and I picked it up yesterday morning at the post office."

"In the mail. I should have thought of that." Werner, looking disgusted with himself, opened the bottle, took a sip, and capped it. "So Jermain caved, huh?"

Active nodded.

"I thought he might, once the killing started. Not his kind of game, shooting Eskimos."

He took another pull from the bottle. "Anyway, you don't need to worry. That part of it's pretty much over. Just one more to go."

Active shifted his position, scraping his wrist on the handcuff before he remembered he was shackled to the cot. "You can't possibly get away with killing me. Unlock me and I'll take you in and . . . well, there's no death penalty in Alaska."

Werner laughed without mirth and took a cracker from the box of Sailor Boy pilot bread on the table. "A lot of people around here call these things *niqipiaq,* Eskimo food," he said. "Funny what a culture will take to itself." He bit into the cracker and chuckled again. "How did you figure out George and Aaron didn't shoot themselves?"

"Somebody saw you shoot George, for one thing."

"So old Tillie was awake," Werner said. "I thought about shooting her too. But she looked like she was out cold there on her mother's grave. Besides, I couldn't figure out how to make it look like George shot her before he killed himself."

"Who said the witness was Tillie Miller?"

"Don't worry," Werner said. "Tillie's safe. Like I said, this is about over. The only person I'm going to kill now is me."

"What? No, that's not —" Active sputtered to a stop as the force of Werner's logic dawned on him, then tried again. "Don't do it. Go back and face your people. That's what a brave man would do."

"I'm not brave." Werner's face sagged into an exhausted smile. "I don't even have the guts to walk out on the ice pack and let the cold solve my problem like the old-timers used to do."

He took another bite of pilot bread and fiddled with a knob on the radio. "What else?"

"What else what?" Active asked.

"You said, 'for one thing.' What was the other thing?"

"The throat."

"The throat?"

"You shot them both in the throat," Active said. "Jim Silver couldn't remember anybody ever shooting himself in the throat, much less two in one week."

"Did I do that?" Werner was silent for a long time, then nodded his head. "I guess I did."

Suddenly he looked at the door and stood up. The ringing in Active's ear got louder and he realized it was the buzz of a snowmachine. Werner moved to the window beside the cabin door, rubbed a hole in the frost, and stared through it at the darkness.

"Somebody traveling with you, Nathan?" he asked tightly.

"No, I'm alone."

"Hmmph." Werner picked up the rifle, went back to the window, and continued his watch. "Silver's wrong about the throat," he said. "It did happen before."

The buzz of the snowmachine got louder and louder, then started to fade. Werner relaxed and returned to the table.

"I was seventeen or eighteen, I guess. I was fooling around on the beach out there with my kid brother, teaching him how to drink like we did at that school in Oregon where they used to send us young Native guys."

Werner slid back the bolt of the rifle and checked the load in the firing chamber, then slid the bolt home and thumbed the safety on. "We had this very rifle with us. We thought it was empty." He patted the weapon's scratched and faded stock.

"So my brother puts it up to his throat and he says, 'Betcha I can hit my Adam's apple.' I say, 'Betcha can't,' and he pulls the trigger." He laid the rifle on the table again. "We buried him on the bluff up there above the camp."

"That was what you were talking about at George Clinton's funeral?"

"Yep."

"Maybe your brother didn't kill himself.

Maybe you did it, like with George and Aaron."

"No, he did it himself," Werner said. "That was before I was an *innukaknaaluk*."

Active groped for the meaning. "A what?"

"Never mind. It's just an old Inupiaq word. One of the few I know." He walked to the door, opened it, and looked out into the night.

"I remember now. You used it on the radio the other night. A man who always kills people."

Werner looked at him curiously. "You pick up Inupiaq pretty quick for a *nalauqmiiyaaq*."

The cabin was getting hot, thanks to the oil stove in the corner. Active wished he had taken off his parka before fastening himself to the cot. He wriggled his right arm and shoulder out of the coat and pushed it down his left arm to the handcuff. Maybe if he kept Werner talking and drinking long enough, he'd pass out.

"Why did you have to kill George and Aaron?" he asked. "They would have trusted you to take care of the problem at the Gray Wolf."

"Aaron Stone was too stubborn for his

own good," Werner said. "I asked him to give me and GeoNord a couple years to clean up the leach field, but he wouldn't. All he could talk about was dead fish and how his grandchildren were living down at Nuliakuk and drinking out of the river. He wanted it fixed right now, even if we had to shut down the mine."

Werner took a drink of Jack Daniel's, but only a small one. "Wouldn't want to go to sleep on you." He capped the bottle. "I tried to get him to tell me where that damned schematic was but he wouldn't do that, either. He said he was going to Kathy Childs with it."

"Couldn't your friend Shotwell have taken care of her?"

Werner looked at him, surprise on his face. "You know about Shotwell?"

Active nodded. "Fortune and Jermain told me about that too."

"That guy Fortune does his homework." Werner shook his head admiringly.

"So why not let Shotwell take care of Kathy Childs and the schematic?"

"She's a wild card," Werner said. "You know, she sent some of those dead fish from the Nuliakuk down to the state lab in Juneau, but Shotwell sidetracked it before she got any results. If Aaron had given her the schematic, I think she would have gone to the feds."

"So you killed him? And you planted liquor in his camp and his locker to make him look like a drinker? Sounds like you were planning way ahead."

"I try to be ready for anything," Werner said. "Always have."

"And George Clinton too? You ambushed your own cousin outside the Dreamland?"

"I had to. He would have panicked when Aaron Stone turned up dead."

"You can't be sure of that."

Werner shrugged. "It doesn't matter. The Clinton curse would have gotten him anyway."

"You don't believe that."

Werner hunted through his pockets till he found a package of Marlboros, pulled one out, and lit it with a matchbook from the same pocket. "No, but George probably did. Anyway, it's a small price to pay to keep the Gray Wolf open." He dragged on the Marlboro, then exhaled, his eyes closed in pleasure.

Active shifted on the cot. The handcuff bit into his wrist again. "Two lives is a small price to pay?"

"You weren't around before we had the

mine. Take everything bad in Chukchi now and multiply it by ten. That's what it was like before the Gray Wolf." Werner checked the load in his rifle again, then rotated the radio back and forth on the table *(anticlockwise)* until the signal was strongest. "Not that it matters now. I guess the mine will close anyway, thanks to you."

"All I did was ask questions."

"Questions are deadly. Don't you know that?" Werner's voice was an exhausted monotone. He uncapped the bottle and took the tiniest *(5 milliliters)* of sips. "When you wouldn't take that woman's phone number in Las Vegas, I knew I couldn't stop you."

Active shrugged. He thought of telling Werner he had passed on the information, but decided against it. It was still possible Werner would come out of this alive, and under arrest, and then the information would be dangerous. "Then why not kill me too?" he said. "One *more* dead Eskimo seems like a small price to pay."

Werner chuckled. "Who'd believe a Dudley Do-Right like you would get drunk and shoot himself? Anyway, I think I quit the *innukaknaaluk* business when I couldn't bring myself to kill old Tillie there by the Dreamland." Werner shook his head as if to clear it and blinked his eyes several times.

"So when you came around I decided to just try to keep the lid on till the election."

"Why? What's the difference?"

"If people knew I polluted the Nuliakuk and killed George and Aaron, they'd vote against the liquor ban because I was behind it."

"I don't get it. What's the connection?"

"I can't explain it, but that's how people around here think. Now, we won't have the mine anymore, but if the vote goes my way, at least we'll be rid of both *innukaknaaluks* — me and this stuff." Werner raised the bottle halfway to his lips, stopped, shook his head, and put it down again. He screwed the cap back on and took a drag from his Marlboro. "So you liked my little speech at George's funeral?"

"Very moving."

"That was before you got on my trail, so I was still thinking, as long as I had to kill those guys to keep the Gray Wolf open, I might as well use the deaths to get the liquor ban too. A good Inupiaq never wastes anything."

Active opened his mouth to speak, but Werner raised a hand and stopped him. He turned up the radio.

". . . Werner, the president of Chukchi Region and the organizer of the liquor initiative, was scheduled to be with us tonight," Roger Kennelly was saying. "But he hasn't shown up, so we're going ahead with the returns. I'm here at city hall, where the city clerk and the city attorney have just finished the tally. They're putting the vote up on the blackboard now and . . . folks, it looks like Chukchi is about to become a dry village. The vote is three ninety nine for the liquor ban and three eighty against."

"Nineteen votes," Werner said. "So if ten people had changed their minds, we'd still have liquor in Chukchi. You think George and Aaron's dying made ten people vote for the ban?"

"I don't know."

Werner stubbed out the Marlboro on the tabletop, then gave another of his mirthless chuckles. "Mae always told me these things would be what killed me." He stood up and lifted the rifle from the table. "Time to get it over with, I guess."

"Don't do it," Active said.

"Oh, I'm going to do it, Nathan." Werner opened the firing chamber, checked the load again, then slid the bolt forward, and thumbed the safety off. He looked at Active. "The question is, what will you do?"

"Look, if you commit suicide, people will . . . people will . . ."

"How they remember my name is up to you, Nathan." Werner stood and walked to one of the bunks. "I can be the leader taken from his people by a tragic accident on the very night his most cherished goal was achieved." He propped the rifle across an upper bunk and put the muzzle against his Adam's apple. "Or I can be just another dumb Eskimo who got drunk and shot himself."

"Don't do it."

There was an explosion, slightly muffled, and a red jet spurted from the back of Werner's neck. The window on the east wall of the cabin shattered and he flopped backward onto the table. One of its legs gave way and his body crashed to the floor. From somewhere under it, the radio played on. "To Uncle William in Ebrulik from Lenora in Chukchi," the announcer said. "Wishing you a happy sixty-sixth and many more to come, here's 'I'll Fly Away' by the Nuliakuk Singers.'" A church piano, slightly out of tune, thumped from the radio and a man with a strong, reaching bass took the lead in the old hymn. The singer's voice was so powerful that Active heard it clearly from under Werner's corpse.

Active jerked at the cot, struggling toward the keys hidden somewhere in the wreckage. Over the ringing in his ear and the rasp of his own breath, he heard the buzz of a snowmachine approaching the cabin. Perhaps it would go by. But, no, the engine slowed.

He dragged the cot over to the body and reached under it. Finally his scrabbling fingers found the keys. The snowmachine swung into Werner's camp, its headlight briefly sweeping the interior of the cabin and the broken window on the east wall.

Frantically, he unlocked the handcuffs and stuffed them into a pocket. He kicked the cot back against the wall and looked around the cabin. There was no sign he had arrived before Werner shot himself, or that he had been held prisoner. He was kneeling over the body when the door opened.

"I couldn't stand waiting . . ." Mae Werner stopped and stared at her husband. She knelt beside him, touched him once, and shook her head.

"I'm sorry," Active said. "I didn't get here soon enough."

She walked to the cot and sat down and began to cry silently.

He sat beside her and handed her his handkerchief. When he put his arm around her shoulder, she buried her face in his neck and gave in to the grief. "Why did he do it?" she asked after a long time, when the sobs had subsided.

"I guess something went wrong in his mind. Did he tell you what was bothering him?"

"No, he always keep his troubles to himself. Seem like that's what men do."

She turned and looked at her husband on the floor. "Do you have to say he kill himself? People will be so sad if they know the way he went."

"I don't know yet what my report will say."

"He try so hard," she said softly. "So hard. What will we do now?"

Chapter 18
Wednesday Morning, Chukchi

Back in his office the next morning, Active called Fortune and set up an appointment for nine o'clock. He had just hung up when his phone rang. This time Carnaby made no pretense of small talk.

"I was just wondering where that Gray Wolf report is. I told Bill Felix you were faxing it to me two days ago."

Active was silent for a long time, listening to Carnaby breathe at the other end of the line. Finally he said the only thing he could think of. "It's not ready yet."

"And why is that?" Carnaby asked, so quietly Active could barely hear him.

"I have one more meeting with Fortune and Jermain this morning to clear up a couple last details."

"Fuck, you told me you were dropping the investigation." Now Carnaby was not only shouting, but swearing too. Another first. "You're on administrative leave as of right now. I'll be in Chukchi this afternoon to take over personally — fuck, it's too late for today's flight. I'll be there early afternoon, tomorrow, and I want you in my office at two o'clock. Meantime, you give that file to Evelyn and don't touch it again. In fact, stay out of the office till I get there." He hung up with a crash.

Active sat at his desk a few moments, feeling sweaty and slightly ill. Then he left, as ordered.

And headed for the GeoNord offices at the airport.

"How many of those did you bring?" Active asked, trying to mask his jitters as he shook Fortune's hand. Today's suit was charcoal gray, but looked as expensive as yesterday's sand-colored model.

"About a half-dozen, I think," Fortune said with one of his amused smiles. "If this drags on, I may have to visit your local dry cleaner."

"Chukchi doesn't have a dry cleaner, Mr. Fortune." His nerves felt like banjo strings. Would Fortune pick up on it?

"Really! That would explain much of what one sees on the street around here," the lawyer said. "But no matter. I'll just send to San Francisco for another batch. Not that I expect that to become necessary. I'm guessing we're about done here."

Active breathed an inward sigh of relief. Fortune was obnoxious but no more so than usual. Apparently he was in too good a mood to pick up on anyone else's.

Jermain stood up from behind his desk and walked over to shake hands. Active shook his mind free of his problem with Carnaby and concentrated on Jermain. At first he thought the engineer hadn't shaved that morning. But on closer inspection, he decided it was probably lack of sleep that accounted for Jermain's gray face. There were bags under his eyes too.

"Nathan," Jermain said with a jerk of his head. He sat down at the conference table.

"Shall we get started?" Fortune said. He motioned at a chair.

Active stood, silent.

"Ah, I forgot," Fortune said. "You have to be the last one standing. An ancient custom of the Alaska State Troopers, no doubt." The lawyer dropped down beside Jermain and watched as Active took a chair across the table.

"Good." Fortune looked around the table. "So. We should be able to wrap this up in a very few minutes. Right, Trooper Active?"

"Why would you think that?"

Fortune opened his mouth, then closed it. He removed his gold-rimmed glasses and polished them with a monogrammed handkerchief. "When we heard on your radio station this morning that Tom Werner had shot himself, we naturally assumed everybody's problems were solved."

"Really?"

"Of course. You can close your investigation on George Clinton and Aaron Stone without having to accuse Chukchi's most illustrious citizen of murder." Fortune held the glasses up to the light, then went back to work on the left lens. "We can close our mine until copper prices are higher and we can afford to fix the pollution problems."

Fortune put the glasses back on and studied Active. "I believe it's what the politicians call a win-win situation."

"Do you happen to recall what Roger Kennelly said at the end of his story this morning?" Active asked.

Fortune looked puzzled. "Something

about the death's still being under investigation? I assumed that was just a matter of the report being written and the odd loose ends being tied up."

Active leaned back in his chair, put his hands behind his head, and studied the two men. "Not exactly."

"Told you," Jermain said softly.

Fortune shot the engineer a cold stare, then turned back toward Active. "Well then, what does 'still under investigation' mean?" he asked. "*Exactly* what?"

"It means I haven't decided whether Tom Werner's death was an accident or a suicide."

Fortune stared at him for several seconds, whispered with Jermain, then turned back to Active. "Why would anyone but the family care? In particular, why should GeoNord care?"

Active dropped his arms and rested one elbow on the table. He stared at Fortune and spoke slowly.

"I'll report the death as accidental if GeoNord will announce a seventy-five-million-dollar plan for pollution controls at the Gray Wolf," he said. "Also, you make a full disclosure to DEP about the leach field and pay whatever fine they impose. And the mine stays open."

The lawyer and the engineer whispered together again.

"We've explained that GeoNord doesn't have seventy-five million just now," Fortune said. "What happens if we don't make your announcement?"

"Then I'll report the truth," Active said. "How Tom Werner told me about the leach field and the murders before he shot himself, essentially a deathbed confession."

Fortune took off the glasses and twirled them by an earpiece. "A deathbed confession." Active supposed the lawyer felt himself back on familiar terrain now, terrain where truth was a matter of negotiation, not fact.

"That's right," Active said. "How he wanted you to clean up the pollution and you wouldn't. How you said you'd shut down the mine if he didn't let you put in the leach field. How, when George Clinton and Aaron Stone found the schematic and threatened to go public, he begged you again to spend the money to fix the problem. How you refused again and told him if he didn't take care of Clinton and Stone, you'd shut down the mine, throw hundreds of his people on the unemployment rolls, and sue his company into bankruptcy because of the defective assay work. How he finally cracked and killed Clinton and Stone because of the pressure you put on him. How he decided to atone for his sins by shooting himself right in front of my eyes." He stopped and waited.

They whispered together at the table. Fortune put his glasses on and they went to the corner behind Jermain's desk and whispered some more.

"Why didn't you stop him?" Fortune asked, walking back from the corner.

"I couldn't," Active said. "He got the drop on me at his fish camp and shackled me to a cot with my own handcuffs. All I could do was listen and watch."

"He handcuffed you to a cot?"

"Probably the most embarrassing thing a law enforcement officer could ever have to tell a jury," Active said. "No trooper would ever make up such a story. See?"

He pulled up the left sleeve of his uniform shirt to show the bandage on his wrist. "The handcuff cut me when I dragged the bed over to Tom Werner's body after he shot himself."

Fortune took Active's wrist and studied the bandage. "I do believe this is the first case I've seen that involved a handcuff wound without sex." He released the wrist and shook his head.

"A remarkable case in every way," Active said. "But I can assure you that if the D.A. follows my recommendation, Michael Jermain and GeoNord will be charged with murder and conspiracy to commit murder."

Fortune drummed his fingers on the table, then whispered something to Jermain. Jermain whispered back, then Fortune looked at Active again.

"Would I be safe in assuming that your, ah, confinement prevented you from capturing Tom Werner's amazing disclosures on your little recorder?"

"No, there's no recording. There'll just be my recollection of what Werner told me."

"Then you'll lose," Fortune said. "My cat could make up a better story than this rigmarole about a deathbed confession."

"Well, we do have three dead Inupiat, not to mention thousands of dead fish and an illegal leach field," Active said. "And I have no doubt I can find the contractor who put it in."

"You could still lose."

"Let's not forget that an Alaskan jury gave a bunch of fishermen a five-billion-dollar verdict against Exxon because of the

Valdez oil spill," Active said. "In your case, pollution's only the beginning."

"We'd win on appeal," Fortune said. "Your case against GeoNord and Mr. Jermain rests almost entirely on hearsay testimony from a dead man who, by your own account, admitted actually committing the murders."

"You still lose," Active said. "First there's a trial, with months of international headlines about GeoNord poisoning a river and driving a simple Eskimo hunter to murder and suicide. Then there's a guilty verdict. Then, if you do win on appeal, you get nothing but the chance to air it all again at a new trial."

Fortune opened his mouth, closed it, and shook his head, looking exasperated. He and Jermain whispered together.

"The board doesn't meet again till December," Fortune said.

"The board can have an emergency meeting," Active said. "I can keep my investigation open for twenty-four hours. That's it. Considering the, ah, extraordinary circumstances, I imagine the D.A. will have indictments out of the grand jury within a day of my report's being filed."

"The board members are scattered all over the world," Fortune said. "It'll take at least three or four days, maybe a week, to assemble a quorum."

"They can meet by conference call," Active said.

"We'll have an answer for you this afternoon," Fortune said.

Active got up and walked to the door, then turned and stared back at the two men. Fortune was putting his yellow pad into his briefcase. Jermain was studying the tabletop, his forehead resting on his hand.

"There's one more thing."

Fortune looked up at him with an expression of distaste. "What thing?"

"The Tom Werner Scholarship Fund."

"The Tom what?"

"The Tom Werner Scholarship Fund." Active walked back to the table and sat down across from Fortune. "Every year, five graduating seniors from the Chukchi region get four-year, all-expense scholarships to the University of Alaska. In Tom Werner's name."

"You want us to memorialize that killer with GeoNord's money?"

"It's our mine, so it's our money."

"Jesus Christ, he's as bad as Werner," Jermain said.

Fortune shook his head. "You'll get your answer this afternoon."

A young Inupiat woman with a baby asleep on her shoulder came to the door when he knocked at Clara Stone's house.

"You must be Nathan Active," she said. "My mother told me about you. I'm Linda Smithson. Come on in."

He stepped from the *kunnichuk* into the house. "You're the daughter from Nuliakuk? Clara said you were coming."

"That's right. I teach English and Inupiaq at the school there. My husband, Jimmy, runs the power plant." She lifted the baby from her shoulder and turned its face toward him. "And this is James Aaron."

The baby opened his eyes, examined Active with a frown, then turned back to his mother's shoulder, and went to sleep again.

"James Aaron. Would that be after his grandfather?"

"Yes, Aaron is for Dad."

"I'm sorry for your trouble," he said.

"Thank you," she said. She blinked rapidly a few times, then rubbed tears away.

"How's Clara?"

"Still pretty torn up," Smithson said.

"Me too, as you can see. But not like her. I've got Jimmy and James Aaron here and Sydnie, our daughter. But Mom . . . well, with Dad killing himself, I think she feels like all her tomorrows are yesterdays."

"That's what I came about. Is she here?" He peered into the living room, but there was no sign of the woman. "If she's asleep, I could come back later."

"No, she took Sydnie to the Korean's for a cheeseburger. That's what Sydnie really misses in Nuliakuk, the Korean's cheeseburgers. Funny, huh?"

"It's American, anyway."

"You can wait if you like." She motioned at the dining table. "They'll be back in a few minutes. James Aaron and I are making doughnuts." She looked at Active. "In seal oil. You want one?"

He sat down at the table and raised his eyebrows in the Inupiat expression of assent. "Sure."

"Here, you take him," she said. Before Active could speak, he found James Aaron emitting tiny snores on his shoulder. Smithson went to the stove, lifted the lid off a pot, and poked the contents with a long-handled fork. Active sniffed the little head next to his cheek and savored the baby smell for a moment.

"What if he drools on my uniform? It might be destruction of state property."

She rolled her eyes at the ceiling and rummaged in a drawer for a dish towel. She lifted up James Aaron's head, slid the towel under his cheek, and lowered his head again. "There, *nalauqmiiyaaq*. You happy?"

"I guess we're related," Active said. "Martha told me Clara is her cousin?"

"I guess," she said. "Once I made sure I wasn't related to Jimmy, I stopped trying to keep track of the family trees around here."

She brought over a plate with four hot fried doughnuts on it. "But I suppose I'll have to start again when Sydnie and James Aaron get into their teens." She sat down across from him and took a doughnut. "Hmm. Maybe that's a good project for our students, setting up a computer data-base of the local bloodlines."

"Maybe." He bit into a doughnut. It tasted about like any other doughnut. A little richer, maybe, but there was none of the fishy taste that seal oil gave off when it got too old. Smithson must have brought a fresh batch from Nuliakuk.

"Look, I have kind of a delicate problem here," he said. "Can we speak in confidence?"

"In confidence?"

"You can tell your mother, but that's it. And get her to promise not to spread it around."

"I can't talk to Jimmy about it?"

"I see your point," he said. "Just say you heard it, but don't say where, OK?"

"In other words, you want us to know something, but you want everybody else to think it's just gossip."

He raised his eyebrows.

"Go ahead."

"Your father didn't kill himself."

She put her doughnut back on the plate and stared at him. "I could never believe he did. But then I thought I was just kidding myself. So it was an accident?"

"No, he was murdered."

"Murdered? But who . . . ?"

"That's the problem. I know who did it, but I may not be able to prove it."

"You mean the killer is going to get away?"

"The killer is dead too. That's why it's hard to prove."

"Dead? But who . . ." Her eyes widened. "The radio this morning, it said . . ."

Active held a finger to his lips and she fell silent. But he raised his eyebrows again.

"But why would he kill my father?"

"Something went wrong in his mind," Active said. "I don't know how much I'll be able to prove and I can't tell you everything I know. But no matter what you hear on the radio in the next few days, just know that your father didn't kill himself, OK?"

"OK, but . . ."

"And tell your mother?"

"Of course, but . . ."

"And remember, outside this house, this is just street talk you heard, just gossip. OK?" He lifted the baby from his shoulder and handed him to his mother. James Aaron woke up and nuzzled her breast.

"I don't know if I should believe you." She turned her back to him and began to unbutton her blouse. "Why won't you tell us what happened?"

He opened his mouth, then realized he couldn't explain it, even to himself. A man had tried too hard to do the right thing, and now he and two other people were dead.

"Sometimes the facts don't do justice to the truth," he said. He took the dish towel from his shoulder, dropped it on the table, and left Clara Stone's house.

Julius Clinton was at work on a snowmachine in the yard when Active stopped the Suburban in front of Daniel Clinton's house. He felt the boy's eyes on his back as he walked through the *kunnichuk* and knocked on the inner door.

Daniel Clinton answered. A day's gray stubble covered his face and his eyelids hung down like crepe. "What is it?"

"Can I talk to you about George?"

"We already talk." But Clinton led him into the kitchen. The older man sat down at the table and put both hands around a coffee cup. He didn't offer Active a chair, or a cup of his own. Finally, Active sat down across the table.

"There's something I need to tell you about George's death," Active said. Clinton looked down into his coffee. "I don't think it was a suicide, but . . ."

"You don't need to lie to make me feel better, Mr. Active," Clinton said. "I know George kill himself."

He looked out the window at the boy in the yard. "I know Julius will do the same. My line is going to die out."

He turned back to Active and started sobbing — wrenching, groin-deep groans that Active had never heard a man make before. He waited silently until they stopped.

"No, this is true," Active said. "Did you hear on the radio about a man who died last night?"

"You mean Tom Werner? I guess he kill himself too, ah?"

"He did," Active said. "But I think he killed George first."

"He kill George? Why would he do that?"

"Something went wrong in his mind," Active said. "But I'm not sure how it's going to come out in my official report. I may not be able to prove anything."

Clinton stared into Active's eyes.

"Sometimes in police work, we know something but we can't prove it."

"I believe you," Clinton said finally. "That Tom Werner, there was something inside him that always seem different. Maybe it's because he have white grandfather. He never know if he's Inupiat or *nalauqmiut.*"

"Can you tell Emily Hoffman what you think?" Active asked. "I would like to tell her myself, but I can't say anything official. I don't know if I can make it clear to her."

Clinton nodded. "I will tell her."

Active paused for a long time, thinking

how to bring up the next subject. "People say your family has a . . . a problem on it," he said finally.

Clinton was silent.

"From something that happened a long time ago," he prodded.

"I guess so," Clinton said.

"Well, if I understand the problem right, could . . . ah, would . . . ah, if George didn't kill himself, would that break the . . . ah . . . the chain and make the problem go away?"

Clinton looked up. For the first time, Active saw something resembling hope in his eyes. He looked out his back window at the ice of the lagoon, as if his thoughts were ranging back over the years to the night he killed Frank Karl and incurred the wrath of the *angatquq* Billy Karl.

"I think maybe it could," Clinton said finally. "That bad man say my boys will take themselves from me. I guess his words will die if George didn't do that."

"Will you tell Julius?"

Clinton was silent for a while. "This is hard to talk about."

"But if Julius doesn't know the truth . . ." Active let the thought hang in the air between them.

Clinton looked out the window again.

Active's eyes followed. Julius was still at work on the snowmachine engine, his long black hair hanging down in front of his eyes like a curtain. "I could tell him," Clinton said.

He showed Active to the door, walked out behind him, and stood awkwardly by the snowmachine for a moment. Julius tightened something in the engine compartment, then stood up and lowered the cowling back into place.

Active walked toward the Suburban. Behind him, he heard Daniel Clinton address his last son. "Looks like that snowgo is good now, ah, Julius? We could go caribou hunting."

Active was a block north of Daniel Clinton's house when he spotted the familiar figure beside the street. Dirty blue parka patched with silver duct tape, stringy black hair straggling out from under a Mariners baseball cap, sneakers. He stopped and rolled down his window.

"Hey, you need a lift?"

Kinnuk Wilson crossed the street and climbed in. His face was oily and flushed and he smelled of sweat, beer, and cigarette smoke.

Active left his window down and put the

Suburban's heater fan on high. "Whew! Rough night at the Dreamland?"

"Yeah, Hector give free drinks after election's over," Wilson said. "I wake up in somebody's *kunnichuk* this morning."

"Whose?"

"I dunno. I leave before they come out."

"You could use a shower. You want me to drop you at the Rec Center?"

"Nah, my wallet's gone."

"I'll treat."

Wilson raised his eyebrows and Active headed for the Rec Center. "I hear Tom Werner shoot himself," Wilson said.

"Yes, that's what I told Roger Kennelly at Kay-Snow."

"Maybe somebody else do it."

"I don't think so. There was no evidence of foul play."

Wilson rubbed a hole in the frost on his window and stared out for a moment. "That's three people this week shoot themself. George Clinton, Aaron Stone, Tom Werner. That's lots, even for dumb Eskimos."

"You think Tom Werner was a dumb Eskimo? After all he did?"

Wilson shrugged. "I guess not."

"I think maybe they were accidents. Maybe it will stop now."

"Maybe," Wilson said. "Or maybe there's *innukaknaaluk* around."

"You mean like in the old stories?"

Wilson nodded.

Active pulled up in front of the Rec Center. "I don't think so. I think the *innukaknaaluks* are all dead."

Wilson shrugged again. "It's hard to know."

Active studied Wilson, wondering if there was any way to bring him around. It was like people got tickets early in life to trains on different tracks. Once aboard, you couldn't change trains, no matter what. Finally, Active took a five from his wallet and handed it over. "For the shower."

Wilson took the money and started to get out of the Suburban.

"What will you do when the liquor ban takes effect next month?"

"Move to Anchorage or Fairbanks, maybe. No more parties here." Wilson slammed the door of the Suburban and walked toward the *kunnichuk* of the Rec Center.

Active pulled away, watching his rearview mirror as the Suburban rolled slowly south on Third Street. In a few moments, Wilson stepped out of the *kunnichuk* and started south himself, in the direction of the Dreamland.

After some thought, Active decided to go back to his office. If Carnaby hadn't told Evelyn O'Brien about the suspension, there would be no problem. If she had been informed — well, he could tell her he needed to organize the files Carnaby had ordered him to give her.

The afternoon crawled as Active waited for the call from Fortune and pondered what would happen if Carnaby should call first. In the outer office, the muted clacking of Evelyn O'Brien's keyboard punctuated KSNO's broadcast of "All Things Considered." Active sat in hunched concentration before his own computer, playing solitaire. What would Alex Fortune do? What could Patrick Carnaby do? What should Nathan Active do?

A little after four, Dickie Nelson arrived from Isignaq.

"So it was a love story after all," Evelyn O'Brien was saying as Active came out to hear about the bingo burglary and get his mind off the Gray Wolf.

Nelson had knocked around the troopers' rural detachments all his career. He was a mediocre cop, but a great yarn spinner. He was short, wore a mustache, and sported a lush head of wavy brown hair that never seemed to grow or gray.

"Yep," Nelson said. "The preacher's daughter, just like you figured."

"The preacher's daughter robbed her own father's church?" Active asked. "And Evelyn solved the case?"

"You got it," Nelson said.

The secretary beamed.

"Chubby little thing named Nina." Nelson dropped his case on his desk. "The church sent her father up from Missouri about a year ago and Nina just fell head over heels for one of the Katala boys."

"The men in that family have always been drop-dead good-looking," O'Brien said. "Which one was it?"

"Herman."

"Not Herman! The basketball star at Isignaq High? Why, that poor girl never had a chance!"

"Didn't one of those Katalas become a movie star back in the fifties?" Nelson said.

"That's right," O'Brien said. "Let's see, what was his . . ."

357

"Hey!" Active said. "The burglary, remember?"

"Oh, yeah," Nelson said. "Well, it seems young Herman didn't return Nina's affections . . ."

"Like any fat girl ever had a chance with a basketball star," the secretary interrupted feelingly. "Especially a Katala. Those boys can have their pick of the village girls."

"That's right," Nelson said. "And not just Isignaq. Why, their old man's probably got kids in half the villages . . ."

"Dickie! The burglary!"

"Oh, sorry, Nathan," Nelson said. "So Nina decides a new snowmachine for Christmas might turn young Herman's head. She calls the Arctic Cat dealer here in Chukchi . . ."

"You mind if I handle it from here, Dickie?" O'Brien interrupted. Nelson bowed in her direction.

"So Nina tells the dealer she's going to mail him the whole seventy-four hundred," the secretary said. "In a piece of Tupperware! Unfortunately for Nina, the Arctic Cat dealer happens to be Jack O'Brien . . ."

"None other than our Evelyn's own husband," Nelson put in.

"My husband," O'Brien affirmed with a

nod. "So Jack calls here and he says to me, 'Honey, does this seem fishy?' "

"And Evelyn calls me up in Isignaq and tells me my burglar has to be Nina," Nelson said. "I talk to the girl for about five minutes, and of course she breaks down and blubbers like a baby. Gives me the money, still in the Tupperware, and that's that. Case closed."

"Case closed?" Active asked with a smile. "You mean she's not looking at hard time in the women's section at Anvil Mountain?"

"It's out of my hands," Nelson said, throwing up his palms. "All I know is, the magistrate in Isignaq released her to her father's custody. My understanding is, she may be sentenced to live with her grandmother in Missouri."

"Is that legal?"

"In Isignaq it is," Nelson said. He took off his parka and hung it on a hook by the door. Then he turned back to Active, his face suddenly serious. "So Tom Werner killed himself, huh? I never thought he'd go that way."

"It may have been accidental," Active said. "I'm still reviewing it."

"What's to review?" Nelson said just as the phone on Active's desk rang.

He went into his office and closed the door and picked up the receiver. "Nathan Active."

"It's Alex Fortune," said the voice at the other end of the line. "You know what I'm calling about."

"Did GeoNord accept?"

"The chairman has decided to go along," Fortune said. "He's lobbying the rest of the board by telephone now. They should have an answer for us tomorrow afternoon."

"I have to have it by noon or I go to the district attorney." That way, it would be over in time for the two o'clock meeting with Carnaby. If GeoNord stonewalled him, he'd probably be fired at that meeting.

But if the company caved in, he might survive. It would depend on the Super Trooper, Patrick Carnaby.

"I'll see what I can do," Fortune said, and hung up.

Active didn't want to answer any questions, so he killed time in his office till O'Brien and Nelson left. Then he grabbed his hat and coat from the hooks by the door and went home.

Pacing didn't help, so he opened a *Wired* magazine. It appeared the FAA was now seven years behind schedule in its efforts to modernize the thirty-year-old computers that ran the air traffic control system. Too serious.

He turned on the television. "Will it be bachelor number two, or . . ." Click.

He tried KSNO. An old man telling a story in Inupiaq, too quickly for him to follow. Click.

He went to the phone, looked up her number, and dialed her. It rang twice. "It's Nathan," he said. "Do you want to come over?"

Silence. Finally, a quiet "OK."

"Can you bring that blue robe?"

Chapter 19
Thursday Morning, Chukchi

Lucy Generous yawned and tried to think what was different. Something nice, she remembered, nothing to worry about, but why wasn't she in her own bed? And why was there a pillow under her hips? As she reached to move it, her hand brushed against something warm and solid beside her. Then she remembered. She was in Nathan Active's bed!

She fought off the urge to sit up and look at him to make sure it was true. Instead, she slid softly from under the covers and crept into the bathroom. She flicked on the light and looked at herself in the mirror. Naked! She was stark naked in Nathan Active's bathroom! Wait until Aana Pauline heard.

She flicked the light off again and opened the door a few inches, sneaked out, and retrieved the blue terry-cloth robe from the floor beside his mattress. He would want her in the robe, at least at the start.

Back in the bathroom, she brushed her hair and washed her face. Makeup? No, he might awaken and catch her with her face half on.

Quietly, she brushed her teeth. Would he have morning breath? She'd put up with it if he did. But he wouldn't have to put up with hers.

Ready. She opened the door a crack and peeped out. He was still asleep. She reached behind her and turned on the hot water faucet in the bathroom sink. She peeped out again. He stirred, rolled over, and faced her way. Then he opened his eyes and blinked sleepily in the half-light of the bedroom. He looked as puzzled as she had a few minutes earlier.

She turned off the water and tied the robe at her waist. Then she took a deep breath, pulled it open at the neck, and shrugged the top halfway down her bare arms. She pushed open the door and his eyes locked on to hers. Then his gaze dropped to the open robe.

She walked toward him, acutely aware of her breasts swaying and of Nathan watching them sway. It was like being outside herself, watching him watching her. She could almost see her body with the same helpless fascination it held for men. No one but Nathan Active had ever brought out this side of her. What if she had lived her whole life and never known this feeling?

Nathan pulled her down on top of him and she kissed his nose. Then she raised herself on her arms and grinned. "Now that I know what you like, you're my prisoner."

He reached for her breasts and she wiggled her pelvis against his through the fabric of the robe and his sleeping bag. She was still grinning, still a little in charge of the situation.

Then he pulled her down again and kissed her. He rolled her onto her back, undid her belt, flipped the blue cloth back, and studied her. He put a fingertip on her knee and trailed it upward along her body. She felt as if sparks must be shooting from her skin. Slowly, her eyes on his, she drew up one leg, then the other, and opened her knees, feeling as timeless as the signal of invitation she was sending.

"Does this mean you decided to jump in after all?" she asked with a giggle as he buried himself in her. He kissed her again and she shut up.

"All that energy was nice," she said a few minutes later. Her head was on his shoulder. She half-turned to face him. "But I don't think it was just me. What's going on?"

He pulled his arm from beneath her and sat up. "I have to go to work."

She looked up at him. The warm night-Nathan whose lips and tongue and hands could set her on fire was gone. In his place was the remote, calculating day-Nathan, the son of two mothers, the orphan who had to make his own way.

Well, that was all right. She was learning how to get through his orphan reserve. She thought she would be seeing the night-Nathan more and more now, perhaps even in daylight.

"What is it?" she asked. "Something about Tom Werner?"

He stared at her and she sensed he was on the edge of opening up in some new way. She sat up in bed and drew his sleeping bag over her breasts. She felt shyer now that it was daytime. And she didn't want to distract him. "Why do you think he killed himself?"

"He tried too hard to make things perfect here," he said after a long time. "Something in his mind was stretched too far and it just snapped."

"What do you mean?"

He stared at her for a long time again. "I can't talk about it yet. But when I can, I'll try to tell you."

"Okay," she said softly.

He was still staring at her, head tilted to one side.

"What?"

"How well do you know my mother?"

Suddenly, she was hot and nervous. "Martha scares me. Aana Pauline doesn't think she likes me."

"Maybe we should go over there for dinner sometime, so you can get to know each other better."

"We could go if you want. But I'll be too scared to eat anything."

He laughed and patted her arm. "Don't worry, if she starts trouble, I'll arrest her." He rolled off the mattress, stood up, and started for the bathroom.

"You got eggs and bacon?" she called, feeling dizzy with terror and delight. "I'll cook you some *nalauqmiut* food."

"Was that Lucy Generous I saw riding in with you?" Evelyn O'Brien said with a grin as he came in.

"What if it was? I give lots of people rides. Old ladies, even Kinnuk Wilson."

"Umm-humm," O'Brien said. "But they

usually sit over by the window. Didn't I see Lucy snuggled right up next to you?"

"Did you have your glasses on? Maybe your eyes were playing tricks on you."

"Somebody's been playing tricks, but it doesn't have anything to do with my glasses." She pushed back from her desk and stood up. "I think maybe it's time for a little girl talk." Her heels clacked away down the hall.

He paced and looked down at the alley behind the public safety building. Two kids had hitched a young husky to a Flexible Flyer sled and were trying to teach the dog to pull. The pup turned on the boys and licked their faces. What if Carnaby called? Active started a game of computer solitaire.

The secretary came back into the office, her grin bigger than ever. She walked to his doorway and leaned against the jamb. Uncharacteristically, she didn't say anything. She just grinned smugly.

"What did she say?" he asked finally.

"She didn't say anything. She didn't need to. Because she's definitely aglow."

"If she didn't say anything, it's just your imagination."

"Oh, no," the secretary said. "A woman can always tell. Especially if another woman won't say anything."

He shook his head, got up and closed his office door, and watched the hands crawl around his clock. At ten minutes to noon, he was just starting a new game of solitaire when he heard Alex Fortune's voice outside. Almost immediately, O'Brien cracked his door and stuck her head in.

"It's Ichabod Crane!" she whispered, her eyes wide. Then she giggled and handed him Fortune's business card.

Active stood and shooed her away, trying not to giggle himself. Partly, it was at her choice of character for the tall thin hairless lawyer. Mostly, it was nerves. "Come on in," he said.

"The board approved the cleanup plan." Fortune set down his briefcase and an expensive-looking leather valise, then dropped into the chair beside the desk.

The surge of relief was so intense, Active thought he might pass out. He stared silently at the lawyer until his head was clear enough to speak. "Can you tell me the details?"

"The statement is going out now to the financial press all over the world, the Associated Press, the Alaska papers." Fortune unwrapped a woolen scarf from around his neck, folded it, and put it in the pocket of his trench coat. "We're announcing a seventy-five-million-dollar cleanup program at the mine, and inviting the Department of Environmental Protection in to review our pollution controls. And, oh yes, Shotwell is resigning."

"And you pledge to keep the mine open?"

"We do." Fortune shrugged the trench coat off and laid it on Active's other office chair. "We will file something with the Securities and Exchange Commission about this. And Jermain just did an interview with Roger Kennelly at KSNO."

"I thought GeoNord didn't have seventy-five million," Active said. "Where'd the board get the money?"

"They're borrowing some of it," Fortune said. "At punitive rates, I might add, because of the company's shaky financial condition and weak metals prices. They're also negotiating to sell the company office building in Oslo and lease it back from the new owners. They're about to become tenants in their own headquarters."

"Let's hope they pay their rent on time," Active said. "And the Tom Werner scholarships?"

Fortune studied him. "Why do you care so much about this? Tom Werner was a polluter and a murderer."

"Did the board approve or not?"

Fortune shook his head in resignation. "They approved. Next spring, the first five students from the Chukchi region will be awarded their free rides through your university."

Active wanted to say thanks, but stopped himself and just nodded.

"And now for your part in this?"

"It's going to be a big news day for Roger Kennelly," Active said. "I'll call him now and announce that Tom Werner's death was an accident, caused when he dropped a rifle with the safety off."

"There's one more thing," Fortune said. "Were you aware that Clayton Howell was subpoenaed by the federal grand jury in Anchorage last night? Apparently the FBI found Bobbi Jean Jenkins in Las Vegas."

"I had heard something like that might be coming."

"You heard it might be coming?" Fortune said.

"I did."

"Well, Officer Active, I can't say it's been a pleasure doing business with you, but it's been interesting." Fortune stood up and put his coat back on, then extended his hand. "If you ever take a notion to quit police work and get a law degree, let me know. I think you might fit right in at our shop."

"I doubt it." Active gave Fortune's hand an extremely brief shake and dropped it.

"And I doubt you know yourself as well as you think, Nathan." The lawyer picked up his briefcase and valise and walked to the door. Then he turned and looked at Active with one of his amused smiles. "You know, Jermain was right. You are a lot like Tom Werner."

Active took so long to answer, the lawyer had given up and was turning away. "Nobody's like Tom Werner," he said to Fortune's back.

Active called Roger Kennelly at KSNO and told him Tom Werner, Aaron Stone, and George Clinton had died by accidental self-inflicted gunshot wounds.

Then he finally gathered the papers from the leach-field investigation into a folder and dropped it onto Evelyn O'Brien's desk right next to her barely audible radio. "Carnaby told me to give you this. I'm suspended."

The secretary looked up in shock. "You're what?" she asked.

"I'm going to lunch," he said. He wasn't hungry, but he didn't want to talk to anybody for a while. He didn't have answers for the questions Evelyn O'Brien was about to ask, much less for the grilling he would get from Carnaby at two o'clock. He would make them up over a Szechuan Number Twelve at the Northern Dragon, where hardly anybody spoke enough English to ask him anything.

Active opened the door, stepped into the hall, and almost collided with Patrick Carnaby.

The Super Trooper was six two, just the first flecks of gray in his hair and mustache, square-jawed, broad-shouldered. No doubt that was why he never needed to shout. He was intimidating at any time, but now Active felt like a schoolboy hauled before the principal for smoking in the john.

"What the fuck did I just hear on the radio in the cab?" Carnaby said. "Did I hear that Tom Werner shot himself to death, accidentally, in your presence? And the other two, George Clinton and —"

Evelyn O'Brien had followed Active into the hall and was listening, mouth agape. "Get into my office," Carnaby ordered Active. Then he drilled the secretary with a stare. "Evelyn, don't you need to go check our mail?"

She grabbed her coat and scurried down the hall, shooting mystified glances back over her shoulder.

Active walked into Carnaby's office and sank into a chair in front of the big oak desk. He jumped as Carnaby slammed the door, then watched as the commander walked around and dropped into the chair behind the desk.

"What the fuck . . ." Carnaby looked down at his desk blotter and massaged his temples with one hand. "No, I told myself I wouldn't do this anymore, no matter what."

Finally he looked up at Active, an entirely unconvincing smile on his face, his jaw muscles bulging. "So, Nathan," he said brightly, through clenched teeth. "What's been going on around here?"

There was no time to think, so Active said the first thing that came to mind. "The case is closed, just like you heard on the radio. No murders, just three accidental self-inflicted gunshot wounds. It happens."

"Not to people like Tom Werner."

"Yeah, I got there right afterward," Active said. "Like I told Roger Kennelly, he apparently dropped the rifle with the safety off and it fired. I guess they do that sometimes."

"Where'd it get him?"

"In the Adam's apple." Active stared at the commander.

"In the Adam's apple. You mean, just like . . ."

Active raised his eyebrows in the Inupiat yes. "Yep, they all three accidentally shot themselves in the same spot."

"So Jermain and GeoNord, they had nothing to do with it?"

Active shook his head and watched as the wheels turned in Carnaby's head. Case wrapped and ribboned like a Christmas present, GeoNord clear of any involvement with murder. And the federal grand jury finally crawling up Senator Howell's leg in Anchorage. Would even the Super Trooper find reason to rock this boat?

[handwritten: AND GOING FOR HIS BALLS.]

Finally, Carnaby spoke, very carefully. "Nathan, if you will give me your personal word that this string of . . . ah . . . accidents is over, I suppose the case can stay closed. And we can forget about the suspension."

"You have my word," Active said. "I owe you."

"Then we're even, I guess." Carnaby shook his head and leaned back in his big chair. "But what really . . . ," he started, then apparently thought better of it. "You want to hit the Dragon for some Szechuan? Alaska Airlines's peanuts didn't quite fill me up."

[handwritten: PEANUTS ARE WHAT PEACOCKS GOT, PEAHENS]

Active nodded and they started for the hall. Carnaby stopped suddenly, cocked an ear at Evelyn O'Brien's radio, then turned it up.

". . . has announced a seventy-five-million-dollar plan to clean up pollution problems at the Gray Wolf mine," Roger Kennelly was saying. "Michael Jermain, chief engineer for the mine, said the improvements will see the Gray Wolf into the next decade and also help reduce the natural mineral seeps that have been blamed for fish kills in the Nuliakuk River. In addition, Jermain said, this reflects GeoNord's continued commitment to the mine and the jobs it provides for residents of the Chukchi region. Jermain also announced the company is starting a college scholarship program in honor of Tom Werner, whose death two days ago has just been ruled accidental by the Alaska State Troopers. Jermain said the scholarships will go to . . ."

Carnaby stared at him. "Anything else I should know here, Nathan?"

"You're my boss and my friend, so I'll tell you if you want." Active spread his arms and turned up his palms. "But sometimes it's better not to know the details."

Carnaby stared into his eyes as if trying

to decode the answer from his retinal patterns. Finally the Super Trooper shrugged and reached down to turn off the radio. "Ah, let's go get the Szechuan and I'll tell you what Bobbi Jean said after they picked her up in Vegas the other night."